FROM TISH'S DIARY:

"It's past midnight, well past. Peter, beside me, is sleeping, looking innocent and untroubled. Incredible how people look so different in sleep . . .

"What I've had to decide is where we're going from here. It's been my decision. Peter, of course, wants to stay together. He wants another chance . . . As for me, I've turned inward a little. I now at last begin to feel something for the Kid. I actually look forward to having him now. The strangest thing is that I've been thinking a lot about a woman's role in a marriage. Maybe I'm becoming pre-liberated. I don't know. I haven't had the guts to say anything out loud. Through fear of losing Peter, of being alone, of being thought tough. But from now on, things are going to change. . . ."

Tish is 16. But she's growing up very fast. She has to. You'll love her. And she just may break your heart. . . .

Other SIGNET Books You'll Enjoy

FOR ALL THE WRONG REASONS

a novel by
JOHN NEUFELD

A SIGNET BOOK
NEW AMERICAN LIBRARY
TIMES MIRROR

This is a reprint of a hardcover edition published by
The New American Library, Inc. The hardcover
edition was published simultaneously in Canada
by George McLeod, Ltd.

Library of Congress Catalog Card Number: 73-75999

SIGNET TRADEMARK REG. U.S. PAT. OFF. AND FOREIGN COUNTRIES
REGISTERED TRADEMARK—MARCA REGISTRADA
HECHO EN CHICAGO, U.S.A.

SIGNET, SIGNET CLASSICS, MENTOR,
PLUME and MERIDIAN BOOKS
are published by The New American Library, Inc.,
1301 Avenue of the Americas,
New York, New York 10019

FIRST PRINTING, FEBRUARY, 1974

7 8 9 10 11

PRINTED IN THE UNITED STATES OF AMERICA

PART I

1.

March 4

It didn't happen again. Maybe I'm too choosy. Sara says I have to let myself go, to let it just happen to me, like waking up in the sunshine. The sun is there. My eyes are open. I stretch and naturally get cozy and warm and smile to myself. Sounds easy enough, but it never, never is.

She, of course, did it with Hank in front of almost everybody. Or would have if there'd been a spotlight. Almost meaning everyone at her house who wasn't doing it themselves. That's me and a few other nervous creeps with no guts. I pretended to be really into it, inhaling so deeply I thought the bottom of my stomach would drop out and roll away.

The good thing about smoking pot when other people are around (and smoking, too) is that they never pay attention to anyone else. That and the fact that when you inhale, you're not supposed to let any of the smoke escape. So, dear diary, if you're nervous like me, you inhale mostly air and then sit there, stretching your spine and sucking in your stomach, head back, pretending like crazy that wonderful things are happening.

My whole problem is that I am nervous. About everything. Not afraid; nervous, which is very different indeed.

Anyway, another party, another day spent in my original state. Virtue by necessity, not by inclination. Does it count in exactly the same way Upstairs?

2.

Propped in bed by two giant red-white-and-blue felt-covered cushions, Tish Davies languidly made her diary entry. She smiled to herself as she wrote. She loved keeping a diary. Who

knew when someone might come across it in an attic somewhere and bam! another Emily Dickinson or, better still, the
early days of a second Xaviera Hollander would be discovered.

Secretly Tish felt that diary-keeping was a way of showing
off. Sometimes she did write down her real thoughts and her
fledgling ideas. But most times, at least once in every entry,
she was conscious of writing *for* someone.

She smiled to herself again and hugged her body, reading
what she had written. She raised her pen and started to cross
out a line. She changed her mind.

From where she sat, Tish reached up and pulled open the
curtains at her window. The month of March seemed to be
starting out pleasantly. No wind, no rain; not tropical warmth
but enough to cause the dirty, muddy New Jersey grass to
begin thinking about turning green.

Tish put her diary into the drawer of her bedside table and
clambered out of the covers. She crossed the room and put
on her robe without allowing herself her usual early morning
appraisal. There was no need. She knew what she looked like.
Ankles just a bit heavy, but long and finely shaped legs. A
body in good proportion to her height; breasts round and well
formed, not too big but certainly not too small, either. All in
all, she knew, not bad for someone her age.

She laughed aloud at her thought. Age? Sixteen, going on
seventy-four sour, virginal years. Ah well.

She went into her bathroom to wash and brush her teeth.
It is true, she was thinking, that by today's standards anyway
she *could* have a last-minute child. When she was thirty, say,
and still a little away from menopause. She could have a child
by some terrific guy she'd just happened to meet on a street
one day. No one would think anything of that. Look at
Vanessa Redgrave. She'd had at least two already.

Back in her room, Tish put on jeans and a bra and sweater
and brushed her thick blonde hair back into a rat's-tail. Idly
she wondered just what the odds were of meeting a Franco
Nero on the streets of Princeton, seducing him in order to
have her last-minute baby. Pretty slim.

"Morning, Mom," Tish said casually, walking slowly through
the dining room and sipping her coffee.

"Hello, darling," said Mrs. Davies, not looking up from
Section Two of the *Sunday New York Times*.

Tish curved toward where Mrs. Davies sat and looked over

her shoulder. As usual. A story about how a Greek shipowner's fashionable wife imaginatively redecorated her fourteen-room Park Avenue apartment. Tish nodded to herself: really important stuff to know.

Tommy Davies was huddled on the carpet in the center of the living room, reading comics, still in his pajamas. He was younger than Tish, barely thirteen, and he steadfastly refused the infusion of culture that the *New York Times* represented to his mother. All he wanted, he said, was a good sports page and some comics. Every Sunday, when Mr. Davies went out for the papers, he was told to return with the *New Brunswick Home News* as well. Kept quiet this way for a few minutes, Tommy required little more.

"Hi, sweetheart," Mr. Davies said, looking up from his section of the *Times*. "Have a nice party?"

"Um-hmm," Tish said. "It was okay." She put her mug on a coffee table and sat cross-legged on the floor, reaching out for a section of the paper.

"Just okay?" asked her father.

"Usual stuff," Tish answered. "Usual people, usual stuff."

"Well, if Sara Wallace is any indication of what your friends are like, Tish, I'd say the 'usual stuff' was pretty lively," guessed her father, not unpleasantly, as he raised his paper up again in front of his face.

Ah, well, Tish thought, what he doesn't know can't hurt him. She turned a page. What a dumb saying. She wondered if anyone, anywhere, had ever been hurt by something he didn't know. Probably. Probably not.

3.

"You're early," said Sara, seeing Tish on her doorstep.

Tish stepped past Sara and took off her coat. "I like to get relaxed a little, before."

"You mean you want a joint?"

"Well," Tish said slowly, "I wouldn't exactly mind. I'm not getting any younger, you know."

"Come on, then," Sara said quickly, clipping her words as though she were angry. "Besides, I think this is the last weekend we can do any of this. My parents are thinking of coming back up."

"You said they'd be away until April," Tish said, surprised to find she felt somehow relieved. Sara was her best friend. She came to every party Sara gave. Still . . .

"It's been raining a lot in Palm Beach," Sara announced.

The two girls walked quickly through a large, elegant living area and down a flight of stone steps. Though Tish had been in the Wallace's house hundreds of times, she never felt easy there. It wasn't just a house. "Sort of a showplace," Sara's mother liked to murmur. That was certainly true.

From a distance, the house was unimpressive. A well-planned, well-planted lawn led straight to what seemed an ordinary sort of ranch house, made of fieldstone. What made the house unusual was that its first floor was in fact merely the top of three. There was a second story that held a dining room, library, master bedroom and enormous bath and dressing room. Below that, one flight down, was Sara's bedroom, a playroom, a bath, and two dressing rooms. For, beyond the glass doors at ground level, was a long, clear, amber-colored pool. And beyond that, Lake Carnegie. Other houses on Riverside Drive were more interesting-looking, on the outside. But none equaled Sara's inside.

"I love where this house sits," Sara had once confided in Tish. "It's absolutely sensational for looking at all that muscle rowing along."

By that she meant the Princeton University crew practice that took place every fall and spring afternoon within viewing distance of her back lawn.

"I go down to the water," Sara had said, "and just watching all those hard bodies exercising gets me all worked up."

She had become sufficiently worked up, and sufficiently brave and clever, to meet and become involved with Hank Rambler, a sophomore on the crew. "I love it when he whispers in my ear: 'Stroke, stroke, stroke!' "

In the playroom, Tish settled down in a comfortable suede-covered armchair, folding her legs up beneath her. She took the cigarette Sara had lit for her and inhaled, deeply, honestly, holding in the smoke and praying two things simultaneously. *Please don't let me cough. Please let it work.*

"So, unless they change their plans, it's just tonight and tomorrow," Sara said, lighting a cigarette for herself. "I invited a little fresh blood over, though. From Notre Dame."

Tish nodded, still holding smoke in her lungs. Quickly a picture of Notre Dame High School flashed through her mind: out on the Lawrenceville Road, a yellow brick prison, enormous, with no beauty. She supposed the Catholics hadn't wanted any distractions for their children.

The doorbell rang upstairs, and Sara left to answer it. She returned leading three girls and two grinning boys. The girls seemed turned on already.

Tish took another drag and looked at the crowd. Fred Kennedy, all pumped up in his muscle T-shirt and cardigan. Jane Something. Lisa Stenner, Wendy Hanson. Charlie Neil, blushing. Charlie wasn't bad-looking, just shy. He and Tish had spent many hours together at Sara's parties, talking about why-they-wouldn't, or how-they-couldn't, or when-they-would-instead-of-now. They supported each other in their unease.

Fred Kennedy, who knew his way around the playroom, began to look less sure of himself, and headed for the stereo for something to do. He selected a tape and within seconds the room was shaking with sound. Within another few seconds, Tish knew that the pot hadn't done what she had hoped it would.

Hank Rambler, huge and pink-faced and happy-looking, jumped down the final few steps and grabbed Sara from behind, putting his hands over her breasts and squeezing them, kissing her neck. Sara laughed and pretended surprise. Tish watched as their two bodies seemed to sink beneath the sounds, moving as though in water, light and fluid.

"Hi," Charlie Neil said, sitting on the floor at Tish's feet.

"Hi, Charlie," answered Tish, giving him only half her attention. "How are you?"

"Pretty good," he said into his folded legs. "I didn't see you much this week. At school, I mean."

"Busy," Tish allowed, watching Fred Kennedy grab Wendy Hanson and begin dancing with her. Tish thought Wendy was wonderfully sophisticated-looking, all tall and streaked and willowy. The two danced apart but clearly they had moved into each other's orbit. Tish sighed.

The doorbell rang again but Sara was too taken with Hank to hear it. It didn't seem to matter, for within a few moments six more people came down into the playroom, shedding coats and scarves and gloves. There were four boys and two girls, the girls hanging onto each other for protection and reassurance.

Sara pulled apart from Hank long enough to greet the new arrivals. Tish could hear the names only faintly. Frank Whateveritwas. Jenny and Carol Whoknewwhat. Mr. X. and Mr. Y. And Peter McSweeny. The last name she heard plainly, for Sara had wanted everyone in the room to know that Peter McSweeny, whoever he was, was here.

He had light brown hair with a shine to it, just long enough without being scruffy. He was long and tall, but not thin. Tish thought he looked "filled out," a phrase her father used with Tommy to reassure him he was growing enough and in the proper ways.

Although Peter's features were well defined, there was a warm, friendly openness about him. To Tish, he looked as though he liked people. Liked almost everyone. Trusted them. Would be honest with them. Suddenly Tish wondered if he had ever been beaten by a nun in school. The thought made her want to cry for him.

But she didn't. Instead, she had only one thought. *Now that is interesting. I mean, that's really interesting.*

Peter McSweeny made himself comfortable around Lisa Stenner on the couch.

Tish sighed again and tried to pay attention to what Charlie Neil was saying. "Sara says if I don't get with it, she's just got to replace me at her parties," Charlie confided. "I wonder how much getting with it she wants."

4.

March 10

The question is, why? Not why he went with her (Lisa), or what they did, or whether it was even any good. But why is it so important for me to have him?

As for Lisa, she's prettier than I am, I know. I'm honest enough about that. And she's pleasant. But I'm "bigger." She's sort of thin, and I always think of myself, objectively that is, as "comfortable." I mean, I should really be a fantastic piece! Ha.

Now I grant there are probably lots of reasons he went off with her. I mean, there I am, sitting with C.N. who

*is going on about something very depressing. From a
distance we probably looked like we were really into
something deep. And the few times I did look up and
catch his eye, I turned away. Not him. And too quickly.
Have got to cultivate some kind of smoldering stare.
But the real question is still why him? Why Peter
McSweeny? (For that, diary, is his name. I still don't
know why Sara is so impressed with him. Maybe it's his
family or something.) Being realistic, which I am most
of the time, there is nothing like "love" involved here.
I didn't even say hello to him. I'll stop and try to think
about this a minute.
Okay. Emotionally, I probably could like him. There's
a nice expectation on his face. He looks solid. He
probably could take care of someone very carefully and
gently. And he's clean. (Also, he's gorgeous, but that's
something else and not objective.)
I could do a lot worse!
For a first, I mean. He looks gentle. He probably has
done it a lot. I mean, he is appealing. Girls probably
break their asses to snare him. (Am I discovering a
raunchy side to me?) I wouldn't, of course. It's all well
and good to want "it," but you have to be fairly
straightforward about it. No point in tricking someone,
or getting all tarted up to lure a poor boy into the sack.
The thing is, being very, very honest, I want him for a
purpose. He seems to be the right "type," and I have
some important research to do. Soooo. . . .
Have made two revealing decisions (hee-hee). I won't
wear a bra tonight. And I'm going to stay as far away
from Charlie Neil as I can. Thirdly, now that I think
of it, I shall stand up all night, too, sort of turned
halfway toward him. He deserves another shot at the
big prize.*

5.

"What would you like?" Charlie Neil asked, struggling
to uncross his legs and stand.

"Anything," Tish said. "No, wait. A Fresca."

"Okay," said Charlie, twisting around Hank and Sara and
snaking between Fred Kennedy and a girl Tish didn't know.

Egad! Am I condemned to do this? thought Tish. *Just like last . . . where is he? Where is . . . ah!*

Tish turned in her chair. Peter McSweeny was standing in a corner, and a girl—Tish saw it was Lisa Stenner again— was talking at him. By her gestures and the way she stood, Tish felt instinctively that Lisa was after more of what she had had, or hadn't quite had, the night before.

Tish dropped her eyes and took a breath, straightening her posture as best she could in her chair. Her right hand crossed beneath her bosom and tightened the cashmere sweater she wore. Slowly, as though counting by numbers, Tish let her eyes raise again until she was looking directly, unblinkingly, at Peter McSweeny.

He looked back, over Lisa's shoulder. He looked back as directly as Tish looked at him. Then, suddenly, he threw back his head and laughed out loud. He put a hand on Lisa's shoulder and moved out of the corner.

"You can't really mean that," he said as he approached Tish's chair. He was still smiling.

"Well," Tish answered, "maybe not all of it. But enough."

"I'm Peter McSweeny. I hoped you'd be here again tonight."

"Like hell," Tish said clearly.

"What?"

"You didn't even look at me last night. I don't mind or anything. I mean, I'm an honest sort of person. That's just the truth."

Peter's face was momentarily blank. "Well," he said, after a minute, "I *sensed* you. You and your friend."

Tish nodded. "I just got rid of him," she announced. "Want to go upstairs?"

Peter's eyes widened, half in honest surprise, half by design. "Gangbusters," he said.

"No," Tish answered. "Just honest, like I said. Want to go upstairs?"

"Now?"

"I won't ask a third time."

"What's with you?" Peter asked, squatting near her chair. "You have to be home by midnight or else, poof! a pumpkin?"

Tish blushed, finally. "Listen," she said, "I'm really not all that experienced. It's just that I figured you might like the direct approach. It's easier for you. No guilt, or anything."

"Do I seem guilty?"

"No. But who knows? You could be."

"And I could be talking to some dimwit who's had two hours of a beginning survey in abnormal psych. Take it easy," Peter grinned. "What's your name?"

"Patricia Davies. Tish. I'm Sara's best friend."

"You are?"

"Of course."

"Of course. Well, Tish, I'll say this for you. You're different."

"Terrific!"

"I meant that nicely."

"Oh."

There was a moment's silence between them, as the music seemed to catch its second wind and come on once more, strongly and louder than before. Bodies in the playroom moved more quickly, from the waist down, and hands and arms waved frenetically in the air.

"You high?" asked Peter at last.

"No," said Tish. "But I've had a few glasses of wine. I hate to feel left out entirely."

"You ever tried meth or cocaine or anything?"

"Are you kidding? Forward maybe, but not dumb!"

"That's good," Peter judged, nodding his head.

"Why? Why should you care?"

"No reason, really," said Peter. "I just think life is pretty good by itself. It's all the hyper I ever need."

"Lisa Stenner's tried some of those other things," volunteered Tish, feeling instantly ashamed. "I'm sorry," she said quickly. "That was unkind."

"Yes, it was," Peter agreed. Then he smiled. "I assume you'd also like to know what we did last night."

Tish flushed. "Of course not! That's your business, and hers."

"That's what I think, too," said Peter.

Egad, ye gods above, what am I doing? thought Tish. Then: *dammit, I would like to know!*

Peter stood up and looked down at Tish. She sat without moving for a moment, ashamed and nervous. Then she looked up at him.

"I am trying to decide," said Peter deliberately, "whether it would be a good thing for us to be involved."

Tish gasped a little, letting the air out of her chest and forgetting to keep her sweater tight against her body.

"I mean," explained Peter, "I like to be honest, too, and try to look ahead."

"Well?" Tish asked.

"Well," Peter said. His eyes scanned the room before coming back to rest on Tish's face. "I guess it might not be so bad."

"Nothing like enthusiasm, I always say," Tish replied sharply, without thinking.

"Easy. Easy. I meant, I even rather like the fact that you were jealous before you could possibly have had any right to be. It sort of fits."

Tish held Peter's gaze a moment before smiling broadly. "You want to dance?" she said, half in jest.

Peter held out his hand to her and helped her stand. "I thought you'd never ask."

6.

March 11

Surprise of the year! He's moral! To a point. That point is that he doesn't want to do "it" around a lot of other people. He says it's something that's private and personal and between two people only. He doesn't want to be part of a circus . . . a sideshow.

I admit I was not disappointed.

Well, of course all this doesn't say what happened, D.D. What happened is that I made contact! Peter McSweeny, Peter McSweeny, Peter McSweeny. Looks nice, doesn't it? So much for Lisa Stenner.

Now that, D.D., almost got me in trouble last night. That kind of remark. No one likes a smart-ass, says Peter. I agree. I don't like myself that way either. But he was able, happily, thank God, to overlook my little failings . . . no doubt in part because of my tits. Hooo! We danced a lot last night. We met and talked and danced until I thought I'd drop. Which, secretly, I desperately wanted to do. How nice it would have been to be that tired and to be able to leave the party, go home, and go to bed . . . with him. Sort of easy and

natural and well adjusted. Is that what it feels like to
be married, I wonder.
Dumb, dumb, dumb! Those kinds of thoughts. Still—
I admit I like him. Really. I like Peter McSweeny. And
Peter McSweeny likes me.
Because it's important (posterity-wise) here's where
we are at the moment. We necked like crazy last night.
I let him feel me, and I liked it. It's quite different with
someone you really like, believe me, O my children. He
has soft, enormous hands. Melting would sound corny,
but that's what I did. I could hardly stand. Thank
goodness the lights were almost out. But I was oddly
proud. I almost wanted people to see what we were
doing, because it would have shown them that he was
mine! (I think I will probably be an incredibly jealous
woman.)
Incidentally, I was pretty busy with my hands, too. I
mean, it wasn't all one-sided with me your usual type
sex-object. I wasn't lewd or anything. But my hands
were under his sweater, and his shirt, and I am here to
say his skin is fantastic! Wow!
I seem to be rambling. D.D., no kidding, I'm going
slightly crazy with all this. I have to finish my English
assignment and somehow pull myself together by four.
He is coming over then and we're going somewhere.
Can you believe that by tonight, March 12th, I'll be a
woman? Only inches away this very minute—tee-hee.
Oh God!

7.

Peter held the umbrella over Tish's head as they ran for his car. Tish pulled the door open and jumped in as Peter ran around in front of the car.

"Well," he said, after he was in, "you get two choices. Either it's a rotten day, or this is romantic weather as ordered."

"Some of us would say rotten."

Tish hurtled around in her seat and looked behind her. "Hi," said a boy Peter's age.

Tish's startled face made the boy laugh. "Relax," he said. "I'm only here for Peter's protection."

"That smart-ass in the back seat," explained Peter, "is laughingly referred to as Poncho Olivera, one of my best friends."

Tish sighed. "About which part do you laugh?"

"The name, please," said Poncho. "I *am* his friend."

"I had lunch at Poncho's house," offered Peter further.

"Oh," Tish said, still at sea.

"It's good to see how the other half lives is what he means," Poncho said. "I'm the oldest of ten kids."

"You're kidding," said Tish.

"Not at all," assured Poncho. "The Catholic Church is largely responsible, of course. That, and the fact that my mother I guess likes it."

Peter started the car, and together he and Tish smiled. "That's a pretty good advertisement, isn't it?" Peter grinned.

"But what does your father do?" asked Tish. "To support you all, I mean?"

"Prays a lot!" replied Poncho.

"No, I'm serious."

"He works at the University. He's in charge of the grounds. A master-gardener I guess you'd call him. Being with Princeton and all, though, he gets a place to live. I guess he just took one look at the house and decided he felt obliged to fill it up."

"It's super, Tish," said Peter. "High on a hill, with lots of land, and a pool out back. Of course, no matter what happens, Poncho's old man can't afford ever to quit. He'd never find anything like it anywhere else."

"No chance of that, anyway," said Poncho. "Princeton is very paternal."

"But what about your mother? How does she do it?" Tish insisted.

"With the help of all of us. That's why Peter met you at Sara Wallace's, and not me."

"What do you mean?"

"Well, every so often I get to feeling sorry for my old man. I mean, with the kids and everything, he and Mom never get a chance to get off by themselves, to do anything special. So, every once in a while, like on a weekend, I take over. They can disappear for a night, anyway, and not worry too much."

"You must like your family," Tish said.

"Pretty much," Poncho admitted.

"The greatest bunch of nuts in Princeton Township," Peter added. "But fun. You'd like them."

The drive was a short one. Down Tish's Linden Lane, right on Nassau, past the campus and out the Lawrenceville Road. Suddenly, Peter signaled and turned off the road to his left. The car began a winding journey up a tree-shaded slope. It passed an enormous white frame house with pillars and swung around behind. Finally, Peter parked before a three-story garage.

"Uh . . . Peter?"

"Yes?"

"Wow!"

Peter laughed.

"Which one is your family's?" asked Tish. "The garage, or the big house?"

"Both," answered Peter, getting out of the car. Tish opened her door herself and stood on the gravel. "I live in the garage, though," Peter went on. "My father thought it was time I had some privacy."

"He really does sick experiments back there," Poncho whispered. "Wait—you're one of them!"

Tish laughed. Sort of.

The three walked up a wooden staircase that was attached to the garage and entered a second-floor living area. Tish took off her raincoat and shook it before she realized what she was doing. "Oh!" she exclaimed. "I'm really sorry. I wasn't even thinking."

"That's okay," said Peter. "Here, Poncho." Peter handed him the keys to his car. "You really think he can do it by seven?"

"Sure," said Peter's friend. "Sidney never promises unless he can produce."

"My car," Peter explained to Tish, "needs a little work. Someone Poncho's father knows at work is really good with things like that. Does it free, because he likes to tinker."

"Wait," said Poncho. "For you, maybe, a bill."

Peter laughed as Poncho opened the door to leave. "It was nice meeting you, Tish. Maybe I'll see you later."

"Bye," said Tish.

The door closed. Without moving, Tish and Peter listened
to Poncho's steps descending. They heard him crunch across
the drive, open the car door. He started the car and turned
slowly down the drive, the sound of tires on gravel
fading.

"Well," said Peter, turning and taking off his coat. "Let me
give you the fifty-cent tour."

Tish put out her hand and grabbed Peter's arm. "That was
a nice idea, Peter," she said softly.

"What?"

"Having Poncho here. Having a third person here to sort of
make me feel easier."

"Maybe he should have stayed a little longer."

"The thought was there, anyway," Tish said. "Now, the
tour."

Peter pulled Tish toward him and his arms went around
her. He did not try to kiss her. "This," he said, "is the living
room."

"Uh . . . right," Tish answered with a sly smile.

"And in there is the kitchen."

"Um-hmm."

"And the bathroom."

"Terrific."

"And the bedroom."

Tish paused a moment playfully. "It's *very* small."

Peter fidgeted. "There's a workroom upstairs, a studio kind
of thing."

"I'll take sugar in mine," said Tish, breaking away.

While Peter went into the kitchen to put water on the
stove, Tish stood in the center of the room. She was pale.
She knew she was. But she wasn't shaking.

She tried to pretend interest in what was around her. The
living room was big enough to hold a couch, an easy chair and
ottoman, and a portable color television set. There was a day-
bed in one corner, and a bookcase full of *National Geographic*.
There were three prints on the walls, all signed by someone
named Miró, whimsical bits of color. Tish turned on her heel.

"I'm going on the rest of the tour alone," she announced
loudly.

"Be with you in a minute," came Peter's reply.

"No. It's all right." Before Peter could reappear from the

kitchen, Tish had mounted the stairway behind the couch and started upwards.

She stood at the top of the stairs, nodding and smiling to herself. Here were all the things one would have expected a seventeen-year-old boy to have around. A desk, cluttered with books and papers. A set of weights in one corner. Hockey skates and a stick thrown in another. A few college pennants on the walls. A dartboard. Bookshelves nearly filled with paperbacks and texts. Lamps; an ash tray clean.

"Ready when you are, C.B.," came Peter's call.

Tish turned. She took a big breath and started back down the stairs.

In the living room, she selected the day-bed rather than the couch to sit on. Carefully, thinking all the time, she sat down, drawing her legs up onto the surface of the bed, lounging at one end. It wouldn't be easy for Peter to surprise her. Then, she remembered that she wanted him to surprise her, in a way. She wanted him to take charge. She sat up, away from the edge, and smiled at him, taking the cup of coffee.

He sat down next to her, holding his cup in both hands. He leaned forward and looked at the floor. "Well," he said. With a half-laugh, he added, "Here we are!"

Tish smiled into her cup. "I'll bet you say that to every girl."

Peter looked up at her questioningly.

"Listen," said Tish seriously, taking one of his hands in hers and putting her coffee down. "I don't know how I can say this, or why, but you know, Peter, we'll both feel better when it's over."

"I know," he said. "This really isn't the most idyllic way to go about things."

Tish frowned. Moral she liked, but not too moral. "Listen to the rain," she said, trying to be alluring. "We could be almost anywhere."

Praying that her hand would remain steady, she lifted Peter's hand to her breast. Peter put his coffee on the floor, and turned toward her. He leaned over and twisted around, putting his other arm around Tish's body. Very slowly and very gently, he kissed her.

Tish leaned back under the pressure of Peter's body, resting against the wall. Peter's mouth was on hers still. His eyes were closed. Her eyes were open. Then she closed them.

8.

March 12

*Why can't I get it out of my head that I've just seen
a movie? All the way home in the car, even at Peter's,
even while doing it, I had the sensation of watching a
film. Watching a typical young girl "awakened,"
as the ads say.*

*Well, world, I'm awake all right. How could I be
otherwise? No one expects me to come home, have
dinner, study, and go to bed for the old eight hours.
(It's now almost eleven p.m. I couldn't any more
not write in you, D.D., tonight than swim to Alaska.)
Well, I hear you shrieking, what happened?
Nosy, aren't you?*

*I feel compelled to write everything down, for posterity,
of course.*

*I know what all this sidewinding is about. I'm as
nervous about finally saying what happened and how
and whether or not I liked it as I ever was before doing
it. There are some words I'll probably never be able to
use.*

*I just sighed. My legs feel weak, even stretched out in
bed.*

Maybe I'm in shock.

*I should be. I was incredible! I seduced him! Which is to
say, I made it easier for him to seduce me.*

*Okay. It happened. It happened twice. The first time
wasn't so terrifically sensational. I was sort of detached.
I was, in the back of my mind, waiting for It. I expected
to be pierced with an awful pain, swimming in blood
and softly crying over the loss of my innocence. No
way. Peter, I guess, knew exactly what he was doing.
I mean he had me feeling things I never even imagined.
I was so busy feeling and trying to think about the
feelings and trying to think what to do to please him
that when It happened, finally, I hardly noticed.*

*Now, that's not altogether true. Yes, I felt something.
Yes, it did hurt, a little, for a moment. But by that time,
honey, it's too late to worry.*

Peter was very clever. I'll never know if he actually had

thought, step by step, how to go about it, but he was
nibbling on my neck and hugging me so hard I had
hardly any breath when It went in. Then he stopped a
minute. I must have gasped, and he clearly knew what
was best . . . to wait a moment, I mean, to let me get
used to it. Does one ever really get used to it? I tried.
I tried to relax. He told me to relax and I did, sort of.
Enough, anyway, for matters to proceed on schedule.
His schedule, I admit, was a bit ahead of mine.
Afterwards, we did *feel better being with each other. I*
admit, D.D., that except for little boys, I had never seen
a grown man in the altogether before. Peter, I am here
to tell you, is beautiful. I won't go on about this . . . it
might seem pornographic.
But I like *his body.*
We had coffee, and it was beginning to get dark about
five or so. We talked a bit. (The reason why Sara is so
impressed with Peter has to be that his father is
self-made and fantastically successful. Sara's mother
probably had Peter picked out and Sara made the
mistake of glomming onto Hank before she found out
how groovy Peter is.)
We laughed about little things. He did most of the
talking, as though he wanted to tell me things he hadn't
told anyone else. (Being honest, is that romanticizing
things?) During all this, we were nude. We touched
each other a little, in friendship. It was all very nice and
soft and every minute I expected to hear music
somewhere. The rain came down once in a while, which
was music enough.
And, D.D., we did it again! It was the most natural thing
in the world. And O so much better the second time!
I began memorizing Peter's skin, special parts of his
back and his sides. I know what his neck looks like, pore
by pore, and what his mouth is like in every corner. I
have to say that everything people say about It is
certainly pretty close to being true. (I'm hedging a bit
there, D.D. Because whatever a climax is, I don't think I
had one. I'm not complaining, mind you. But I just think
it didn't happen. No zings or anything where it is
supposed to count.)
One of the nicest things is that Peter didn't just roll off

and go to sleep, the way people in books are always
doing. He's too considerate for that. He cares too much
about the other person. Of course, I was dying to talk
about things that really mattered . . . like how many
times he'd done it, and with whom, and how I compared
first time around. I couldn't naturally. I'd be terrified
of the answers. But in my heart of hearts I'm starving to
know all that. Maybe sometime, years from now, if we
meet in New York or somewhere and have a drink
together, I can ask if he remembers those things. I'm
certain he will. He strikes me as the kind of boy who
remembers everything.
Anyway, here I am a woman at last! And you know
what, I don't feel so different. It's sort of disappointing,
this part of it. No one can just look and tell I know
about things. That I'm part of the grown-up world for
real now. My father asked the usual questions at dinner,
and I gave the usual answers. My mother was intent on
some sort of club meeting she has to entertain tomorrow
for lunch. Tommy, as always, is somewhere deep inside
his own head. And I just floated through as I usually do.
Except, of course, that I am different now. I wonder
how Peter feels . . . about me. I wonder how I feel
about him. I was right, D.D., in picking him to be the
first. Maybe the reasons were a little weak, but the
decision was the right one.
Guess what? I'm happy. And tired. Good night, D.D.
Good night, Peter. Good night, Chet. Good night,
David.
Hello, World!

9.

Tish walked briskly out of Bellows, smiling to herself, feeling very much the April Fool for having bought what she did.
She didn't need anything, really. But life had been too good
lately not to have celebrated in some sort of juvenile fashion,
she felt. The long skirt under her arm was just right for
Peter's apartment: sexy but sensible. It made her feel ultra-
feminine, and she liked that feeling since she had decided
that clearly that was what she was. Peter McSweeny was still
hers.

She shook her head in wonderment and secret delight as she passed Gene Seal's Flower Shop. On an impulse, she walked in and ordered two bunches of freesias to be delivered to her mother.

That took most of what money she was carrying, but she still had five dollars, more than enough for the sophisticated lunch she anticipated with Sara at the Annex. A Bloody Mary (after a bald lie about her age), and then a hamburger and coffee.

She knew what Sara wanted to talk about. Knowing this made her feel very secure and grown-up. Of course, she wouldn't say anything personal. What she and Peter did was strictly between themselves, as two mature, affectionate adults. Let Sara eat her heart out.

Tish frowned. At least she hoped Sara would remember to bring the pills.

She walked down the steps into the darkened restaurant slowly, unbuttoning her coat. She stood at the doorway of the room, looking through the half-light for the familiar face. She found it: Sara had snagged a table along a wall and was waving at her.

"You're being cruised," Sara whispered as Tish sat opposite her.

"Where?" Tish asked, looking around as nonchalantly as she could.

"Over there. That boy, with his parents."

Tish looked where Sara directed. A man and a woman and a younger man were seated finishing their lunch, lingering a moment over coffee. "Probably going to the baseball game or some dumb thing," Tish decided aloud.

"He's not bad," Sara estimated. "Probably just a freshman, though. Too young."

"Not for me," Tish said laughing. "Mine is younger still!"

The waitress came and winked at the girls when they gave their orders. Sara took a pack of cigarettes from her purse and lit one. "It's ages since we've really talked," she said, exhaling.

"I see you every day in school."

"No, I mean *really* talked."

"You mean about Peter and me."

"Exactly."

"There's nothing to say, Sara," Tish said solemnly.

"Oh, come on!" Sara was annoyed. "I'm your oldest and dearest friend. It's me you have to thank for even meeting him."

"I did thank you."

"Yes, you did. Well, I mean, what's he like? Come on!"

Tish smiled. "He's a very nice person."

"Argh!" Sara exploded, just as the waitress approached with their drinks.

For a moment neither girl spoke, as the woman put down their Bloody Marys, still smiling to herself and amused at their pretense. Finally she walked away.

"You're really going to hold out, aren't you?" Sara guessed.

"Come on, Sara," said Tish. "Really. It's not as though you haven't done these things yourself."

"But people do things differently!" Sara explained. "I mean, if there are a thousand positions, there are probably a thousand more we never heard of."

"Well," Tish relented, "for your information, we're fairly standard. So far."

"Is he . . . is he . . . big?"

"How would I be able to say? I have nothing to compare."

"You are the most exasperating person in the world!"

"I'm sorry," Tish said, half-meaning it.

"If I tell you all about Hank and me, and about him especially, will you share Peter with me? Verbally, of course."

"Sara," Tish said slowly, "you already *have* told me about Hank."

The waitress returned with their sandwiches. In silence both girls began to eat.

Tish stirred her coffee. "Did you remember the pills?"

Sara sat back in her chair with a thud. "My God!" she said. "I completely forgot! Are you desperate for them?"

"No, not desperate. I'd just feel a little better. It was terrific of you to offer."

"I still don't see why you don't get your own."

"You know my mother," Tish replied. "She'd die if she even suspected her little baby was busy on the side. And Dr. Nelson and I just never developed that kind of relationship where we could talk about these things."

"Well, I'm sorry I forgot. I'll bring them to school Monday. You'll be okay till then?"

Tish laughed. "I *am* okay, Sara. Really. I had my period. Everything's in working order. After all, Peter and I don't do it every day, you know."

Sara sighed. "I don't know how you do it, making up all those stories for your family and all."

"It's not as hard as all that."

"I mean, with me it's different. My mother thinks it's just too, too divine that I'm seeing someone from *the college*. She loves it when I say I'm going to a play or a concert at McCarter or something with Hank. She thinks it's just wonderfully healthy."

"Isn't it?"

"Well, *I* think so. You know, Tish, the part I like best about everything is that it's supposed to get better all the time."

"Like how?"

"Well," Sara began, "I'm enjoying it now, of course. But I was reading a book the other day which said that women reach their sexual peak at about thirty. Just think, all that time to warm up!"

"It seems to me you're already pretty fiery."

"Well, I suppose I am. Aren't you? Don't you like it? I mean, just thinking about it before, doesn't it get you all worked up? Don't you feel sort of flushed and weak and then empty until you've done it?"

"Egad!" Tish laughed. "You should write all that down for *Cosmopolitan!*"

Sara nodded. "I'm very purple prose, that's true."

10.

April 11

Enough of all this babbling. I've just read your last few pages, D.D., and it's pretty soapy. There are other things happening in my life. I'm sure there are.
Oh! A bit of trauma in English today. Problem: longish assignment on Milton, 2,000 words. Pretty steep and heavy, especially if you're not fond of Paradise Lost. *When I told Mother about it, she positively gaped. She hadn't even looked at Milton until she was a sophomore*

*in college. Helpful as always though, she went up into
the attic and found some of her old papers. It just
happened there was one about Milton and imagery, for
which (admittedly 21 years ago) she had gotten an A–.
Who's to know, we decided. I recopied it, and reworded
some parts. I mean, I am devoted to the study of the
English language (which is to say I like reading and
words), but the relevance of J.M. is somewhat distant.
Handed it in on Friday, confident of snowing ye olde
teacher-e. Hah!*

*No need to tell you what the actual mark was. Enough
to say I snuck by, with comments like "sounds infantile,
coming from you"; "are you sure you mean to use this
word?"; "seems incompletely developed." My mother
doesn't know, of course. It would kill her. Ah well . . .
crime still doesn't pay.*

*Just a little about Peter now. He is absolutely dreamy!
That sounds infantile, but it's true. I am getting to be
very fond of him (which is a good thing!). Note, D.D.,
I'm hedging again. "Love" is a word that is simply not
going to be used until I'm absolutely sure. (Is anyone,
ever?) I keep finding out about him when we meet. For
example, he's much brighter than I am. The books he
reads I've never even heard of, let alone heard the names
of their authors. Here's one: Carlos Castaneda. Mean
anything to you? I thought not. Anyway, he's into a lot
of weird things, like "existential time," whatever that
means. Arthur Clarke. He can tell you the names of
every Nobel winner in physics for the past fifteen years.
He's dying to be eighteen so he can get into politics.
Even now he drives people to the polls, and mails letters,
and makes telephone calls. He's very McGovern, which
he says drives his father wild.*

*But for all the head-things he does, he's normal, too.
Of course, he's that way in bed. I mean, he's about
where he should be for his age. In spite of the fact that
he's Catholic, he's just like people at my school. He's
an end on Notre Dame's football team, though he says
he's not really that keen on football. The problem is he's
tall and pretty fast and to say he didn't want to play
would sort of be turning away from an obligation, a
duty. He's the only person I've ever met for whom I*

*could use the word "altruistic." What he really likes is
swimming. He's a superstar in a pool, and he swims
dashes (are they called sprints?) and relays, both. He
says he loves the freedom he feels gliding through the
waves. Probably very embryonic or wombish or
something, floating around in fluid.*

*He's decided to go to Yale, and then to Harvard Law if
he can get in. Then again, half the time he gets confused
and says it the other way around, which would be
terrific, too. He's very serious about becoming "an adult,"
a word he uses a lot and I never do. And, also, I think
he is getting to be very fond of me. I hope so. It's not as
though my world revolves around his. Not in any way.
I'm still my own girl. But the idea isn't as frightening as
all that. And I don't think that if the idea has occurred
to him, too, that it frightens him, either. Tomorrow I
am meeting his parents and having dinner at their home.
It's a good thing I'm clearheaded, or I could assume a
lot of things and get myself in a hell of a lot of trouble.*

11.

The bumper sticker on the rear of the Mercedes told her
a lot, but Tish admitted silently that she was unprepared for
Mr. McSweeny's lapel pin.

She and Peter had had a glass of wine above the garage
before walking across the gravel and in the back door of the
McSweenys' house. Jokingly, Tish had suggested perhaps this
would be the time to share a joint. But only half-jokingly.
She told herself that there was no reason to be nervous, but
she was. In the back of her mind, practical and pragmatic
though she knew she was, was the thought that this might
very well be her first visit with her future in-laws. She shook
her head and tried to empty it of such romantic fantasies,
but in vain.

Mr. McSweeny held her hand in his longer than Tish was
prepared for. She withdrew it after a moment and then, for
only the first time, she looked straight up at him. She had
to, for he was as tall as Peter.

"No need to be shy, young lady," said Mr. McSweeny pa-
ternally. "Peter's mother and I like to meet *all* his friends."

He looked down at Tish thoughtfully. "I suspect you *are* the shy type, though."

"No, I'm not," Tish said quickly. "But I like to observe before committing myself."

Mr. McSweeny laughed, turned, and led the two young people into the dining room. "That's good," he said. "That means you can still be educated. That your ears are still clean and empty of a lot of the junk Peter has in his."

"Hello, Tish," said a sleek woman through a swinging door from the kitchen. "I'm Peter's mother."

"How do you do?" said Tish politely, trying to look quickly and carefully at Mrs. McSweeny without seeming obvious.

"We thought instead of having drinks first, we'd go right in to dinner, and then, later, perhaps we can have a brandy," Mrs. McSweeny said, moving toward a large mahogany table at which four places were set. "Tish, you sit here, on my right."

While Peter's father asked him something about school, Tish studied Mrs. McSweeny at the head of the table. What she saw was an attractive, well-kept woman, somewhere in her forties, Tish guessed, with natural black hair and a lineless face which somehow still had a tan; looked as though it had had color all through the winter months. She was dressed simply, and Tish felt expensively, pearl earrings her only ornament.

Tish had the feeling that Mrs. McSweeny was looking her over, too, or perhaps had even done so in the few seconds they had all been standing. Tish felt very young.

The swinging door opened and a woman in uniform appeared and began to serve the soup. Tish looked down at her place setting, calming herself. Then she looked at Mr. Mc-Sweeny.

He was looking at her. "Relax," he said with a smile. "We're the most ordinary people in the world."

"For a self-made man," Peter added mockingly.

"My son tells me that I announce my background, or lack of it," Mr. McSweeny laughed, "to everyone I meet. Right off. So there should be no mistake about who's who and how good."

"Peter's quite right, dear," said his wife. "You do. Both Peter and Bosey just like to beat you to the punch."

"Bosey's my girl," Mr. McSweeny told Tish. "She's a bit

of her mother, though. A sometime snob."

"George!" said Mrs. McSweeny laughing.

"Well, it's true," he said. "You and she care about a lot of things I don't. Even Peter here sometimes gets delusions of gentility."

"I think Peter is genteel," Tish said defensively.

"Thank you, ma'am," Peter grinned at her.

"Where is your daughter?" Tish asked Mr. McSweeny, knowing the answer.

"I'm told at a fashionable boarding school. In Washington."

"Where she is studying Affectations One, just to get Dad's goat at vacation time," offered Peter.

"I'll give her the goat if she is," said his father. "You see, Tish, my career is a little checkered. I wasn't always a loud, successful reactionary Republican. I started small."

Tish smiled, and then began to nod her way through the soup, listening to Peter's father. The end of the Depression. His first job. His first bankruptcy. A moment of comparative flush, when he had two-not-one-but-two Cadillacs. Unfortunately he hadn't money enough to pay for gas for either. His first successful job with Montgomery Ward's.

Mrs. McSweeny sat smilingly through it all. From time to time, when she dared, Tish looked across at Peter, who winked back at her. She felt oddly comfortable and warm among strangers. Peter's wink.

Lamb and baby potatoes and LeSueur peas and mint sauce, accompanied by Mr. McSweeny's narration of moving west, working in some dimly discussed position at Twentieth-Century-Fox. Beginning to put a little aside for emergencies, feeling a little more solid. Coming east for a holiday. Meeting Mrs. McSweeny, née Payson, and marrying her.

"Correction, George," said Mrs. McSweeny at this point. "You didn't marry the boss's daughter. She married you!"

Mr. McSweeny laughed easily and admitted this was true. That his wife had pursued him without shame.

"Why?" asked Tish, realizing instantly that her question had been unbelievably rude.

Mrs. McSweeny looked blank a moment, but then she smiled. "Because of George's untapped potential," she said. "He didn't know what he could do, but I did. Also, at that point, I convinced myself he needed me. Of course, he did."

"My wife, coming from a fairly impressive sort of family,

was used to buying and training horses. She simply continued to use that talent."

"George, I also loved you."

"Ah, true, true," said Mr. McSweeny. "Still do, too."

Mrs. McSweeny smiled softly then, for the first time, and Tish felt her question hadn't been as far out of bounds as it had seemed.

Dessert was accompanied by the rise of George McSweeny, investment counselor and stock wizard.

"George," Peter's mother interrupted over coffee, "one of the reasons we asked Peter to bring Tish around was to find out something about *her*."

"We have," said Mr. McSweeny quickly. "That she's a wonderful listener. A very important trait, young man, if you're looking into the future at all."

Peter blushed.

"Come, Tish," Mrs. McSweeny said, standing. "Tell us about yourself in the library. We'll have our brandy there."

Tish stood, frantically wondering what to say that could possibly be of interest to Peter's parents. She looked at Peter as they walked together, following the older couple, and shrugged her shoulders.

"They really would rather hear about you," Tish whispered.

"You're doing just fine," Peter whispered in return, pinching her arm a little to reassure her.

"Suppose I tell them," she whispered back, "that you're a terrific lay?"

Peter's eyes opened at the same time his mouth did. "I dare you!" he said laughing.

What she did instead, in the library over brandy, was ask the McSweenys questions about Peter and Bosey. Both McSweenys happily recalled events and accidents and ideas of their children without seeming to be aware that they were monopolizing the evening further. Whenever a pause threatened, and Tish worried lest one or the other remember that they had asked to hear about her, she would lean forward and earnestly ask something else.

"She's quite a young lady," said Mr. McSweeny to Peter as the evening ended. The four were standing on the back porch. "Bring her back again, son," he added.

"I probably will," Peter admitted, "after she's recovered."

"If she recovers, you mean, sweetheart," said his mother,

playfully kissing Peter's cheek. "Tish, do come again. I'm sorry we rambled on so, but getting us to do that is quite a feat in itself. It was lovely seeing you."

Tish shook hands with Mrs. McSweeny, and the older woman smiled warmly at her.

"It's a soft night, for April," observed Mr. McSweeny. "Don't be too long taking this young woman home, Peter." He winked at his son and patted his shoulder. Then he turned and followed his wife into the house.

After the short drive, during which Tish had comfortably leaned against Peter's shoulder but said nothing, Peter pulled his car to a halt before Tish's house. She roused herself and sat up, looking at him. Then she smiled.

"I don't think I've ever been so tired," she said.

"You were sensational," Peter said. "I know how hard it was."

"My ears are hoarse," Tish confided with a giggle. Then she kissed Peter quickly and ran up the walk.

12.

Tish nearly stumbled and plummeted down the stairway. The phone had rung three times. She was home alone, but had forgotten.

"Hello?" she said breathlessly into the receiver.

"Tish?"

"Oh Sara, hi," said Tish, trying to catch her breath.

"You sound like you're just out of the tub or something," Sara said.

"I was working on that damned French assignment. I don't think I was ever intended to speak French with any kind of accent whatever."

"Listen, are you and Peter busy Saturday?"

Tish thought. Smiling to herself, she made her voice sound disappointed. "Oh, damn, we are! Why?"

"Well, Hank and I thought we'd do something, nothing special or anything, just fool around somewhere. I sort of wanted company."

Something in Sara's tone pulled Tish to attention. "Why?" she asked. "What's up?"

"Well, I don't know. It's just that . . . Listen. Have you,

have you ever . . . well, I mean, have you ever . . . done Peter?"

"What are you talking about? Done Peter?"

Sara sighed. "I mean, have you ever, uh, taken him in your mouth?"

Tish reddened. "Sara Wallace, I am a junior in high school. What would I be doing that for?"

"Well, I only wanted to ask, is all."

Tish thought a minute. Something more was in Sara's voice. "Sara," she said quietly, "what's the matter?"

Sara sniffled over the phone. She did not speak for a second. "Well, I guess it's not unusual or anything," she said finally. "Unnatural is what I really mean, I guess."

"All right," Tish said encouragingly. "So what?"

"Well, it's just that Hank sometimes . . . sometimes likes to do it that way. Have it done that way, I mean."

"You don't have to do it, you know, Sara. Just tell him."

"Oh, I couldn't. It would upset him. He thinks I'm terrifically free and liberal and all that."

"Well, set him straight, then," advised Tish.

"No, no, I just couldn't. I want him to think I'm a wanton woman. Sort of. It's just that . . . well . . ."

"Yes?"

"Well, Tish, I just want to say that that is a highly over-rated practice. And—" Sara's voice broke. "And . . . it's very unsatisfying for the woman!"

There was a "click" and Tish held a toneless receiver in her hand.

13.

April 23

> *Today is Sunday, and I'm writing in the right space at the wrong time. But I couldn't write last night. I needed time to come down.*
> *You're frowning, D.D. Relax. The McSweenys went into New York for a show and dinner afterwards, which meant that Peter and I could stay in his house for hours and hours without worrying. About anything.*
> *So we did. He picked me up around three. I told Mother*

*we were all (Sara and Hank and Peter and I) having
dinner somewhere and then going to see a play at
McCarter. (Doubly guilty that made me, insofar as Sara
seems to be in extremis with Hank . . . again.) I was
clear that way until almost midnight, at least, and
maybe, depending on how tired Daddy was, until even
longer. (Good old Daddy. His question and my answers
are still the same. "Usual stuff?" "Usual stuff." Oh,
wow!)*

*Anyway, I set about cooking supper, if you can believe
it. I picked something fairly cheap but that made a lot,
that was sort of splashy and yet just needed to be put in a
casserole. Chicken and dumplings, if you must know.
The most awful thing, though: after Peter and I spent
about twenty dollars at Davidson's, getting everything
the* New York Times Cookbook *called for . . . on our
way out, in the frozen food department, we saw a
Checkerboard Square Frozen Dinner—chicken and
dumplings for four for something like $1.49! Terrific.
Anyway, I followed directions and did everything I
was supposed to and we put the top on the casserole and
that was that. Well, then what do you think? Peter
pulled out some pot. We were at home, he said, and
didn't have to do anything, and neither one of us had
ever had sex after smoking. I was game enough. I mean,
even after I told him that I'd been smoking for years and
nothing that terrific ever seemed to happen. He said just
relax. Stop sucking in and holding and going through
all that show biz stuff. Just smoke. So I did. I probably
had three or four joints all by myself. Surprise, surprise
—something finally happened.*

*Not wild colors or anything, or fantastic visions, or
voices out of the night. Just sensible things: like time
standing still. Peter and I made love. For ages, it seemed
—loose, free, happy. We laughed and snuggled and
dozed and got hungry. I touched him in places I'd never
even planned to. He is so soft! (most of him, tee-hee!)
Anyway, dinner couldn't help but be a smashing
success. Which it was. D.D., you should have watched
those Bisquick dumplings grow. Unbelievable! I think I
could be a fairly accomplished cook if I put my mind*

to it. I mean, if you can read, you can cook, right? It's a
good thing I'm beginning to take an interest in that,
anyway. Because, D.D., I fear a worm is in the apple.

14.

Sara and Tish walked slowly out of Buxton's, daintily nibbling at their ice cream cones. They turned, carefully avoiding
pedestrians in more hurry than they. The plan was to check
Thorne's for new cosmetics, then see if anything interesting
could be had more cheaply at Woolworth's, or at the discount
drugstore farther along Nassau Street.

"I still don't see why I couldn't just have come by your
house," Sara said, her mouth half-open, rolling ice cream
around in it.

"I just wanted to get out," Tish replied. "Besides, I wanted
a treat of some kind."

"Ice cream is a pretty chintzy treat," Sara observed.

"True," Tish admitted, "but I figure I better hold on to
what I've got for a while." She looked sideways at Sara, who
was looking straight ahead. "I think I've got the big disease."

"Poverty?"

"Not if you mean physically."

Sara stopped and turned to look at Tish. She examined her
friend's face carefully. "Are you telling me what I think
you're telling me?" she asked finally.

"Only if you're thinking that I'm telling you what you
think I'm telling you."

"You're pregnant?"

Tish began to walk ahead. She nodded, squinting into the
warm May sunlight. "All precincts haven't reported yet, but
on the basis of Voter Profile Analysis, it certainly looks that
way."

"Where can we talk?" Sara wondered urgently.

"Right here, as we're walking. Less of a crisis atmosphere
that way."

"No," Sara objected. "We have to sit down and really have
a *talk!*"

Tish nodded. They turned out walked silently a while, then
crossed Nassau Street and then Washington Road, entering the
Princeton campus.

The ground was dry. Buds were rapidly becoming honest

leaves, and the air as they walked toward the Library cleansed itself of the soot and exhaust of Nassau Street. The noise around them abated until the only disturbing sounds were steps of others around them, or an occasional shout. At a wall of a dormitory, they saw a boy trying to scale the stone, grip over grip, to reach his room.

"What's he doing that for?" Tish asked. "Why doesn't he just go in the front door?"

"It's a weird craze," Sara explained. "Hank says that everybody's doing it. It's exercise. Shows how strong and resourceful you are, or something."

They walked further, each thinking her own thoughts. Finally, on the grassy side of a Henry Moore sculpture, they sat on the ground. Tish sighed and leaned back, lying fulllength, her legs crossed at the ankles. Sara sat upright but turned anxiously over Tish, looking down at her. "When did you find out?" she asked.

Tish smiled to herself, her eyes closed against the sun. "It wasn't apocalyptic or anything," she said. "I mean, after a while, all the signs added up."

"You missed your period?"

"Yes."

"How long ago?"

"Three weeks, maybe a little more."

Sara sat quietly a moment. "It could be something else," she murmured.

"Cervical cancer, a good cold, intestinal blockage," Tish nodded to herself. "It isn't. Other than this one tiny little thing, I'm in perfect health."

"But sometimes your system gets clogged. Things slow down. Your period just doesn't come right on schedule."

"I know all that, Sara," Tish said, opening her eyes and looking at the branches over her. "Listen, believe me when I say I know I'm pregnant."

"Did you go to your doctor?"

"Are you kidding?"

Again both girls were silent.

"What can I do?" Sara asked gently.

"You could ask Hank," Tish said. "I mean, with girls at the college and everything, someone must know the name of a . . . of a good doctor in New York."

"You want to abort?"

"Probably," Tish said emotionlessly.

"Have you got the cash?"

"How can I know until I know what it costs?" Tish answered. "Maybe Hank could research that, too."

Sara threw herself down on her stomach, crossing her arms beneath her and leaning on them. "Are you going to tell Peter?"

"I don't know," Tish answered honestly.

"Shouldn't you?"

"I should," admitted Tish. "I mean, I know I really should. But I don't think I want to."

"He would want to know."

"Why?" Tish asked, leaning up on an elbow to look at Sara. "What could he do?"

"Well, two things I suppose," Sara said. "He could give you the money you need. He could marry you."

"I knew you'd say that," Tish frowned. "I knew it."

"Well, it's true, isn't it? Both things."

Tish nodded.

Sara let her head fall onto her arms and closed her eyes. "It wouldn't be so bad, you know. Marrying Peter. I mean, you'd be fantastically provided for."

Tish remained silent.

"Do you love him?" Sara asked after a moment.

Tish played with the grass. "Who knows?" she asked in return.

"Does he love you? Has he ever said so?"

Tish moved her head negatively. "But I think, probably, he does. A little."

"He'd have to, a little, wouldn't he?" Sara asked.

"I don't know," Tish wondered. "Does a boy have to fall in love with every girl he sleeps with? I doubt it."

"But to do it a lot," Sara encouraged. "I mean, there would have to be some feeling there. Hank has some feeling, I think. I hope."

Tish grinned suddenly and punched Sara in the ribs. "Between his legs, anyway!" she laughed.

"Tish Davies, this isn't something you can laugh about!" Sara said angrily.

Tish shook her head. "Yes, it is. It is, it is! You have to."

Sara sighed and rolled on her back.

Tish rested her head on her hand, looking down at Sara now. "You have to, Sara. I mean, here we are, two perfectly intelligent people. It's not as though neither of us knew nothing about sex. I mean, about . . . about preventing these little accidents."

"Well," said Sara, "it couldn't have happened recently. I mean, you've had the pills for a while now."

"Yes, it could. The pills aren't foolproof," Tish laughed, but not bitterly. "Nothing is proof against a fool, Sara."

Sara sat up quickly. "You mustn't blame yourself."

"Why not?"

"Well," Sara said slowly, "you just shouldn't. Peter's as much to blame as you are."

"Sara, he's *Catholic*."

"Would the Pope have known?"

15.

"Notice how the days are already getting longer?" Peter asked, as he and Tish stepped around a puddle. The Raritan Canal trail led them over fallen winter logs and through brown, grassy thickets, small and friendly ones with few thistles, along water that mirrored freshly green trees and a swiftly moving sky.

"I'm glad," Tish said, grinning. "I like to play outside after supper."

Peter put his arm around Tish's shoulder. "Why do I keep getting the feeling you're brittle?"

"Brittle?"

"Wit, with only an ounce of wisdom."

"Very funny."

"And grouchy."

"Well, it's just that I've got something on my mind."

Peter laughed. "You're pregnant! You've been in a funk trying to figure how to tell me!"

"Are you serious?"

Peter lifted his arm from Tish's shoulder and tousled her hair. "Relax, can't you? Everybody's got problems. What is it? Another assigned saga on Milton?"

Tish stopped walking and turned to face Peter. Her expression was calm, but also severe. "No, it is not Milton again. What it is, smart-ass, is that I *am* pregnant!"

Without waiting for Peter to speak, Tish strode ahead,

briskly walking through struggling new clover and crushing it underfoot. It seemed to her a very long time before Peter finally found his way to catch her.

When he did, it was his face that had become calm, solemn and thoughtful. He grabbed Tish's hand and turned her around to face him. Without speaking, he then let her go and took off his jacket, spreading it on the damp, canalside and, with one hand, he pulled her down to sit with him on it. For a long moment, they simply stared at one another.

"You look like you're going to cry," Tish observed. "It's not your fault."

Peter's face struggled to realign itself into something resembling an expression of hope and strength. "I'm sorry. I was just sort of . . . well, I mean irony is one thing but . . . does it sound stupid to say I wasn't really expecting you to say that?"

"Yes," Tish answered firmly. "To me, not to you." Peter nodded that he understood. "It's not your fault, Peter. I'm not blaming you or calling you dirty names or anything like that."

"I thought you were on the pill," he said lamely.

"I was, most of the time."

"Then it was early, before . . .?"

"I don't know," Tish admitted. "Who can tell? The pill isn't infallible, you know. It could have been when I was taking it."

Peter sighed. "Oh, wow," he said under his breath.

"Don't get all tensed up. I'm not going to have it."

Peter's head snapped up. He looked hard at Tish. "Yes, you are."

"Peter," Tish began, remembering to speak slowly and patiently, "think what that would mean. I'd have to drop out of school. Make up all kinds of incredible excuses. Disappear for a while. Come back as though nothing had happened, and never know where the child was or what he looked like or whether he even survived. There's no question of my having it and bringing it home to raise it as a part of our family. My parents would die of shame. They will anyway, if they ever find out." Tish stopped and drew a big breath. "I am not forgetting the other possibility, Peter. But I'm not pushing for it, or holding you in any way responsible. You have your future to think about, too, and your own family."

Peter's eyes had not left Tish's as she spoke. But they had widened in surprise. "You really have thought all this out, haven't you?" he asked.

"Yes, I have," Tish's answer was firm and not defensive. "I've had a couple weeks to look at it in every light. Sara and Hank are lining up a doctor for me. I've enough money in my savings account to do it in New York. I'm not asking you for a thing."

Tish sat back and smiled a little. "So, you see, Peter McSweeny, you're perfectly free and clear to go on being the wonderful Peter McSweeny you are. No bitterness, no recriminations, no scenes now that this one is over."

"What makes you think it's over?"

"Well, it is, that's all," said Tish. "Now you know. And now it's up to me to follow through."

"All right," Peter said. "Is the performance finished? Everything you rehearsed you've said, right?"

Tish blushed.

"You really think I'm small, don't you, Tish?"

"What on earth do you mean?"

"Your opinion of me is so low that you just naturally assume I wouldn't lift a finger to help, or take the responsibility." Peter wasn't angry, but disappointed. Tish knew the difference.

"Look, Peter. All I'm trying to do is set your mind at rest. I got myself into this, and I can get out. No sweat, really."

A piece of underbrush snapped. Peter and Tish turned, startled, to see another young couple walking along the canal trail, arm in arm. The newcomers smiled and reddened as they stepped around Peter and Tish and then continued on the path toward Griggstown.

"Cute, aren't they?" Tish said, in spite of herself.

"Is the performance finally over, Tish?"

Tish looked back at Peter, and smiled. "Yes."

"Good. First of all, you have to have the baby."

Tish started to shake her head "no."

"Yes, you do, Tish. It's my child. I want to see whether I'm any good at this."

Tish grinned automatically. "You are," she said. "Oh, boy, are you ever!"

Peter smiled in return. "Apart from that, I like kids. I like the very idea of having kids."

"And naturally you don't care about the very ideas of Yale and Harvard? About all the other plans you've told me? That's all make-believe?"

Peter's face clouded. "No, it wasn't. I wanted those things. I still do. And I'll still have them."

At the same time, they both said, "It will just take a little longer, that's all."

They were surprised to be so in tune and they laughed after a startled moment.

"All right," Peter began, his eyes moving very quickly, stopping frequently to look deep into Tish's to see, almost, whether she believed what he was saying. "The first thing to understand is that I'd *like* to marry you. I might even have fallen in love without this little push. With it, loving's a necessity. We both can accept that, I think. We don't have to get married. We want to. You don't have to have the child. I want you to."

Peter took one of Tish's hands in his and spoke even more earnestly, as though to convince himself as well as Tish. "In time, the idea of having a baby and living together— all of us, as a family—will really grab you. I know it will. It does me. The idea of being a father, though the reality may have come a little early, really really appeals to me."

"What about the reality of being a husband?" Tish asked. "The reality of dropping out, of having to get a job instead of floating through college?"

Peter smiled with just a hint of condescension, as though in the past few minutes he had had more than enough time to make decisions, to select the important thoughts from a barrel of inconsequential ones. "Listen, there are such things as responsibility, too, you know. And things like duty, and honor, and cherishing each other. They must be as important, more even, than giving up those things."

"That scares me, Peter," Tish admitted suddenly. "Looking at something like this philosophically. Duty and honor. Peter, this is a practical problem!"

Peter nodded. "I know that," he said. "But you have to let

me solve it my way, Tish. If I have to fall back and believe things I was taught as a little boy, about love and duty and responsibility, better that, for God's sake, than arranging a marriage for ten months and then planning an annulment."

Tish's eyes opened in surprise. "Who mentioned that?"

"No one. But one or the other of our parents will, I promise you. We have to make them understand we are grown human beings, and as such, perfectly capable of making our own decisions."

"Like deciding to have a child."

"Yes!" Peter said very firmly. "Like that. That and living together and marrying and working together."

"Peter," Tish interrupted. "Can I ask you a personal question? And do you promise to answer honestly if I do?"

"Go ahead."

"Does having the child have anything to do with . . . your religion?"

Peter stared at Tish. Then he shook his head. "It didn't even enter my mind, the sanctity of human life and all that. What did enter it was that the child is mine, and yours. That I want to see it, to see it grow up, to grow up with it."

"Will it, he or she, be Catholic?" Tish asked softly. "I mean, are your parents going to want to insist?"

"I doubt it. It's only Mother who pretends any more to care about that. I've always thought her feelings had more to do with her image of herself as a Catholic Gentlewoman, whatever that is, than with anything else. Also, I guess she felt it important to give Bosey and me some sort of training. It's the easiest kind, you know. No decisions, no questions, no options."

"My mother will care," Tish said. "The more we don't, the more she will."

"There's no point in saying this will upset both our families," decided Peter. "The whole thing depends on how we present it."

Tish smiled sadly. "I don't think, in the end, that that's going to soften the blow any."

Peter took Tish's other hand then, and tightly held them in his. "We like each other, right?" he asked. Tish nodded, noting to herself how very fast Peter was talking. "We understood each other, from the very beginning. We have fun together. We're good in bed together. And now we have a common concern. I'd say that was a lot to start a marriage with."

"You don't have to, Peter. Seriously! You don't! I can go to New York. Your life can go on. Mine can. We can start all over again, when we're ready, or not, as we choose. It's not such a big thing."

"You sound like Lieutenant Calley," Peter said. "It's one of the biggest. Tish, I want to do this." He paused, and then suddenly smiled. "Will you marry me?"

In return Tish smiled, a little. "Well, if you're going to ask me, I guess I'll have to. Yes. Yes, I will."

Peter stood up and helped Tish to stand. He looked into her face and then, chastely, he bent down and gave her a gentle kiss.

Tish opened her eyes. "You really think we know what we're doing?"

"I may not know what you're doing, dummy, but I sure as hell know what I'm doing!"

Tish laughed a little and then turned, taking her first steps back along the water. Peter put an arm around her shoulder, and they turned toward Rocky Hill.

They had been walking only a few minutes along the canal's edge when Peter clasped Tish more tightly to him.

16.

May 24

Well, D.D., it finally happened. I cried. Not because of the baby, or because I'll probably end up married at seventeen (there is still a chance that won't happen; we haven't said anything to our parents yet. Peter wants to wait until the time is right. It's all I can do to keep from reminding him that that time has already passed!) Or even because I know what this will do to Mother and Daddy and Tommy.
What it is, and what happened was: I was sitting up here at my desk after school today, hammering away at some ditsy assignment . . . and I suddenly realized that I, Patricia Anne Davies, am going to be a Drop Out! That these last few weeks of school are all I'm

*likely to get, at least for a long time to come. That I'll
probably have to send off the top of some dopey
matchbook cover for Study at Home! Earn Your High
School Equivalency in the Comfort of Your Own Home!
And then I realized, I guess for the first time ever, that
I really liked going to school. That learning is pretty
terrific. That secretly I must have felt all along that
going led naturally into leading a meaningful life as you
get older. That it did prepare you, it did mean
advantages, a better chance for being useful and a part
of things later.
So, of course, I cried like hell. Great huge sobs. For
hours, or so it seemed.
Being clearheaded, though, I know that some of the
tears weren't for that alone. But that's what started me
off. I'm over it all now. I've adjusted, I think, to what's
going to happen. Worse, to what isn't going to happen.
I won't even graduate! I won't have to ever meet Milton
face to face again! (Now there, being honest, I'm not
exactly despondent over that!) Being truthful, I guess
you'd have to say that today, for the first time really, I
began to understand what Peter and I are up against.
Before, when I thought back over what we've done and
said about it, it all seemed very low-key and
matter-of-fact and, I suppose, a little cavalier, too.
(Peter, especially. How can he accept so much
responsibility and so many changes as easily and happily
as he seems to?) It seemed very mature at the time.
Sensible, logical, unhurried, adult. I'm not so sure of
that, any more. Not tonight, anyway.*

17.

It had taken less than five minues for Tish to realize that
she had made a mistake. Not a small error; a major mistake.
Every time she felt as though she were getting the hang of it,
she would again be surprised to be the only person standing
instead of kneeling. Almost worse, she would find herself
sitting down when the rest of the congregation had slid to
its knees.

She had thought her idea a good one. To show Peter's
family, his mother in particular, that she was flexible—better.
eager to learn and share new things. After church, there
was to be a brunch at the McSweenys'. Peter had finally
decided that it would be then that he would announce their
plans to his family. Tish's idea had seemed inspired and
perfectly natural to her at the time.

Clearly now it had not been. The Mass was nearly over.
She had been perspiring for almost an hour, struggling to do
as others did, wishing that Peter had sat with her at the back
of the church rather than in front with his mother. At least
in the back row no one behind could see how confused you
were. But Peter had answered, and rightly Tish felt then, that
if she was going to do this thing, she should do it properly.

He had taken to grasping her hand during the service,
hoping that by putting pressure on it he could signal the
appropriate physical response. But by the end of the Mass,
he had been reduced to smothered giggles. In fact, he had
given up and needed all his energy to keep from bolting the
church altogether, standing on the front steps and roaring.

Mrs. McSweeny went about her devotions entirely ab-
sorbed. She neither noticed Tish's confusion nor commented
on it if she did. Tish was grateful for that, but feared the
casual remark she felt certain would come during the ride
back home.

But there was no casual remark in the car. Mrs. McSweeny
talked cheerfully about the plans she had made for Bosey
during the summer, the things she hoped to do with her
daughter, acknowledging at the same time her daughter's
independence and the likelihood that more often than not
Bosey would probably have other, competing plans.

Tish's stomach during the drive seemed to grow further
and further down. It felt empty. She smiled to herself, knowing that *that* wasn't true at all, but nonetheless she felt hollow
with fear. She hadn't asked Peter how he was going to approach his parents. She had thought he would be insulted if
she questioned his decision, or made suggestions of her own.
But she did wonder. She hoped he wouldn't wait until she
fainted from the tension. That, she felt, was a real possibility.

Then she smiled again. Fainting would be exactly what

happened in movies. And in movies, when a woman faints everyone around instantly understands what the trouble is. Terrific.

Inside the McSweenys' home, the sideboard was overflowing with food. Sausages, bacon, minced ham, scrambled eggs, toast, popovers, homemade sweet rolls, coffee, milk, and juice. Mrs. McSweeny's cook was a middle-aged English woman who had come to America after the war, used to cooking enormous meals for her previous, very social and intensely horsey employers. On Sunday, she served a hunt breakfast, enough for thirty healthy riders after a morning of flying after foxes and hounds. Mrs. McSweeny smiled as she explained all this to Tish, and shrugged her shoulders. "Better a habit kept than a spirit broken," she said philosophically, filling Tish's plate for her.

Tish thought she might have an answer for that, but decided against offering it. Instead, she sat demurely at the table across from Peter. Catching his eye, she tried to smile.

Mr. McSweeny drained the last of his Bloody Mary and put the glass aside. "Know what I'm thinking, Kate?" he asked his wife.

"What, dear?"

"I'm thinking about what I'd like to do when I retire."

Tish looked quickly at Mr. McSweeny. "You look a hundred years away from that," she said diplomatically.

"Well, I'm not," Mr. McSweeny replied, a grin thanking Tish for her kindly estimation. "What bothers me, always, is to see the waste of good people when they've stopped working hard."

"You could join the Executive Peace Corps," said Peter. "Or whatever it's called. You could go to Nigeria, for instance, and teach the natives how to buy and sell stocks and bonds." Peter laughed at his own thought.

"Very funny, young man, making fun of people less fortunate and able to meet the demands of the modern world," admonished his father.

"I wasn't doing that," said Peter. "I just had a picture of you, in khaki and pith helmet, talking about bulls and bears."

"What would you do, dear, if you stopped working?" asked Mrs. McSweeny.

"Well, now that you ask, I've got some ideas. The thing

to do, I figure, is do something you've always wanted to do and yet never had the time or ability to do before."

"Like what, Dad?" Peter asked.

"I've always thought South America was undeveloped, a last frontier of sorts," said his father. "And I've always been interested in geology."

"You have?" asked his wife, surprised.

"Yes, I have," said Mr. McSweeny defensively. "I just might study mineralogy in earnest sometime. I understand there's a crackerjack school in Colorado. Then we could spend a couple years in the Andes perhaps, prospecting, sharing what we've learned."

"What who's learned?" Mrs. McSweeny wanted to know.

"There's no reason you couldn't come with me," said her husband. "After all, in a few years Peter will be out on his own. Bosey will have finished school. What else have we got to do that's half so exciting?"

"You mean that first of all you expect me to be some sort of coed, after all this time, working to put you through school. And *then* to disappear into the wilds of South America to talk about rocks with whatever Indian stumbles into town?" Mrs. McSweeny laughed in disbelief.

Tish and Peter were staring at each other across the table. Peter nodded almost imperceptibly.

"South America isn't all jungle and disease, Kate," Mr. McSweeny said. "Buenos Aires is called the Paris of the South."

"I know," said his wife, "I've been there." And she laughed again, but kindly.

"Dad," said Peter.

"Yes, son?"

There was a silent moment. Tish knew instantly that Peter couldn't think how to say what he wanted to.

"Dad," he said again, finally, "Tish and I are going to be married."

Mr. McSweeny did not say a word. He looked at his son. Then he turned toward Tish. Mrs. McSweeny was already looking at her.

Mrs. McSweeny wadded up her napkin and put it beside her plate. She lit a cigarette. Tish wished desperately that she, too, smoked.

"I don't mean to offend you, Tish," said Peter's mother,

looking down at the table, "but are you sure you want to have the child?"

"Yes," answered Peter quickly. "We are sure."

"Peter, darling," said his mother, leaning toward him, "it's so easy to arrange things differently now. It's quite sanitary and safe. And it's legal, in New York. We're not judging. We're just looking a little further ahead than perhaps you've had the time to do."

"I understand that, Mother," Peter said. "But we've thought it all through. I want Tish to have the child. We want to do the right thing."

"That's entirely commendable, dear," said his mother, smiling as best she could. "But both your futures are too precious to be given up so easily."

Tish straightened in her chair. "Mrs. McSweeny," she said, "without being disloyal to Peter or anything, you ought to know that, at first, I said the same thing. I am still willing to do that, if it's necessary. I don't want to ruin Peter's life."

"I'm sure that's true, Tish," said Mrs. McSweeny. "And I appreciate both your honesty and your concern."

"It's more than that," Tish went on. "Peter and I are very fond of each other. I wanted always to be honest with him. We've discussed abortion. Peter won't have it. I've suggested I could go away and have the child, and then give it up for adoption."

"And?" asked Peter's mother, brightening.

"And I said no to that, too, Mother," Peter answered. "What Tish is trying to say is that she hasn't trapped me into marrying her. That she *has* honestly told me I can turn away and that she feels she can handle things. But it's my responsibility, too, you see. What we did was an adult act. The consequences are adult. We have to face them as adults."

"Oh, Peter," sighed his mother, leaning back in her chair and stubbing out her cigarette. "Dear, dear Peter, don't you see what this does? How this changes everything you've always said you wanted? College is going to become only a frustrated dream if you go ahead this way."

"Why should it?" asked Peter. "It may mean that I don't ease my way through as I might have, but it doesn't necessarily mean that sometime, somewhere, I can't pick up things again and do them."

"At night, I suppose," guessed his mother, "after you've

come home from work. You can't expect your father and me to support you both—you three, indefinitely."

Tish's face felt suddenly hot. "We have never even considered that," she said quickly.

Mr. McSweeny coughed. "What does your family think, Tish?" he asked gently.

Tish looked down at her plate. "We haven't told them yet."

Mr. McSweeny nodded, as though he now understood something clearly. He turned to Peter. "What is it you want us to do, son?" he asked, just as carefully as before.

"We're not really sure yet, Dad," Peter said honestly. "Ideally, we'd like to stay here, above the garage, for a while. Until I get organized and can set us up somewhere we can afford on what I'll be earning."

"And how much will that be?" asked Mrs. McSweeny.

Peter smiled ruefully. "I know what you're saying, Mother. What kind of job can I hope to get without even finishing Notre Dame? I don't know. But I figure if a man wants to work, there's always a job for him somewhere. At least, Dad's favorite President is always saying that's true."

"And his favorite Vice-President would say this is all the product of a permissive age," snapped Mrs. McSweeny, ignoring the smile on her son's face.

"Now, Kate," Mr. McSweeny cautioned. He turned in his chair so that he faced Peter more squarely. He was also sitting closer to Tish. As he spoke to his son, he reached beneath the table for Tish's hand, and held it. "Well, son, I'll tell you what I think," he began. "I think this is a damned shame, that's what."

Tish tried to pull her hand away from his, but Mr. McSweeny gripped it more tightly. "And I will probably feel that way for the next few years," he said. "There's no point in trying to hide that."

"We can understand that," said Peter evenly.

"That's good. I'm not saying I disapprove of what you're doing as much as I just wish it had come a little later. That's all. As for not going to college, that upsets me less than your mother. I've never been to college. It hasn't been an enormous handicap. Life goes on. We do the best we can with what we have. Besides,"—and here Mr. McSweeny couldn't help but smile, just a little—"I've always thought that not everyone benefited from going to college. Some people just weren't cut out for it. Some go and learn nothing. And in view of all the rabble-rousing that seems to be part of freshmen orientation everywhere, it's probably just as well you're not going. What we don't need, especially if we're going to have a grandchild, is some activist radical father who spends his wife's delivery night in jail."

"Well, you don't have that to worry about, anyway," said Peter in return. "Not now."

Mr. McSweeny moved his chair again, so that he could look from Peter to Tish easily. For a moment he said nothing. He looked down the table at his wife, who avoided his gaze.

"I'll tell you something else, young people," he said. "I'm sorry this is happening. But I'm proud of the way you're handling it."

"George!" Mrs. McSweeny objected angrily.

"Well, Kate, I am," protested Peter's father. "I think there's something important here we don't want to forget. Regardless of the situation, these kids are two fine young people. And I don't want to lose sight of that, or begin to treat them as failures or criminals."

In order to swallow her tears, Tish coughed. Mr. McSweeny turned to face her directly. "Is there anything I can do, to make your next . . . family conference any easier?"

"No, Dad, thanks," Peter said. "We've got to do things the way we think is right. It's our duty. Our responsibility."

Mr. McSweeny nodded. Then he stood up and pushed his chair back from the table. "Then what we had better do, and we may as well do it now, is check the garage. It can't have everything a pair of newlyweds need."

Tish stood up quickly, happy to be leaving the table. She looked surreptitiously at Mrs. McSweeny who sat now rigid in her chair, looking out a window onto the front lawn. She made no move to rise. She had lit another cigarette.

Tish took a few steps and found Mr. McSweeny's heavy arm across her shoulder. His other arm held his son. The three of them started to walk into the hall, to turn toward the back door.

As Mr. McSweeny pulled open the door for Tish and Peter, a sudden shattering crash was heard from the dining room.

All three stood motionless. Then, smiling again slightly, Mr.
McSweeny pushed Tish and Peter through the door, and
followed them out onto the gravel.

18.

May 28
D.D., this may all be too much for me. I'm upstairs
again, with you, hiding out. Peter is due in about half
an hour. In theory, we're supposed to be going to the
movies. I've had dinner, with the family, and am
supposed to be doing my homework for tomorrow,
which I've already done. Actually, what I'm doing is
losing my mind.
We told Peter's family today. Mrs. McS. tried hard,
but it finally got her. Peter's father was a dream. Is it
all going to be this easy? Are my parents going to be
real human beings, too?
One of the things in the back of my mind is whether or
not Peter's conception of duty and the right thing is
mine as well. Secretly, D.D., I'm hoping like crazy that
my parents will fight like hell. I do, in my own way,
love Peter. I know I do. But I'm just not certain it really
wouldn't be better to abort (why doesn't that word
bother me? because I haven't any feeling at all of a
child, a real baby with hands and feet, growing inside
me?).
There is another solution, too. Peter and I could just
live together; have the child, and then see how we felt
about being married. I don't really think that would
traumatize a tiny baby, as long as we both showed him
(her?) we loved him. The other thing that bothers me
is the thought that since I can't seem to make up my
mind about what I want to do, maybe I shouldn't be
doing any of this. Maybe I'm not as ready for Life as
I thought. Or as Peter thinks. Sometimes I look at
him and have the oddest feeling that he's sort of playing
at being manly. That's probably unfair, I know. But he
always seems to do the right thing, or know the right
thing to say. He's too perfect. (Of course, I knew he

was perfect when I first laid eyes on him. That was the reason I picked him.) I suppose I should be happy he's as strong and reliable as he is. One of us has to be. Apart from all this doubt, D.D., I'm afraid I'm still the same dissolute girl. I had the craziest idea this afternoon, when Peter and I were finally left alone in his apartment. I knew, I just knew without saying why, that whatever flack my parents send up they would be certain to insist that Peter and I not see each other (until the wedding, if there is one; ever again, if there isn't). One of my weirdest fantasies has always been being laid in a car. That's sort of sick, I admit, especially since Peter and I can go at it in perfect privacy, peace, and comfort in his apartment. There's no point in trying to rationalize this. It's just something I've always heard about and wanted to try. Well, my dear, I had to nearly beg! (Which isn't all that surprising, since Peter's the sane one of us two.) I tried to explain it to him, and show him how important it was that we do it now . . . later, what earthly fun can there be in having your own husband in your own car? (I can't believe I'm actually writing all this down. It's a good thing, D.D., that you're a liberated lady yourself.) I mean, some of the fun has to be in the danger of discovery, or the discomfort, or the ingenuity and heat of the moment. After about twenty minutes' scene, I got Peter into the garage and into his car. (It wasn't as safe as you might think. His father or mother could always have come out to get one of their cars.) I admit to having to work a little to get Peter in the mood. But happily, after a little, there we were, sprawled out across the front seat—his legs dangling outside the car, my left leg over the back of the front seat, all set and ready to go. It wasn't too uncomfortable. After a while, I mean, you're so far into it that it wouldn't really make any difference if it were. Anyway, we're just about to do it and I get the giggles. What floated into my mind was that I couldn't remember any more whether you were supposed to do it in the front seat or the back. I tried to pull myself together, to ask Peter what he thought, which he would prefer. And of course that did it. He couldn't concentrate at all any more. He

*started to laugh, too. Pretty soon, we were both
hysterical, our clothes lying (hanging, actually) in odd
pieces from odd limbs, tangled like you wouldn't
believe. My giggling set him off, and his set me off again.
Finally, of course, we had to give up. We went back
upstairs and tried to look put together again. And then
set off here for Round Two.
Which all goes to prove that the best-laid plans of mice
and men and so forth. Maybe you shouldn't try to plan
these things. The problem is that sometimes, when I
haven't anything special to do, I can't help but plot little
seductions and scenes to play later.
So here I am, waiting. And scared to death. And hopeful
and fearful and wanting to put on my sweater and just
walk out the front door and disappear. Peter would
say that that was an infantile reaction. I would too.
I feel like a baby. I am one.*

19.

Tish was still upstairs in her room when she heard the
doorbell downstairs. Without thinking, she grabbed her
sweater and her purse and ran down the stairs, just in time
to hear her mother say, "Come in, Peter. Have a cup of
coffee. Tish didn't expect you until eight, I think."

Tish stood on the final step and watched her mother lead
Peter into the study where she knew her father was, too.
Oh, God, she thought. *Now what?*

She crossed the hallway and walked through the living
room as quietly as she could, standing in the shadows outside
the study.

"Well, Peter," she heard her father say. "Have you got a
job lined up for the summer?"

"Yes, sir," Peter answered. "I've been lifeguarding the last
couple of years. I'll do that again."

"That's certainly a healthy way to spend the time," said
Mr. Davies. "I've always wondered what a lifeguard does
when it rains, though. I mean, there are some little tykes
who will swim in any weather."

Tish moved into the doorway and motioned at Peter. He
saw her and stood. Mr. Davies looked around.

"Come in, Tish," said her father. "We're just having a cup of coffee and a little chat."

Tish nodded. "I'd like to speak to Peter for just a minute, Daddy. Alone."

Mrs. Davies nearly collided with her daughter as she carried in two more cups and saucers. "You're not going so soon?" she asked both of them.

Peter smiled and nodded knowingly. "Tish has something urgent on her mind," he explained. "We'll be right back."

Mrs. Davies gestured that she understood and thought romance was wonderful, and disappeared into the study.

"Peter!" Tish whispered, though they were by now in the hall. "I can't do this to them!"

Peter's smile faded.

"No kidding!" said Tish. "I just can't! Look, I've got the money. It's easy to do. Let me do what I wanted to do. I don't want to ruin your life! Or theirs!"

Peter frowned. He opened his mouth to speak but changed his mind. Taking Tish by the hand, he turned and walked back into the study.

"Just sugar, Mrs. Davies," he said as he pulled Tish down onto a couch to sit beside him. "One," he said, as Mrs. Davies handed him his cup, saucer and spoon.

"Tish, dear?" Mrs. Davies asked, pausing after she had poured another cup of coffee.

"Black, please," muttered Tish without looking at her mother.

Mrs. Davies sat back with an expectant smile on her face. "What film are you two seeing?" she asked interestedly.

"Mary, Queen of Scots," answered her daughter swiftly. "We'll probably be late if we don't get going." Tish started to stand but Peter held her down.

"Actually, Mr. Davies," said Peter, "I have another plan for the summer."

"What's that, son?"

Tish sank back into the corner of the couch.

"I'd like to marry your daughter," Peter announced.

Tish peered up and across the room at her father. He said nothing, but the color in his face drained. Slowly then, it returned, florid and fast, starting at his neck.

Mrs. Davies coughed. "Now, Peter," she began, forcing a smile into her voice, "I think the way you young people mature so fast these days is a wonderful thing. But Tish is only seventeen. Don't you think you could afford to wait just a little?" Mrs. Davies added a genteel little chuckle at the end of her question, and leaned forward for her coffee. "Of course," she went on, leaning back, "there are a number of things to be considered in a step of this kind. I mean, for example, you're Catholic."

"Annie, for God's sake," sputtered Mr. Davies. "Are you some kind of idiot? You daughter is pregnant!"

"That's true, sir," Peter said quietly.

"That's true, sir!" mimicked Mr. Davies. "By God, young man, you'd better be on your feet and out of here by the time I stand up, or I'll punch you senseless!"

Peter did not move. Mr. Davies rose from his chair with difficulty. Tish suddenly saw her father as middle-aged.

"Daddy!" she said quickly. "Daddy, that isn't going to help."

Mr. Davies looked sullenly at his daughter. Tish knew instantly it was she he wanted to strike. But without knowing why he did so, she watched her father turn away instead. He stood a moment, facing into the living room, trying to breathe normally. Suddenly, Tish heard her mother's crying.

She looked at Peter, imploring him to say something, anything, the right thing whatever it was.

Peter nodded. "Mr. Davies, sir," Peter started, "I know this is a shock. And a disappointment."

"You're goddamned right it is!" Tish's father answered, without turning around. "And I'd appreciate it if you would just shut your goddamned mouth a minute and let me think!"

Mrs. Davies' sobs grew. "Anne, for Christ's sake!" said her husband without looking at her. But she didn't stop.

Tish and Peter sat on the couch, Tish clasping Peter's hand so hard he could hardly feel circulation in his fingers. Together they waited.

"How could you?" came Mrs. Davies' broken question. "Oh Tish, how could you?"

Tish did not answer.

"After all we've done," Mrs. Davies got out. "After we've tried to give you . . . we've always tried to teach you the right . . . how could you just go ahead and break our hearts like this?"

Before Tish could try to soothe her mother, and now she wanted to, her father had turned back into the room. "All right, Anne," he said. "There's plenty of time for that. Let's try to be a little practical now, shall we?"

Peter cleared his throat. "We'd like to tell you what we hope to do, sir," he said.

"I'm listening," said Mr. Davies, still standing.

"Well," Peter began, "we'll get married, of course. Then, I've spoken to my father. We can live where I do now, in a fairly big apartment over our garage. Naturally I won't be going back to Notre Dame next year. I'll spend what time I have this summer looking for a steady job somewhere, something to make enough money to support Tish and pay for the baby."

"Just hold it right there, young man," said Mr. Davies. Tish looked up at her father.

"First of all," he said, "there isn't going to be any marriage. I won't have Tish ruining her life that way."

"Daddy," objected Tish. "Who says I'd be ruining my——"

"I do," said her father. "I never thought, I never thought in my wildest dreams, that I'd be saying this to any daughter of mine, even to any young women I knew, but Tish, you're going to have an operation."

"Harry!" gasped Mrs. Davies.

Peter smiled thoughtfully. "That's impossible, sir. The child is mine as well. And my religion——"

"Screw your religion, buddy!" shouted Mr. Davies. "I couldn't care less. Let's get one thing straight. We'll take care of our little girl. We'll stand by her and see that what needs doing she'll do. You, buster, are not even the smallest consideration at the moment. As far as I'm concerned, you can get up and walk out of here, a free man. No guilt, no shame. Nothing! But let me tell you this: if you ever lay a hand on Tish again, singlehandedly I'll start a whole new chapter of the Ku Klux Klan! And I ain't just whistlin' Dixie, you better believe it!"

Tish stood quickly. She planted her feet firmly beneath her. "Daddy," she said, "you're being unfair and unreasonable. Don't I have anything to say ab——"

But she didn't. For her father had reached out instinctively and slapped her, backhandedly, across her face. Tish gasped, but did not put a hand to her face. "Harry!" Mrs. Davies screamed.

Peter stood. "Mr. Davies, that was unworthy of you or

Tish." He put his arm around Tish's shoulders and drew her toward him.

Mr. Davies grinned scornfully. "Was it, indeed? Well, baby boy, if I'd done that regularly all these years, that one moment would never have come!"

"Harry!" Mrs. Davies cried, standing up at last. She had stopped crying, and her eyes were wide with worry. "That's enough. That's just enough."

"Like bloody hell," said her husband.

"I said," Mrs. Davies insisted, "that that is enough!"

There was a moment when no one moved.

"Now, Harry," Mrs. Davies said, effortfully keeping her voice controlled, "if you'll just sit down a minute, perhaps we can look at this as adults."

"Adults, my ass!" said her husband beneath his breath. But he sat down.

"Now," Mrs. Davies sighed, seating herself as well. "Tish, Peter, sit down. Please."

Peter looked at Mrs. Davies and hesitated a moment. Then he pulled Tish back down onto the couch with him.

"Well, at last," Mrs. Davies said with another sigh. "Maybe we can be sensible now."

"Mrs. Davies," said Peter, "Tish and I are truly sorry to have to present you with . . . with all this. Believe us, the last thing we ever wanted was to cause you or your family any pain."

"Bullshit," muttered Mr. Davies.

"I know that, Peter," answered Tish's mother. "Harry and I both understand. Now, let me clear one thing. Tish, you don't want to have an . . . an operation?"

Tish stiffened. "I thought so," she said. "At first."

"It would be much the best thing to do, you know," said her mother. Tish nodded that she knew.

"Mrs. Davies, Tish and I both discussed that," Peter said. "It would be running away from ourselves. From our responsibility. Also, of course, my religion"—and here he nodded at Tish's father—"doesn't allow it."

"Your religion isn't Tish's, Peter," said Mrs. Davies. "I really think, since it is Tish who has to go through it all, whatever you decide, that she should be free to make up her own mind about this."

Tish turned to look at Peter. His features were set. She knew he knew what she wanted to say. She turned back toward her mother. "We think it's better to have the baby, Mother."

Mrs. Davis nodded. "Of course, you could marry now and have the child. An annulment is not such a difficult thing to arrange afterwards."

"We've thought about that, too, Mother," said Tish. "That isn't what we want to do. It wouldn't be giving us, or the baby, a fair chance."

"You can't really think that this is giving either of you a fair chance?" said her father in a new tone. "Not seriously?"

"Still, Daddy," Tish answered, "that's what we've decided."

"We behaved as adults," added Peter. "We both knew what we were doing. What we wanted to do. Now it's simply a matter of carrying the thing through, to its natural conclusion."

"That sounds wonderful," Mrs. Davies said with an edge to her voice. "Very mature, but a little more complex I think than perhaps you realize."

"In any case, ma'am, we're determined to be as honest about this as we can. We're not asking anything from you. We don't expect to live on charity. All we want is your consent to live the way we feel we have to."

The front door slammed. The sounds of feet running into the hallway, stopping, and then running through the living room were heard before Tommy appeared. "Hi, everybody!" he said, a carefree smile on his face.

Mr. Davies stood up quickly. "You just march upstairs, young man," he said, pointing. "It's past your curfew, and past your bedtime too for a school night."

"But, Dad," Tommy objected, "it's not even eight o'clock yet!"

"You heard me!" Mr. Davies shouted, taking a threatening step toward the boy.

"Okay, okay," said Tommy, looking into the study with puzzlement at his mother.

When Tommy had disappeared, and his footsteps overhead could be heard, Mr. Davies turned back into the room and sat down, leaning forward in his chair. "I want to get a few things straight," he said. "You won't have an abortion?"

Tish shook her head.

"You won't go through the motions and then separate?"

"No, sir," said Peter.

"But you do need our consent to get married?"

"Yes, sir."

"What about your family?" asked Mr. Davies. "Have they consented?"

Peter tried to smile sympathetically. "Yes, sir. Reluctantly."

"And you're going to live with them?"

"In the garage, sir. It's a separate building."

"Well equipped?"

"Yes, sir."

Mr. Davies leaned back. "All right," he said sadly. "All right."

"When were you thinking of, for the ceremony?" asked Mrs. Davies.

Tish coughed. "Right after school, Mother," she answered.

Mrs. Davies nodded. "We'll have it here," she said. "Just Peter's immediate family, and ours. Is that understood? No celebration, no bridesmaids, nothing of that sort."

"That's what we want, too, Mrs. Davies," said Peter.

Mr. Davies stood again. "I just want to say a couple more words to you both," he announced. "I gather Peter McSweeny here comes from a pretty well-off family. I think that's fine. But Mrs. Davies and I have no intention of trying to keep up with them, or of supporting you with surprise gifts of any sort. When you're married, you're on your own. You chose this. You live with it."

"That's all we expect to do, sir," Peter interrupted.

"I'm not finished, young man," said Mr. Davies, taking a step backwards toward the doorway. "We'll do the right thing, too. You have our consent. Have the child. Ruin your lives. Whatever you want. But depend on us for nothing!"

Abruptly he turned and left the room. The three remaining heard the front door slammed behind him.

Mrs. Davies stood up. "I suppose, under the circumstances, it would seem silly to ask you not to see each other too often between now and . . . and the wedding," she said. "I can only ask you to use what little judgment you have left . . . about whom you see and what you say. It will be difficult in any event for us all. There's no need to make things more complicated."

Peter stood. Mrs. Davies was at the doorway between the study and the living room. "Tish," she said, "I am married to your father. We are part of the same team, in a way, but he's supposed to be the captain. Afterwards, if he doesn't want me to see you too often, you'll understand I hope where my first responsibilities are."

Tish held Peter's hand. She nodded.

"You have disappointed us very greatly," said her mother, as she turned.

Neither Peter nor Tish moved. They were alone in the study. Finally, Tish pulled her hand away from his. She went toward a bookshelf and reached up to take from one of its shelves a porcelain figure of a shepherdess. She studied it a moment. Then, casually, she stepped back a few inches. Her hand, still holding the figurine, jerked up in the air, its fingers loosening.

But Peter grasped Tish's wrist and closed her fingers. The statuette was held still, though not because Tish wanted it that way.

Exhausted, Tish leaned back into Peter's chest, and closed her burning eyes.

20.

June 1

I took the long way to school today. Down Linden, along Nassau, up Moore. Ever since I can remember, though I rarely take the trouble, walking that way gives you the best view of the building. It was warm and sunny today. Not as warm as to put you off with a sweaty vision of the summer to come, just pleasant. As I came up the hill and saw the towers, my throat filled. Suddenly Princeton High School looked like a palace. Rather, a castle. With turrets and ivy and dark red brick with white casements. All I could think was that inside that castle were things I would never have. I guess you could say that I'm a little depressed lately. Getting over last Sunday's scene wasn't so bad. I mean, I don't blame Daddy at all. But it really took a lot out of me. And, being truthful, even though I've finally been to see the

*doctor and he says I'm in great shape, I suppose my
system must be changing a little. I'm probably not
geared up right now for a lot of tension and emotion.
Which is a pity, because that's about all one has now for
breakfast, lunch, and dinner. Today, for example, I
discovered that Sara, like, I suppose, anyone else's best
friend, can't keep her mouth shut. I didn't really expect
her to, I guess. But at lunch I was surrounded by a lot of
giggling, snickering, sympathetic teenie-boppers
wondering how I felt and what I was going to do and
did I want baby showers and all that. It took all my
resources not to simply open my mouth and scream at
them. I'm glad now the wedding will be so small. It will
teach Sara a lesson—although, honestly, I know she'll
be hurt, too, which really isn't fair. Oh, well.
Peter says he's told only Poncho, but that even if
someone else found out, he says it's not something we
need be ashamed of. We should be happy and proud and
ready for anything. Easily said, from his point of view.
All this shows is that he's virile, and that I'm dumb. Sigh.
I walked away from all the commotion finally and sat
outside in the sun, eyes closed, pretending to be carefree
and interested only in grabbing a few early rays. But I
looked around. Mostly at the boys standing in groups,
posing for girls, kidding each other, pretending to be
nonchalant and worrying all the time about their
masculinity. Mentally I compared them all to Peter.
They lost. I mean, how can you find some six foot string
bean sexy in white jeans that no matter how often they're
washed and shrunk are still too baggy? Or someone
who's so tiny he looks like a twinkie? They look so silly.
They're barely able to get excited and they begin to
pretend they know everything. (A sudden thought: I
could have said that about myself a few months ago.)
What it is, D.D., is that I'm growing old and sour. Will
getting married arrest the disease? In one way, of course,
it will. But what about one's spirit, if one has one. Do
I have the strength to bounce back the way I want to, to
be happy and busy and good to Peter?
To be honest, what I want right now is that Peter be all
those things to me.*

21.

Peter kicked open the door with his foot and backed into the living room. Tish, arms as full as his, staggered in behind him and dropped her parcels flat on the floor. She leaned back, closing the door. "Thank God for Alexander's," she said.

Peter put his packages on the couch and stood, straightening his shoulders, loosening them up. He dug into his pants pocket and pulled out a crinkled memo. He read it silently.

"I don't want to exhaust you, sweetheart," he said. "But we did forget a few things."

Tish kicked off her shoes and flopped into a chair. "Maybe on Monday the discounts will be even greater. That's soon enough for me, anyway."

Peter nodded that he agreed, and began carrying boxes and bulging sacks into the bedroom. Tish sighed and struggled out of her chair to follow. In the doorway, she leaned against the jamb and folded her arms, watching Peter. Suddenly, her face lit. "Peter?" she said.

"What?" He did not look up from his work.

"Take off your shirt."

Peter stopped what he was doing and looked at her. "What for?"

Tish smiled at him. "Just do it, to please me," she said. "I like to see your body doing things."

Peter shook his head. "If you had your way, I'd walk around here with no clothes on at all."

"That's quite right," Tish admitted. "I like to see the way your muscles work. I don't think that's obscene or anything."

Peter smiled, and continued to unpack.

"Please, Peter," Tish insisted.

He laughed then, and took off his jacket and the shirt he wore beneath. "There. Now, do you mind if I straighten up this mess?"

"No," mused Tish. "Just keep the bed clear."

"I wonder if all pregnant women are so overheated," Peter said as Tish helped him clear the top of the double bed.

"I'm sorry," Tish said. "I don't feel overheated at all. I just happen to think you're a beautiful-looking human being, and I like touching you."

She stood close to him and ran both hands down from his shoulders to his hips.

Peter smiled thoughtfully and allowed Tish a tiny kiss on the lips. Before he could move away, Tish embraced him firmly and trapped him in a long, plainly sexual kiss. Peter stood immobilized a moment before allowing his arms to encircle her body in response.

Tish smiled as she felt her triumph approaching, and leaned back on her heels, slowly sinking down onto the bed with Peter on top of her. His hands began pushing her sweater off her shoulders, and then unbuttoning her blouse.

Tish closed her eyes as Peter pulled himself up and away from her body, rolling her on one side and then the other to pull her upper clothing from her. Then he sank back on top of her and while kissing her again, began playing with the zipper on the side of her skirt. Tish sent both hands down under Peter's belt, beneath his blue jeans.

"Oh, Peter," she said as his hands massaged her breasts. "I love feeling desirable."

Quickly Peter stood at the side of the bed and took off his remaining clothes. With one easy motion he half-lifted Tish out of her skirt and panties, and then lay down again, half across her, his hands roaming where they wished. Tish's body began to move in subtle anticipation.

Peter moved over her, kneeling between her legs, kissing and nibbling her breasts, the soft skin along her sides, moving rapidly and skillfully down her body. Tish's hands never stopped reaching for him. She held his shoulders and caressed them. Let her hands slide down his sides, gently touch between his legs. Peter made love upwards again, sinking gradually down on her with all his weight, not yet penetrating, drawing out the play and affection and discovery.

Peter bit gently on Tish's neck, her shoulders. "Ah, Superstud," Tish whispered. "You know . . . ," but Peter's kiss interrupted her. As his mouth moved and he began to nibble the other side of her neck, she continued.

"You know, my hands *feel* you. I mean, even when we're not together. The palms of them. I can feel your skin on the palms of my hands. The idea just comes and suddenly, there you are, in my hands. Oh, Peter. Peter—!"

Without warning, he was into her, plunging into her with eyes clenched, again and again.

"Peter!" Tish started to cry out, but he quickly pulled his right hand up from beneath her body and covered her mouth.

Tish was terrified. He had never taken her this way before. Her eyes wide open, she sensed a new fury in him, an anger, a need to hurt. Then she remembered the child.

"Umph!" she tried to call out. She twisted her head to escape his hand, fleetingly thinking of biting his fingers. She thrashed and tried to sit up, but Peter pushed her down with the force of his own movements.

Not knowing why, Tish suddenly lay still, clenching her teeth, her eyes still watching Peter's contorted features as he banged into her. He didn't seem to care that she had stopped moving in response to him, or that she had ceased struggling to lift his hand. His body heaved more violently, his strokes now longer and harder, as though he were trying to crush something deep inside her.

It was over as suddenly as it had begun. Peter's sweat-drenched body shuddered once, and then again. As though halfheartedly, he pushed into her for a second more, and then rolled off, lying on his back. His left hand and arm were hidden under Tish's still body. He brought his right up and over his eyes, and lay there, trying to breathe regularly.

Relieved, Tish did not move, the ceiling above her hard and cold and smooth and threatening.

22.

June 16

Well, D.D., this is nearly it. Today was the last day of school. Tomorrow is another one, another last, I mean. How do I find myself on this eve of eves? Pretty shaky, I don't mind saying.

Daddy wouldn't allow us to have a prenuptial dinner tonight. He still won't meet the McSweenys. Tomorrow is soon enough for him, he says. So you can imagine all the light, bright, and breezy conversation and laughter around our table. Peter was with his parents, too. How do they ever expect us to survive if they're going to fight every step of the way? Mother and Daddy, I mean. Sudden thought: maybe they don't expect us to survive. Maybe this is just the beginning of what Peter and I

can expect. Maybe they don't want us to make a go of
it. But how stupid—can't they see that a failed marriage
would be as bad as no marriage at all? As far as their
precious neighbors are concerned, I would think the
scandal of divorce would be even greater than what we
already have. I keep trying to tell myself that I'm as
grown up as Mother and Daddy are, and yet I don't
begin to understand what motivates them.

We've told everyone we aren't going away after the
wedding, but we are. We've made a reservation for one
night only at Cherry Hill. Peter says he doesn't want me
to feel deprived. I suspect he's more romantic than I am.
He certainly is something more than I am. I just have
to remember, all the time, that he has strains and
problems, too, adjusting. It's true I have to go through
the bloody part of this myself, but how unsettling it must
be for him, too. (If I said, D.D., that sometimes he
surprises me—oops! I'm hedging again, still—sometimes
he scares me, would you say that comes from my own
inexperience? My own fright and uncertainty about life?
I hope so.)

I've just stopped and taken a sip of brandy. I snuck it up
with me from the kitchen, so I could make one toast at
least to myself. Here's to you, kid!

I just had a blinding flash. (No, it was not the brandy!)
I'd be willing to bet anything that tomorrow, when he
gives me away, my father will be crying!

If he does, I know, I absolutely know, that whatever I
do, I'll start too.

You know what? Suddenly I can't remember what it
was like being a child.

PART II

23

Poncho drove slowly up the McSweenys' drive and pulled around toward the garage. He put the car in park, and gently pushed twice on his horn. He hoped that Tish was listening for him. He didn't want to awaken Mrs. McSweeny or Bosey. Or Peter, on his day off.

He sat staring at the outside staircase, watching for Tish. He had agreed to pick her up and take her to his house for the day because Peter had decided that Tish needed a day around kids.

Poncho tapped his fingers lightly across the top of the steering wheel. He guessed he understood what Peter had in mind: get Tish used to kids a little. See how an expert handles crises. Help get lunch, or change, or referee battles, or talk with. Poncho smiled to himself. Or help make beds, clean up rooms, load a clothes washer, and then the dryer, try to keep neat and happy while every nerve screamed to be allowed to snap.

He saw the door above open and then quickly close, Tish coming down the wooden slats quickly but carefully. He leaned across the front seat and opened the door for her from inside.

"Hi, Ponch," Tish said, sliding across the seat. "How are you?"

"Punchdrunk," Poncho answered, shifting into drive. "It's been almost a month since I've even seen daylight."

At the foot of the drive, Poncho turned slowly right, onto the road heading back toward Princeton. "I don't see how you people face it, day after day. Sunlight, I mean."

"It's really that bad?" Tish asked laughing. "Your job."

"Not if you're a dog lover," Poncho grinned back. "They've got some of the most beautiful and mean dogs around that store you've ever seen. The whole first week I spent trying to make friends with four Dobermans. My only hope is that if someone does try to rob the place, those damned dogs can tell friend from foe."

They passed the Witherspoon Street light, heading east. "I'm not kidding, Tish," Poncho went on. "The first few hours I'm there, every night all I do is sit there and sweat."

"I thought you liked animals. Peter says your house is full of them."

"It is, it is," Poncho said. "Seven full-grown dogs and, depending on the seasons, from three to twenty puppies. Two ponies, four scattered bowls of goldfish. One aquarium for fish of a more special, expensive kind. One goose, one Sardinian ass, one ordinary donkey, three cats, and an indeterminate number of rabbits. But these animals are something else!"

Poncho turned the car onto Washington Road and headed for Route #1. Tish sat with a pleasant, relaxed expression on her face, watching the trees and being watched, covertly, by her chauffeur.

"Was Peter up yet?" Poncho asked. "I tried to be as quiet as I could. Wouldn't want to disturb the country club's own Mark Spitz."

Tish laughed. "He's not only up, he left before you even got there."

"On his day off?"

"Yes, Ponch. He's got something in mind he thinks could be terrific. He's out now, scouting around."

"What is it, or can you tell?"

"I can tell, I think. Last week we went into New Brunswick to the flicks. It wasn't quite dark yet, and we got stopped at a light outside a store called Pack-a-Camp. Right on Twenty-seven. I'd never noticed it before."

"It's newish," Poncho supplied. "Camping gear, backpacks, skis. Things like that."

"Right. Anyway, we were sitting there, traffic was fierce. End of the day. So we had time to look around at this spot. It had mountains of stuff inside and out, and hundreds of cars in a lot nearby. The place was crawling with customers. But what grabbed Peter was the way the clerks looked. At least from a distance."

"I don't get you," Poncho said.

"Well, from what we could see, they were sort of hippie-ish."

"So what?"

"That's what I said. Who cares? Well, Peter did, for one.

He started thinking out loud about how he didn't know a lot about camping, but he wasn't altogether dumb about people. He thought that no matter what was being bought or sold, people would rather do it, always, with someone who looked neat. Looked neat and was dressed properly and knew how to approach people as an adult. Peter decided that the kids Pack-a-Camp was using were all greasy and sloppy and probably couldn't care less about what they were doing. If the customers began to feel that, he said, they'd get up and move and spend their bread elsewhere."

"It's that kind of insight," said Poncho, "that probably made whoever's head of General Motors head of General Motors."

"I said it was too bad Peter hadn't just gotten off a boat all fired up with the American Dream. He didn't think that was funny."

"So what's he doing now?" Poncho pressed.

Tish sighed. "He's gone to get a haircut. He took some clothes to the cleaners yesterday, a blazer and a pair of slacks. He's going to present himself to the manager today. Straight to the top."

"That's swell," Poncho said, "but if he doesn't know anything about the camping business, I don't think the manager is going to be all that impressed."

Tish nodded. "Peter says it has to do with how you operate. If you know your psychology, you can sell anything."

"Well, I suppose he's got a point there."

"I don't know," Tish wondered, as Poncho turned onto Route #1. "He has so many inspirations. Nearly every day he comes home from the club with a hot new idea, all on fire to start taking over the country, or writing the Great American Film, or starting a new self-help program for handicapped kids. He's positively frantic with ideas." Tish looked sideways, and seriously, at Poncho. "He seems sort of . . . of fragmented to me, Ponch. I mean, his mind zaps all over the place."

Poncho looked straight ahead. "Probably premature middle age setting in. No doubt he forgets things, too," he said with a chuckle.

Tish stared at him. "He does, Poncho," she said quietly. "He really does!"

Poncho looked at Tish as he turned off onto River Road.

He could see she was serious and worried. "Well," he ducked, "that's enough about me. Tell me about you."

Tish's face did not relax immediately. After a second, she gave a little shrug, turned to face forward again, and smiled. "Oh, me," she said, "I'm busy trying to feel like an expectant mother."

"That hardly sounds like a full-time job," Poncho said.

"And what would you know about it?" Tish snorted. "It's no easy thing."

"Is that all you're doing?" Poncho asked. "I mean, the kid can't have started to kick yet. You don't look a pound heavier. You must have just a little time on your hands, every once in a while."

"Well, I do, that's true," Tish admitted. "I *am* trying to learn to drive. That's one thing."

"Oh, my God," Poncho said loudly. "I can see it now. Peter will turn out to be Chase Manhattan's youngest president, and every morning you'll get up, hair in curlers and bathrobe wrapped around you, put on your coat and drive him dutifully to the station."

"If he's the president," Tish said, "he can drive himself. I'll be too busy with fittings and figure classes and Junior League and Cub Scouts and entertaining simply but fantastically four nights out of five."

"It sounds like you both just got off the boat!" Poncho laughed, pulling into a long, uphill driveway.

The car chugged up the rise and then was turned toward the left, following a lane that was bordered by coarse grass and fences on one side, by rows of crops and flowerbeds on the other.

Tish's first view of the Oliveras' house surprised her: it made her think of an old-time whaling captain's house, only it was three times that size. There *was* a widow's walk on top, but the house had what seemed to be three full, livable floors, and it spread out over a considerable expanse of lawn.

As Poncho's car swerved to avoid several alarmed-sounding dogs, Tish saw a VW wagon begin backing out of a turna-round.

"That's my dad," Poncho said, waving as the two vehicles passed one another.

Tish nodded, looking ahead as the car slowed. There, standing with either hand on top of two small children's heads, was

Mrs. Olivera: short, petite, a nice figure, and still sharp, youthful features. Sharper features than Tish would have thought possible after having ten children. Further, and this thought came as a surprise to Tish, Mrs. Olivera looked happy.

Poncho stopped the car and let it shudder into silence. He got out, and Tish did the same. Mrs. Olivera came forward with her hand outstretched.

"Hi, Tish," she said easily, with a smile. "I'm Poncho's mom. Mary Margaret Olivera, née Callahan, if you want to know. Nearly killed my old man when he showed up. He, incidentally"—and she indicated the disappearing VW—"is very cute. You'll meet him sometime soon. He's cute, but he has absolutely no sense of humor. Don't ever rib him. He simply doesn't understand he has to take as good as he gets."

"Hey, Mom," Poncho said, walking toward the house, "before you pull out the bear-rug pictures, I'm hitting the sack. Wake me around three, will you?"

"All right, Rip," Mrs. Olivera called, as the screen door slammed behind her son.

"This is a lovely spot," Tish said, trying to sound appreciative and alert.

"It is, it is," said Mrs. Olivera. Before she could say anything more, her skirt seemed to fall forceably from one hip. One of the two very small children she had been standing between was now hidden behind her, looking out wide-eyed at Tish. The other held his mother's hand. Mrs. Olivera laughed and pulled her skirt back to her waist. Then she felt around behind her and grabbed a hand, pulling the child forward.

"This is Kevin," she said. "And this is Kerry. Say hello, boys."

"Hello," they both said, eyes quickly falling again to the ground after looking up for a fraction of a second at their visitor.

"Hello," Tish replied. "I'm pleased to meet you."

"Wait, wait," Mrs. Olivera cautioned. "Never say that to anyone, even a child, until you're absolutely certain that's true. These two are passive enough now, but wait!"

The two little boys looked across their mother and decided to escape. As though pulled on one string, they turned quickly around and ran off toward the house.

"They are adorable," Tish said approvingly.

"From time to time," Poncho's mother answered. "Listen, before we go any further, let's get one thing straight, shall we?"

"Of course," Tish answered, a little embarrassed by the older woman's openness.

"Don't look so stricken!" Mrs. Olivera laughed. "All I wanted to say was that my name, what everyone around here calls me, besides Mom that is, is M.O. Poncho's father insists that that just stands for Mary Olivera. My own suspicion is that it stands for the first two letters of 'mouth.' Anyway, that's what you're to call me, too. Don't be embarrassed. Really, I'm serious." Mrs. Olivera started to turn to follow her children. Tish took a step and then halted. "M.O.?" she tried.

Mrs. Olivera turned around smiling. "See," she said. "That's not so hard. What, dear?"

Tish blushed. "I've always wondered," she said hesitatingly, "Peter won't tell me, and Poncho swears he'll keep it secret till he dies. But what's his real name? Poncho's."

Mrs. Olivera reached into her skirt pocket for a cigarette. "His real name is Henry. Henry Elihu Olivera. And he would die if you ever used it."

Mrs. Olivera lit her cigarette and moved again toward the house.

"M.O.?" Tish said again.

"Yes, dear?"

Tish walked to where Mrs. Olivera was standing, and together they began to enter the house. "*My* friends all call me . . . Mrs. McSweeny."

Mrs. Olivera stopped and looked darkly at Tish, but the confused expression that met her gaze told her Tish was almost as surprised as she was. She laughed aloud. "Poncho never told me about your bitchy streak, Tish. But that's good. We all need it from time to time. We're going to get on just fine!"

Tish sighed inwardly. What she had said hadn't sounded right when it came out. She had meant to say that what mattered to her most was being recognized as Mrs. Peter McSweeny.

She nearly ran into M.O.'s outstretched arm as they entered the kitchen.

"Ooops!" said M.O. "Heads up. I nearly forgot to ask you something."

"What's that?"

"What do you want with your coffee?" M.O. asked slyly. "A beer, or a martini?"

Tish felt relaxed enough now to laugh.

"Go on, go on," said M.O. "Laugh! Wait a while, honey, you'll find you need all the help you can get!"

24.

Late that afternoon, M.O. sank into a chair near the pool and called to Tish who was still inside the house. "Make yourself a drink!" Tish came through the screened porch and pushed open the door. She was carrying a can of Fresca.

M.O. lit another cigarette as she watched Tish sink into a canvas lounge chair. A form went flying past her, hurtling through space and landing with a loud *thwap!* in the pool behind her.

Tish smiled. "It's good to sit down. I feel like I've been working in a hospital all day. I don't see how you do it."

M.O. inhaled. "The secret of good management," she confided. "I let everyone help. If you hadn't been around today, I'd have conned Tommy or Susan or Patrick into working. I'm the only mother around, but there are ten of them."

Tish nodded and grew serious. "But how can you find time for yourself?" she asked. "I mean, there must be times when you want to get away from everything, and do just what pleases you."

"You're not paying attention, honey," M.O. said kindly. "I let the kids help. I have time for things, for the things that I think are important, anyway."

Tish's question was unasked, but understood. "I like reading," M.O. explained. "That's about the cheapest, most satisfying way to escape into someone else's world. There's a guy who works with Poncho's father who buys books like crazy. Once a month or so he comes for dinner and brings what he's finished. Keeps me up to date, fictionally, anyway."

Tish swallowed some of her Fresca. M.O. regarded her a moment. "You know, Tish," she said, "it's almost too bad you're already married. You and that friend of mine would get on like a house afire."

"Married only a couple of months," Tish laughed, "and already I'm being solicited."

"Don't get me wrong," M.O. said. "I'm crazy about Peter. He's like one of the family around here. I just have the feeling that somehow, well, you're more mature than he is." M.O. thought a minute. "Maybe that's because you're pregnant. Pregnant women have to mature pretty damned fast!"

A small typhoon erupted from the pool. Without turning, M.O. shouted over her shoulder. "Patrick! Cut that out!"

Tish smiled at the boy as he sank beneath the blue-green water, pushing off from poolside to glide out a few feet.

"No kidding," M.O. said, "You and Bernie would really like each other. He's a little older, of course. But he's stable, and bright. I've been trying to push him off onto somebody for years."

"Why? Isn't he happy as he is?"

"Of course, *he* thinks he is," answered M.O. "I've always felt that he was missing something. The surprises and delights of living with a woman. He thinks he understands all of life. I think he could be astonished any time."

"Well, assuming I were interested, which I'm not, what else has he to recommend him, besides being pigheaded?"

"He's cute," M.O. chuckled. "About as tall as Peter, with curly blond hair he's let go wild, being very with it. He's responsible and works hard and has a nice laugh."

"It sounds to me, M.O.," Tish said slowly, "as if you've got your eye set on him for a little extracurricular entertainment."

"Hooo!" shouted M.O. "No way! I've known him for so long that we'd only be able to lie there, looking at the ceiling, and giggle. Never."

"M.O., how does it feel?"

"How does what feel, honey?"

"Having a baby."

"Oh. It's not so bad as all that."

"I thought of talking to my mother about it, but she's only had two. Her memories wouldn't be as clear as yours."

"Wrong," said M.O. "We're not allowed birth control, but no one has ever said no to anesthetic. I figure if I'm doing it, I deserve as much comfort as I can get. I can't tell you anything but foggy memories."

"Did you ever think about natural childbirth?"

"Once," M.O. said. "But two things held me back. One, I don't see why I should ache if I don't have to. And two, Poncho's father would pass out in the delivery room. He ducks his head in movies if there's blood on the screen."

A flying form ran past the two women and disappeared beneath the water.

"Who was that?" Tish asked.

"Sandy," M.O. answered. "There's real trouble. She's suddenly busty and wise. A dive like that is only the final echo of childhood."

"Do you trust her?"

"I have to," said M.O. "I can't go around spying on the kids. They're supposed to have been brought up sensibly and with some idea of right and wrong. If they choose not to exercise that, that's their problem." M.O. paused, and lit another cigarette. "That's not exactly true, of course. I mean, if there ever was any trouble, the old man and I would fight like crazy for the kids. But I can't smell their breath, or look at their pupils, or check their sheets."

"You know, M.O., I worry about me."

"Why, honey?"

"Because I don't feel at all maternal," Tish replied. "I'm not looking forward to this happy little package. I don't care one way or the other whether it's a boy or a girl, though Peter wants a boy. I haven't started buying cute little things, or worried about a nursery. Maybe I'm trying to hide from everything. Maybe it's just that I'm not really that crazy about being a mother. Wouldn't it be terrible to have a child you didn't care about?"

"That won't happen, Tish," M.O. said somberly. "Your problem is that you weren't given the option of having or not having. Suddenly, there it was. You didn't spend much time dreaming about what it would be like to be married, or thinking about a family and what fun it could be. You couldn't have. You're simply too young."

"I wanted an abortion," Tish said, looking to see whether M.O. would be shocked. She wasn't. "That's all well and good, honey," she said, "but stop a minute and think. Suppose the operation hadn't been clean. Suppose somehow you'd been damaged in the process and found, later, that you couldn't *ever* have a child. That's a pretty big piece of reality to have to hang on to and try to be happy and whole."

"Yes, but I didn't think about that," Tish explained. "I didn't want Peter to feel trapped. I didn't want to be trapped."

"You told him, didn't you?"

"Yes, but—"

"Then clearly you wanted something. I mean, if you'd wanted to, you could probably have arranged the operation and Peter would never have known."

"But it was his baby, too."

"He would never have known that, dear. It was up to you."

Tish nodded. "I guess you're right. Psychologically, that's probably very sound."

M.O. smiled and tried to break the mood. "It's all that reading," she said. "I'm one of the best lay practitioners around. You got a problem, bring it to M.O. I've seen 'em all."

"I think I'll do that," Tish answered thoughtfully. "If you really don't mind. You're much easier to talk to than my mother is, or than Peter's mother would be."

M.O. looked steadily at Tish. "I think I know what's really eating you," she announced.

Tish smiled wanly. "What?"

"You're afraid you don't love him."

Tish was silent.

"Deep down," M.O. pressed, "isn't that what's troubling you?"

Tish nodded, but then spoke quickly. "Maybe I just don't know what the word means. I mean, I was crazy about Peter, from the very first. But now, it seems so . . . so, well, childish, I guess. What I had was natural. God knows he's gorgeous. He just . . . he just . . ."

"What, honey?"

"Well, M.O. he just sometimes scares the hell out of me."

"What has that to do with love?"

"I don't know," Tish said, sounding suddenly exasperated. "But every time I stop to think about it, and think I'm really there, really in love with him, with my *husband,* for God's sake, he does something that makes absolutely no sense at all."

Tish leaned back in the lounge, closing her eyes, looking to

M.O. as all the strain she must have been feeling had finally been allowed to surface.

"I tried, a little, to talk to Poncho about it, this morning," Tish said, keeping her eyes closed. "But I sensed he felt he shouldn't get involved."

"Honey," M.O. said brightly, "there isn't a man in the world who doesn't seem crazy sometimes."

"Did Poncho's father ever try to get you to miscarry?" Tish asked coldly, opening her eyes.

M.O. stared at Tish. "No," she said. "Did Peter?" Her voice betrayed astonishment and concern.

"I think so," Tish answered, closing her eyes again. "Before we were married. We were . . . we were making love, and he just went berserk. He was so violent I honestly thought I would miscarry. There wasn't anything I could do. I tried. But I couldn't reach him suddenly. He was so deeply into his own head, he couldn't have stopped, I think, even if he'd wanted to. I can't tell you how frightened and helpless I felt."

M.O. stubbed out a cigarette. "Did you talk with him about it?"

"No. I decided better not to. Maybe I was reading the thing wrong. But I'm almost certain I wasn't."

M.O. sat thoughtfully. "And since then?"

Tish shrugged. "Sometimes he's the perfect husband. Solicitous and charming and warm. Other times it's as though he's forgotten I'm around. As though he had forgotten who I am and why I'm there."

"You know, Tish," M.O. said after a pause, "maybe Peter feels some of the same things you do. About not wanting to be a parent, perhaps. Or about how suddenly he was forced into becoming an adult, some of his childhood simply erased from the big board. It seems I was right before, in what I said. You are more mature than he is. And if you are, Tish, it's like I'm always telling Poncho and Tommy. They're older and they should know better. You're older in some ways, and the responsibility, I'm sorry to say, for keeping things on an even keel will probably be mostly yours. For a while, anyway. That's one of the unpleasant facts about becoming a woman. It *is* the woman who works harder at making a marriage go."

"We have more to put up with," Tish said with bitterness in her voice.

"No," objected M.O. "Women's Lib goes only so far. There are responsibilities you take on because your husband has neither the time nor the talent to deal with them. And you accept that."

Tish stood and took a few decisive steps. "That word again," she said hotly. "Every time Peter wants to impress someone, he goes on about responsibility and duty. Who the hell does he think is having this baby?"

M.O. studied Tish walking near the edge of the pool. The children were huddled at a distance, near the far end of the pool. Their voices could scarcely be heard. Tish walked steadily around a corner of the pool, then turned and walked back to her chair, sinking into it with a fatigued smile.

"I'm sorry, M.O." she said. "I'm tired, I guess. I'm tired a lot of the time lately. The baby, probably."

M.O. smiled gently. "Long walks and vitamins," she advised.

25.

Tish turned to wave goodbye to Poncho below, and then pushed open her door. She stepped into the living room and threw her purse onto a chair.

"Well, about time!" Peter half-shouted at her, emerging from the bathroom wrapped in a towel.

Tish smiled and tried to squeeze past him in the short, narrow hallway. "I didn't want Poncho to make two trips, so I waited until he was ready to leave for work," she explained.

Peter had put his arm across the hall, barring her way. He smiled down at her, expectantly and a little triumphantly. He said nothing. Tish looked into his face for a clue as to what was expected.

Finally, after a moment in which he stood absolutely motionless, he shrugged and dropped his arm. "The honeymoon's over, I guess," he said in mock despair, moving ahead of her into their bedroom.

"What's the matter?" Tish asked following him. "I don't understand."

Peter whipped off his towel and threw it over the bedpost. He stepped into his shorts. "Well, madam, it used to be that the very sight of my bare, bronzed, beautiful skin would drive you wild with desire. I mean, at least you used to say so."

Tish grinned with effort. "My desire quotient is at a low ebb, I guess." She began to undress, putting on her robe and starting toward the bathroom. "Don't you want to know about it?" Peter called.

Tish stopped in the doorway. "About what?"

"About what happened in New Brunswick," Peter supplied.

"Oh," Tish said, leaning against the door. "I completely forgot. You mean Pack-a-Camp?"

Peter stood in triumph. He wanted to be coaxed.

"Well," Tish obliged. "What happened?"

"You are about to learn all there is to know about duofill sleeping bags, and duck down and virgin polyester fiber," he announced. "Sounds sexy, doesn't it? I got the job!"

"What job?"

"Well, that's a very clever question, actually," he said, posing. "In fact, there wasn't a job till I got there. I walked in and bulled my way into the manager's office. I told him what I could do. *And* about what I thought of the way some of his people worked and looked. I convinced him to try me out, part-time, for two weeks. At night. Extra. I'll go from the club there, and then I guess we'll eat late. Two weeks is all I need to really show that guy what he can do if he tries."

"Is he going to pay you?"

"By the hour," Peter said. "Nothing staggering, but it'll come in handy. In two weeks, I figure I'll be full-time and probably on a commission as well. We can really make something out of this, Tish. No kidding!"

"But what about the club?"

"That's why I made it a two-week thing. I'll give Clark my notice tonight."

Tish smiled. "You sound pretty sure of yourself."

"I am," said Peter. "Just listen to this. Coleman coolers, Bernz-o-matic lanterns, Camptrails Skyline Frames. In two weeks I'll not only know what the hell all those things are, I'll know what they cost and how to use them. And how to suggest to customers that if they're buying Item One, they really should have Items Two, Three, and Four to go along with it. I'm going to be terrific!"

Tish walked back across the bedroom and kissed Peter on the cheek. "Hooray for you," she said sweetly. Then, teasingly, she lifted her right hand and let it rest on Peter's shoulder for a second before bringing it down sensuously and slowly along his side. She pinched his waist.

"Easy!" yelled Peter.

Tish winked. "I might be persuaded to feel you up, after all. Later," she said, turning again toward the bath.

"How was your day?"

She stopped and turned to face Peter. Dramatically, she let her shoulders droop, her posture go slack, her mouth hang open, her eyes cross. Then, as Peter's laughter erupted, she turned and shuffled arthritically away.

Dressed and finally ready for the evening, Tish went into the living room. Peter was sitting in an easy chair, reading a camping equipment catalog, his lips moving as he memorized items and prices. He looked up, and then he stood and smiled. "For a pregnant lady, you look terrific! No one would ever know."

"How gallant," Tish said, curtseying. "What time do your parents want us over?"

"They're not driving us," Peter said. "I said we'd take our own car. That way we can leave when we want to." He grinned suddenly as he stood at the door. "Maybe we can even go somewhere and play around in the back seat. Just like old times."

Tish smiled thinly. "Old times," she mused. "All of one month. Besides, we never did that 'in the old times.' "

She passed him as he held open the door for her, and led him down to the driveway.

At the club, what would once have astonished and interested Tish didn't. Suddenly, she felt oddly uncertain who she was. Mr. McSweeny and his wife, she and Peter sat at the table, having attacked the club buffet at will. No one wanted to dance immediately. The orchestra played largely for its own amusement, having been paid in any case.

Tish looked around the large vaulted room. She recognized friends of her parents. Parents of her friends. Without understanding why, she began to consciously envy some of the people she watched. They seemed secure. They knew how to behave and what to say. They understood the insignificant chatter that was required, and the meaningless flirting that went on between people forced to sit together for a few hours of "entertainment."

Mr. McSweeny was solicitous. He was Tish's host, as he had been the first time she came to the club. He introduced her as his new daughter, and Tish liked that. People came to their table and stood talking, saying unimportant things and looking at Tish and Peter with a mixture of amusement (if they knew) and curiosity, or surprise (if they didn't) and more curiosity. Tish began to feel visibly inflated. As though her state had become so immediately identifiable that she had ceased to be a young woman and had become instead only an expectant mother.

Peter was constantly standing at his place, shaking hands and smiling politely. Mrs. McSweeny sat erect and flawless, smiling softly at the men and openly welcoming the women's comparative glances. Tish simply sat and tried to fit action to required response. She felt automatic. Her face hurt from holding her smile.

"Mrs. McSweeny?" came a voice from across the table. Tish turned to look at Peter's mother. "Mrs. McSweeny, Junior?" the voice clarified. Tish started. It was her father-in-law. "Would you like to dance?"

Tish blushed. She looked out at the dance floor. She had no intention of dancing alone, where she would be conspicuous beyond her worst dreams. But a few couples had ventured out now, and she could hear other chairs being scraped back from their tables, and sense a more general movement. She nodded.

They danced silently. Mr. McSweeny held Tish firmly but not too close, understanding that she needed to find the moment in which she could relax and have her own fun. They danced a slow waltz. Then they stayed on the floor for a fox-trot.

Tish was suddenly conscious of her silence. Fearing it might seem more like rudeness than thought, she leaned back away from Mr. McSweeny and looked up into his face. "You dance very well," she said. "Much better than Peter does."

Mr. McSweeny acknowledged the compliment with a wink. "One of the jobs I held before Mrs. McSweeny—Kate—decided I was more honestly employable," he said, "was a gigolo. If you couldn't dance, you didn't eat."

"Really?" Tish asked. "Were you really?"

Mr. McSweeny laughed and spun her around quickly. "No," he admitted. "I just wanted to see you cheer up a little. For a new bride, you're rather glum and disappointed-looking. Are you disappointed, Tish?"

Tish's face grew red. "Oh no," she said. "No. It's just that . . . well, maybe I'm coming down with something."

Mr. McSweeny squeezed Tish to him and rubbed her back. "Not twins?" he asked in mock surprise.

Tish smiled. "Just a cold," she said. "I feel kind of weird, is all."

The music stopped. "Let's go outside," Tish suggested.

Mr. McSweeny led her by the hand through the crowd, weaving among tables and chairs until they passed through French doors onto a terrace. He leaned against a railing and took out cigarettes, lighting one and handing it to Tish. She shook her head. "I don't smoke."

"I know that," Mr. McSweeny said. "But it looks very grown-up." He smiled gently.

Tish understood his smile and reached out for the cigarette. She held it a minute between her thumb and forefinger, and then shifted it into the proper grip. She smiled a little as she waved it about, trying one pose and then another.

"You know, Tish," Mr. McSweeny said, lighting another cigarette for himself, "that's the hardest thing for Kate and me to remember."

"What?"

"That you and Peter are still only seventeen."

"Oh," Tish said. "It's not so hard for me to remember."

"I wouldn't think so. It seems unfair, doesn't it?"

Tish looked puzzled.

"Go ahead, Tish," Mr. McSweeny urged. "I'm not going to bite you, if you want to say something."

"You're a very nice man, Mr. McSweeny," she said.

"I know," he laughed. "But I was worrying the other day. Unless I find something new and exciting to fill up a little time, I'm well on my way to turning into your usual everyday prying mother-in-law."

Tish chuckled a little. "What about South America?" she asked.

"Well, that's true," Mr. McSweeny remembered. "It's not easy, Tish, being on top of everything and having less and less honest work to do. You know, you work terrifically hard at something for years and years, and one day you find there's no further up you can go in that spot. You're there, and younger people, who deserve a chance, are hot on your heels."

"Well," Tish considered, "you've got your garden."

"One well-tended rosebush a horticulturist doth not make," Mr. McSweeny replied.

Tish was aware again of the music from inside. With a surprised ease, she flicked her cigarette into a clump of bushes below the terrace. "George," she said in a surer tone than she had used all evening, "you sure know how to please a lady."

Tish moved close to Mr. McSweeny and took his arm, turning him in the direction of the music. They smiled honestly at each other and went in.

On the dance floor, Tish searched over her father-in-law's shoulder for Peter. She found him, surrounded by slowly dancing older people, doing some sort of lazy frug with a young girl Tish didn't know.

Tish looked at the pair a moment before she was turned in another direction. Nothing to worry about, she decided. Peter had a preoccupied smile on his face. It didn't seem to her as though he was having the time of his life.

Mr. McSweeny swerved to avoid bumping into another couple. Over his shoulder, Peter and the girl again came into focus. Tish could see now that Peter was smiling in a forced fashion, and sweeping the floor with his eyes. No doubt, Tish felt, looking for her.

In another few seconds, she and Mr. McSweeny were within a few feet of Peter. Tish looked directly into Peter's face, brightening and lifting a hand from Mr. McSweeny's shoulder, blowing a kiss across the floor at him. Peter seemed unaware of her, or the gesture. He stared through her.

An hour later, after they had thanked the McSweenys and said good night, Peter escorted Tish down a long hallway toward the front of the club. Suddenly, from a side room, an older couple appeared: the man with white full hair and erect, his companion tiny but ramrod straight, dressed in flowing purple.

"Peter!" said the man, recognizing him.

"Hello, Dr. Perry," Peter said, sticking out his hand and shaking the doctor's hand firmly. "Mrs. Perry," he added.

"How's one of my most notable deliveries?" the doctor asked. "Having a good time?"

"Yes, sir, we certainly are," Peter said. "I'd like you to

meet . . ." He turned to Tish and she saw a suddenly panicked expression on his face. His mouth was still open, but he could find no words to speak.

"Hello," Tish supplied quickly. "I'm Tish McSweeny. I'm awfully glad to meet you."

She shook hands with Dr. Perry and smiled nicely at his wife. Peter laughed with embarrassment. "Had a little blackout there, I guess."

Mrs. Perry looked coldly back at him and then turned to Tish. "You're very lovely," she said. "I hope you'll be very happy."

Tish smiled in gratitude.

"Gracious," exclaimed the doctor. "I must be older than I thought!"

"Good night, Peter," said Mrs. Perry stiffly. "Good night, Tish," she said more gently, guiding her husband past them and along the corridor.

Peter stood in shock, shaking his head. "Wow," he said. "How could that happen? I'm really sorry, Tish."

"That's all right," Tish said evenly. "I'll wait here while you get the car."

"Right," Peter said, patting her on the shoulder and disappearing through the doors onto the circular drive beyond.

Tish stepped through the doorway after a moment, and breathed deeply, looking at the stars. She was as thoughtful now as she had been before, but the frown and the crease between her eyes deepened.

She was talking to herself. "It's not so strange," she said in a whisper to the night. "It hasn't been very long, really." But what she didn't say to the darkness was that Peter's sudden forgetfulness was an instant replay of the same thing only a week before.

They drove directly back to the garage.

In bed, although Peter seemed not to care particularly, Tish turned away from him without explanation.

Tish cared. It was the first time she had done so.

26.

One morning, after she had finished giving Peter breakfast and seeing him off, cleared and cleaned the dishes, and straightened up as much as she wanted, Tish sat lazily having a cup of coffee in her living room. Expecting no one, she heard suddenly the sound of wheels on gravel.

She stood, thinking that Peter had come back for something. She looked around for a strayed catalog or a half-hidden price list, but saw nothing.

Remembering that it could be Mrs. McSweeny or Bosey coming back from an errand, she sat again and crossed her legs, somehow not hearing the light footsteps on the stairway outside. The knock at the door came as a complete and unwished-for surprise.

She stood, looking quickly down at herself in her robe and closing it more tightly around her. Then she went to the door and opened it.

"Mother!"

Mrs. Davies smiled encouragingly and waited on the step without entering.

"Come in," said Tish after a second. "I wasn't expecting to see you."

"I know," replied her mother, coming through the doorway as Tish stood aside.

Tish stood behind her mother, trying desperately to see the room as she imagined her mother would. Mrs. Davies said nothing but held her smile. She turned to face Tish, an eyebrow raised in expectation.

Tish smiled. "Of course," she realized. "Come on. I'll give you the tour."

Grateful that she had made some effort at least with the house, Tish led her mother from the living room into the kitchen, the bedroom, and a quick doorway inspection of the bathroom.

Mrs. Davies said nothing. Tish had made only the slimmest of comments. "This is the kitchen. This is the bedroom. Here's the bath."

They stood again in the living room. "What's up there?" Mrs. Davies asked, breaking her silence.

"Oh, that's Peter's domain," Tish said. "That's where he used to study and read and listen to music. It's a workroom now, of sorts. He keeps his catalogs and stuff there."

Without being invited, Mrs. Davies walked to the stairway and went upwards. Tish stayed below waiting. When Mrs. Davies came down, she was shaking her head. "I must say, it doesn't look like an office to me," she exclaimed. "Looks more like a little boy's playroom. Even after all this time."

Tish was defensive. "It's not been that long, Mother," she said. "After all. We've been trying to think how to fix it up. The problem is that it's too far away for a nursery, for the first few months in any case."

Mrs. Davies looked quizzically at her daughter. Tish understood the glance. "And I've been going to classes, too," she said. "At Peter's church. For new mothers."

Mrs. Davies frowned. "Would you like some coffee?" Tish asked.

"Yes, dear. I would."

"You stay here. Sit there. I'll get it," Tish said quickly, leaving her mother with relief. When she returned, bringing Mrs. Davies' cup and saucer, cream and sugar on a tray, pot in hand, Tish could tell her mother had been crying silently. Mrs. Davies stuffed her handkerchief quickly into her purse and reddened.

Tish put the tray down before her mother and straightened up. "For God's sake," she said with a smile covering her irritation, "it's all over now, Mother. I mean, we've already been through that."

"I know, dear," Mrs. Davies said. "I just couldn't help it. It was only for a second."

"Okay," Tish said pleasantly.

Mrs. Davies put what cream and sugar she wanted into her coffee and took a hesitant sip. "Why, it's very good, dear," she said, not trying to hide her surprise.

Tish smiled thinly. "Thank you," she said. "I try."

Mrs. Davies then smiled for the first time. "How are you as a cook?" she asked, as a mother.

"Not too bad," Tish answered, folding up on the couch. "I've been taking classes in that, too, at the Y. And exercise classes."

"You certainly sound busy," said her mother. "I'm glad. One thing I worried about, you know, was what you'd find to do with your time. It's all very well for Peter to be off being successful, but what does it mean unless you're happy, too, during the day."

"I'm happy, Mother," said Tish, knowing as she spoke that

that was the one sentence her mother both feared and waited to hear. "Believe me, things are just fine."

Mrs. Davies nodded shortly.

"How's Daddy?"

Mrs. Davies arranged her features carefully. She coughed. "As well, I suppose, as he could be. He was very disappointed, you know."

Tish knew.

"He still insists you could have done things differently."

"And you don't?" There was a sharpness to Tish's question. "Mother, you may as well stop holding your breath. It isn't going to happen."

"No matter what?"

"What does that mean?"

Mrs. Davies blushed. "Well, of course we all hope this doesn't happen, but suppose . . . just suppose . . . something should happen to the baby. Or that——"

"Mother!" Tish said loudly, pulling her feet from under her and standing. "That's the most horrible thing I've ever heard!"

"It is a possibility, dear. You have to face it."

"No, I don't. I don't at all."

"Every woman does, darling."

Tish stood at the window looking down into the back lawn and Mr. McSweeney's garden. She turned after a moment.

"Mother, I am not angry. I am not cruel. But if you ever have any intention of even seeing that child, I'd advise you to stop thinking along those particular lines."

Mrs. Davies put her cup and saucer on the table and leaned back in her chair. "You've become quite a strong young woman, haven't you, Tish?"

"Mother," answered Tish, exasperated, "I don't want to talk about things like this. Can you possibly stop being bitchy a moment, long enough to be a mother?"

Mrs. Davies gasped, turning her head as though she had been slapped across the face. She drew her handkerchief from her bag.

Suddenly, Tish felt years and years older than her mother. She crossed the room and knelt beside her chair. "Mother, I love you. Really. Besides that, the feelings I have for you as my mother, I've always *liked* you. As a person. You're making it hard for me to continue, you know."

Mrs. Davies cried in earnest then, sobbing openly into her handkerchief and turned away from Tish.

Tish stood with a sigh. She wished suddenly that she were dressed, on her way somewhere. She waited in silence.

"I'm sorry, darling," Mrs. Davies said, trying to choke her sobs down into her chest. "I promised myself, I made one promise after another that I wouldn't come here and say these things. I just couldn't help it."

Tish said nothing. She knew there was nothing she could possibly say.

"There," Mrs. Davies said. "I think it's stopped." She reached up and took Tish's hand. "I'm trying, dear. I am, really."

"I know, Mother," Tish allowed, patting her hand. Then she let go and walked into the kitchen, returning with heated coffee. She poured it for her mother and herself and then walked backward across the room, smiling tentatively. Seated on the couch, Tish took a careful swallow.

"Mother, I know you're trying. But we may as well face a few facts. I am not a virgin. In fact, I'm pregnant. Happily, I'm married, too. That much is taken care of. And what I am now, most of all, is a human being, another woman. Can't we be friends that way? Can't we, Mother?"

"Yes. Yes, dear," Mrs. Davies said very quickly. "Of course."

"Good," said Tish. "How's Tommy?"

Mrs. Davies tried to smile, but it was a pale effort. "Just the same. Full of beans. And very excited in his own way about being an uncle."

"That's nice," said Tish, beginning to feel easier. "He'll be terrific."

"How are you feeling, dear?"

Tish smiled. "If you mean do I get sick, or dizzy, or eat crazy things, I'm just fine. None of that. The only thing that makes me uncomfortable is the heat." Tish gave a short laugh.

"What's that, dear?"

"Nothing, Mother. Except I remember, for years, seeing pregnant ladies on the street in the summer and vowing, never ever, to be that pregnant, really heaving, between July and September. And here I am, staggering around, exactly the same way."

"You're not so heavy, dear."

"No, but I'm getting there. And it's beginning to show, just slightly. It's not attractive, you know."

"I think you look wonderful. Perfectly healthy, really."

"Well, thank you for that, anyway. As long as Peter thinks so, too, we're okay."

"How is Peter?"

"He's fine. A huge success in New Brunswick."

"He seems like a nice boy," Mrs. Davies offered.

"Mother, he is."

"I mean, he's so young."

Tish nodded. "Just like me."

Mrs. Davies coughed. "Is he . . . is he . . . does he make you . . . happy . . . in bed?"

Tish stared at her mother. "Mother, that is positively obscene!" Then she laughed. "From Sara I could expect that, but not from my own mother!"

Mrs. Davies smiled calmly. "Well, dear, if we're going to be women friends, I don't feel so awful as that for just asking."

Tish acknowledged her mother's nondefense with a grin. "That's fair," she said. "If you must know, I think he's terrific."

"Well, that's important. I'm glad."

"So am I."

There was a sudden clumping on the stairway outside, getting nearer. The knock on the door and its opening were simultaneous. "Hi!" Bosey said, bursting into the room.

Peter's younger sister resembled him strongly: her coloring was identical, and she was slightly taller than the average fifteen-year-old girl. Her features were as fine, but her face was far from soft, as Peter's was. She had inherited some of her mother's look of fine inbreeding.

"I'm Bosey McSweeny," she announced, sticking out her hand at Mrs. Davies. "We met once before, remember?"

Mrs. Davies took the hand for a fraction of a second and then let it go. "At the wedding," she said.

"Right!" Bosey answered. Then she turned to Tish. "How *are* you? I haven't seen you guys in ages!"

"Not since yesterday, anyway," said Tish smiling.

Bosey reddened. "Actually," she said, "to be perfectly honest, when I saw your mother drive up, I thought I'd come over and get acquainted. We are sort of related, you know."

Mrs. Davies stood from her chair and smiled icily. "Perhaps some other time we can chat," she said. "I only stopped by to say hello. I was on my way to the Farmer's Market, in Trenton."

"Don't they have terrific stuff?" Bosey enthused.

"Some of it is very good," Mrs. Davies agreed, moving toward the door. "Tish," she said, her hand on the knob, "you look wonderful. I'll tell your father. He'll be very pleased."

Tish walked quickly to her mother's side and kissed her cheek. Mrs. Davies made the gesture in return, kissing the air near Tish's ear. "Thanks for coming, Mother. It was really nice of you."

Mrs. Davies took a moment to look again at her daughter, then turned and opened the door.

Tish closed it after her and stared at Bosey, who stared back, as they listened to Mrs. Davies' footsteps on the stairway outside. After a moment, Tish turned to the window. "Oh, God," she said aloud.

Bosey walked to Tish's side. Below, they could see Mrs. Davies' hands coming to her face as she sat in the front seat of her station wagon. In a moment, the car's engine was ignited, and Mrs. Davies made a slow descent of the McSweeneys' driveway, stopped, and turned back toward Princeton.

"Trenton, my ass!" Bosey said happily, turning away.

"Oh well," Tish said, following her.

"I just knew she came over to bug you," Bosey said. "I just knew it. Did she moan and look around, feeling sorry for you all over the place? Did she offer to bring a lot of things over?"

Tish smiled. "No."

"Didn't she even ask you if there was anything you needed?"

"No."

"What a cheapie!" Bosey said. "Honest to God!" She walked into Tish's kitchen and flung open the refrigerator. She returned with a can of Coke in hand. "No kidding," she announced, flinging herself on to the couch, "I don't see how you stand it."

"It's not so hard," said Tish. "That was only her first visit."

"Really?"

Tish nodded.

"Then I wouldn't waste a minute more," Bosey said firmly, sitting up.

"What do you mean?"

"Hanging around here," Bosey answered. "If that was the first visit, watch out. Follows the deluge!"

"I'd be pretty surprised," Tish said.

"I wouldn't. Not at all," said Bosey positively. "You can tell about these things. That woman is only days away from making your life really miserable."

"Bosey, she's my mother."

"That only means she's better at it than someone would be who wasn't," said Peter's sister. She paused a moment. "You really should have a place of your own, Tish. No kidding."

"Why? We're comfortable here. At least for a while. We like it."

"Peter, too?" asked Bosey.

Tish was surprised. "Well, I think so."

"That isn't what he said the other day."

"What did he say?"

"Well," Bosey said, drawing the word out, "he sort of gave me the impression he was getting nervous around here. I think he has some sort of image of himself as father-provider. It's tough to keep that up if your own father is always around."

"Peter is a father-provider," Tish said a little sternly.

"Well, you know what I mean," Bosey said. "He gets these weird ideas, sometimes, and then has to set the stage to make everything come out right."

Tish sat down in her mother's chair.

"You noticed that, haven't you?" Bosey asked. "I mean, Peter loves to . . . well, to sort of play scenes. Right now, his favorite is father-provider. Stern older brother. Knower of the greater world."

"Well, he is older and knows more."

"Of course he is," Bosey said easily. "That's not the point. The point is that he feels he needs props. Things around to reinforce his self-image. Listen, didn't they have any psychology courses at Princeton?"

"I don't know," Tish said. "If there is one, it's mostly to do with rats."

"There you are!" Bosey said in triumph. "The old territorial imperative. Peter needs his own territory. He feels he's encroaching on Daddy's."

"Has he said all this to you?"

"In so many words. He'll probably get around to telling you, too, as soon as he's got everything figured out."

"I hope so," Tish said, trying to sound lighthearted.

"I admit," Bosey raced on, "that I wouldn't be altogether disappointed to see you all clear out. I've had my eye on this place since I was knee-high."

"You mean to live here?" Tish asked.

"Absolutely. Have I got plans!"

"What about St. Timothy's?"

"Oh, that," Bosey said, frowning. "I meant for the summertime. And vacations."

Tish smiled then, feeling stronger again and a little wiser. "If I were you, Bosey, I'd sort of forget about that. After what happened to Peter and me, I'm not so sure your mother would think your taking this place over was such a hot idea."

"Never fear, my dear," Bosey said. "I know all about *that*. I've been on the pill since I got home."

"Whatever for?"

"For just in case, of course," Bosey said. "I mean, here you and Peter are, object lessons to the world. I'm no dummy!"

"I admit that possibility never entered my mind," Tish said, astonished that suddenly, for some reason, she felt something like resentment toward Mrs. McSweeny and her daughter, two people she had until then liked openly.

27.

Leaving Tish to sleep late, Peter had dressed silently and gone out to the club with his parents, playing nine holes of early morning golf with them. Seated now in his chair in his own living room, he was studying the real estate section of the *New Brunswick Home News*. Tish, not long out of bed, still dressed in her robe, was having coffee across the room, not clear-eyed enough yet to want to do anything but stare out at the heat that seemed to be solid and blown between branches of the McSweenys' trees.

August was coming to a close, and Tish was eager for the first gusts of autumn air. Though she hadn't gained much weight, she now *felt* heavier and, standing sideways facing into the mirror, she could discern clearly the bulge that would soon grow into what she felt was an unsightly, ungainly, unattractive signal to the world.

She was about to get up, refill her cup and take it into the bedroom for a bout of frenzied exercise, when Peter looked up from his paper. "New Brunswick isn't so far," he said.

"So far from what?"

"From here," he answered. "I mean, we could live there. It's near my work. There's Rutgers around the corner. We could have some sort of stimulation because of that."

Tish sighed. She had been waiting. "You're saying you'd like to have a place of your own."

"Wouldn't you?"

"I suppose so," Tish said unenthusiastically. "Maybe I picture day-to-day life the same way I play chess . . . badly. I've never been able to visualize the whole board."

"I didn't know you played chess."

"I don't."

She stood and walked into the bedroom, deciding as she went that tomorrow she would exercise. Today, after all, was Sunday.

Tish bathed quickly and dressed. She felt as though she should do something, but what she couldn't decide. Maybe learn to cook something. Something that would be served chilled. Then she thought about driving down to the beach. For the air, and the sun, and the change. Or she could make an effort with her family. Invite her mother and father over for a dinner. Invite Peter's parents, too, and let them slug it out. They had met only once. It was time, she felt, for them to behave in as adult a fashion as she and Peter were being forced to.

Maybe she would call Sara. Check in and see what was new in her life. Was Hank still around, or had Sara moved onto someone more sophisticated? Tish smiled, remembering one particular conversation she had had with Sara before she was married. She hoped that maybe Sara would find someone who wasn't quite so sophisticated as Hank was, then, in his way. It was too upsetting for Sara.

Or the Oliveras. It might be fun to have them over for a picnic in Mr. McSweeny's garden. Just the parents, not the kids. Tish had been meaning to phone M.O. for days.

Tish shrugged tiredly and stood in the middle of the bedroom, facing the unmade bed. "Gleep," she muttered and then, slowly, began to smooth the sheets, fluff the pillows, and pull the bed together neatly.

"Hey, Tish!" Peter shouted from the other room.

"What?" Tish answered unenthusiastically.

"Come here," Peter called.

Standing slowly and straightening, her hand pressing the small of her back, Tish sighed and turned away from the bed.

"What's the matter?" she asked, standing in the doorway of the living room.

"Nothing's the matter. But listen to this: 'Fully furnished, five-rooms downstairs, historic house near campus. Two bedrooms, full bath. Sublet, September fifteenth through April. Near bus, all transportation. Responsible replies only. AX 7-4651.'"

Tish said nothing. "What do you think?" Peter asked her.

She shrugged. "What does that mean, 'five rooms downstairs'? And how come there's no price listed? It must be a fortune."

"It wouldn't do any harm to call," Peter suggested.

"Go ahead."

"Well, why not?" Peter wondered, excitement creeping into his voice. He stood and went to the phone.

Tish turned away and headed back toward the bedroom. If the house was any good, it would already have been taken. No need to get too revved up.

She bent back over the bed and smoothed out the spread. Behind her, she heard Peter say, "Could I bring my wife over to look at it now?" That meant going out in the hundred-degree weather and trying to be excited for Peter's sake. As far as she was concerned, Tish wanted air-conditioning and enough room for the baby, period.

She went to her bureau and put her lipstick and brush and a little money into her purse. Peter came into the bedroom. "It's still available," he said happily. "Let's drive over and just take a look."

Tish nodded. Would she ever be happy when October hustled in.

"You want to drive?" Peter asked as they walked down the stairs.

"No, you go ahead," Tish answered, inserting herself carefully into the front seat and fastening her seat belt—something she had only lately begun to do.

They drove along Route #27 toward New Brunswick, moving slowly as they passed through Kingston and Kendall Park and Franklin Park, having to stop twice as churchgoers crossed the highway under the watchful look of patrolmen.

"I should have had something to eat," Tish announced at one point.

As they neared New Brunswick, passing the commuter's bus terminal, Tish turned suddenly to her husband. "Peter, have we got enough money to move? To pay rent and everything?"

Peter smiled knowingly. "Of course," he assured her. "I've got nearly six weeks' salary saved."

"You have?"

"Sure," he said. "After all, we haven't had to pay rent or electricity or water. Telephone bills aren't bad. What have we done, besides buy a few things, send you to the doctor, and eat?"

"Where's the money?" Tish asked.

Peter grinned at her, as he signaled a left turn at the railroad station and went beneath the overpass and up Easton Avenue. "It ain't in the mattress, honey," he said. "I've had a checking account for almost a month now. I have everything sent to me at work, so there's nothing for you to worry about."

He drove slowly through the usually busy neighborhood, the avenue studded on both sides with shops. He pulled a wallet from his back pocket and handed it to Tish. "Look what else I got," he said.

Tish opened the wallet. In the card section she found a Bank Americard with Peter's picture on it. "Where did you get this?" she asked, surprised.

"The bank," Peter replied. "I didn't really ask for it. But I have a feeling it's going to be a good thing to have. Everyone else has one."

He slowed and signaled a right-hand turn, easing the car

slowly around a corner and onto Morell Street. "Well, at least there are a lot of stores within walking distance," he observed.

"How much farther is it?" Tish asked.

"Not too much," said Peter, slowing again for a turn onto Sicard Street and driving a block farther. "Let's see, number seventy-three should be . . . just about . . . there!"

The house was frame, carefully painted and shuttered. It seemed small across the front. Tish wondered how far back into the property it extended. If the ad in the paper had been accurate, it must go back at least a hundred feet. The lawn was tiny but well-cared-for, flat, with few bushes and fewer flowers. It seemed, from a distance, a nice house, Tish decided, but interesting, no. Instantly she preferred her garage.

Together she and Peter walked slowly up the cement walkway. Peter stepped onto the stoop and rang the doorbell. After a moment, the door was opened. "Come in," said a voice whose owner Tish could not see.

Peter stepped inside, and Tish followed, looking at an old man who held the door for her. He was thin, very thin and stooped, but with high color to his face. "Mrs. McSweeny?" he asked pleasantly. Tish nodded.

Peter held out his hand. "Peter McSweeny, Mr. Wilson. We called a little while ago."

Tish turned to watch. Mr. Wilson closed the door and nodded slowly. "Yes, of course," he said, looking sideways at Peter, a lopsided grin creeping across his mouth. Tish shivered.

"Well," Mr. Wilson turned. "As I told you, I'm looking for a responsible couple to take care of the place. My son, in Florida, has an extra room where he lets me live during the winter. And I take no chances, not at my age, no sir. The minute summer is over, I'm off."

Mr. Wilson walked a few steps into the darkened hallway and stopped. "At my age, you can't be too careful."

"No, sir," Peter echoed, "you certainly can't."

Mr. Wilson nodded. "Now then, as I said, this is the living room." He pointed behind him. Tish craned her neck to look in. A long shadowy room was there, heavily furnished in thick velvet upholstery and Oriental rugs, ungainly tables and lamps made from cider jugs and candlesticks. The room extended almost twenty-five feet, from front to back, and Tish was not surprised. But it seemed more funeral home to her than a home for the living.

"There's the dining room," Mr. Wilson pointed, across the hall, "and the kitchen behind it."

Tish stepped past the old man and led Peter in the dining room. A polished mahogany table stood in the exact center of the room, with two chairs only at either end. There was a sideboard, a hutch arrangement, shelves totally empty. A Tiffany-like lamp hung above the table. On the far wall were gauzy white curtains, yellowed with age. Tish tried to smile and nod approvingly. Then she walked into the kitchen.

"Of course," she heard Mr. Wilson say to Peter behind her, "as I said before, the kitchen isn't the most modern feature of the place." Tish took one look and silently agreed. The refrigerator could be called an icebox, but only if you were insistently generous. A bare bulb hung above the sink, which was yellow and gray with stains. There were shelves along the wall where the stove stood, and pegboard above the stove itself from which hung copper-bottomed frying pans that Tish knew instantly hadn't been polished in twenty years. Light fought its way into the room through a cardboard-patched window.

Mr. Wilson walked with sudden speed past Tish and opened a door beside the stove. "And here," he muttered swiftly and under his breath, "is the bathroom. Has two doors."

He disappeared quickly as Tish and Peter followed, walking through the bathroom, feeling rather than seeing its chipped floor tiles and peeling paint above the tub. There was a hand-shower attachment to the nozzle there.

"Come in," Mr. Wilson motioned. "I made the bed today, young man. Here, Missus, is the master bedroom."

Tish looked puzzled as she stepped past Peter into the room. A double bed cringed in the middle of the floor, with two walnut side-tables at its head. Mr. Wilson threw back a large, heavily grooved wooden door and pulled a string. "Walk-in closet," he announced proudly.

Tish did not look into it. She was beginning to feel uncomfortable, and a little angry. What a waste of time.

"One terrific thing, Tish," said Peter brightly. "There's a bus that runs down Easton, and one on College. I could bus back and forth to work and you could keep the car when you needed it. And the shops are so fantastically close."

Tish nodded, and walked past Mr. Wilson. She found herself in the darkened hallway again, facing another door. Quickly and decisively, wanting to leave as soon as possible, she pulled the door open and walked directly into a sunflooded smaller bedroom, empty entirely but for the heat which seemed to spring from a crouch at her. She reeled.

Peter saw Tish stagger, and rushed into the room. "Are you all right, honey?"

Tish nodded weakly, and took a careful step toward the dank hallway.

"Probably all the walking," Peter explained to Mr. Wilson.

"Well," said the older man, "that's where the little one would go. It's not so bad in the winter. You need sun for a baby."

Peter supported Tish toward the front of the house. Mr. Wilson was only a pace behind. "What about the upstairs?" Peter asked over his shoulder.

"Well, like I said, they don't move in till after Labor Day," Mr. Wilson answered. "Won't have the back stairs finished till then, anyway. Nice people, though," he added.

"What do you think?" Peter whispered to Tish.

Tish looked slowly at Peter in astonishment, and screwed up her face to say silently, "You must be joking!" But then she saw an expectant smile on his face and stopped in midmessage. Something was happening over which she not only had no control but of which she began to feel the victim.

" 'Course," said Mr. Wilson, "the main feature is how close it is to the college. You'd have only a five-minute walk to class, and you could come home every day for lunch. Probably save money that way, too."

Tish watched Peter. His eyes were bright with enthusiasm, and there was a half-formed smile on his lips as he listened and nodded in agreement with the old man.

"Why don't you wait in the car, Tish?" Peter suggested, opening the front door for her. "Can you make it?"

Dazed, Tish went into the clearer, hot air.

She walked down the sidewalk and stood a moment at the side of the car. She looked back at the house. In any case, she thought, the rent was probably nothing. And it was only for a few months.

Then angrily she jerked the car door open and sat in the front seat, feeling her pulse quicken and hot perspiration form in the small of her back and between her shoulders.

"He thinks you're a student at Rutgers, doesn't he?" Tish asked as they drove back toward Princeton.

Peter smiled. "Must be used to students, I guess. Probably everyone who ever stays there is."

Peter swung the car off the road and Tish found herself suddenly staring at the glass front of Pack-a-Camp. Peter steered the car among the crazily parked, more nearly stacked cars of customers and stopped.

"Peter," Tish said, trying to sound firm but not unpleasant, "I'm hungry!"

"Just a minute, honey," he said, turning to give her a warm smile. "You've never seen the inside of the place. Wouldn't you like to see where your ever-lovin' husband spends so much of his time, and does so fantastically well?"

Tish stared at Peter a minute and then smiled weakly. "All right," she agreed, beginning to swing out of the car.

They walked across the cinder-stubbled parking lot, threading their way through groups of people bent over piles of merchandise, and entered the electric-eyed doors of the store. Tish almost pulled back as the roar of sound hit her: people talking, wondering, asking, bargaining and buying, feeling and trying on, lifting and settling, assembling. The place was alive with sound and sight and color, and banners draped across the entire width of the store advised that not only was this a once-in-a-lifetime-sale, but that it was currently in progress at seven other locations, as well.

The enormous warehouse-like room was divided and labeled into departments. Sleeping bags. Tents. Packs and Frames. Camping Accessories. Sporting Goods. Fishing Gear. Peter guided Tish through, waving twice at store personnel he knew as they walked.

"Pretty impressive, eh?" he whispered happily.

Tish's answering nod was honest; it was.

"Stay here a minute," Peter said eagerly. "Maybe I can make our first month's rent."

Tish started to object but was too late, as Peter moved swiftly away toward the Tent department.

Left with nothing to do, Tish moved slowly to follow Peter. He had already engaged a youngish-looking couple in conversation. She stood behind a pile of wooden stakes, and tried to hear what Peter said.

"Of course," he said, in mid-sentence, "if you're looking for something a little more substantial, we've got this terrific screen house, which is still, believe it or not, portable. Forty-nine ninety-nine, which is about thirty-five off."

He bent down and pulled a bag out of a counter shelf, tearing open the drawstring top and pulling things out as he spoke. "Comes with poles . . . stakes . . . and carrying bag, like this one. Duocom fabric roof, as you can feel, and terrific netted sides, made out of nylon."

The young woman who stood near Peter, her hands folded beneath her bosom and her face creased in thought, muttered, "I think that's a little steep, though."

Peter looked up at her and grinned. "Could be," he admitted. "Could be, but I've got this one, too." He bent down and pulled up another parcel. Tish moved nearer to hear more clearly.

"Now this," Peter began, "is sensational, a real bargain. No kidding. Less than thirty dollars. Weighs under four pounds and has four-way ventilation, which is important. Not only that, it has a screen door plus vents in the walls. Nylon floor, zippered rear window. And the carry-bag, of course."

"How much under thirty dollars?" asked the young woman's companion cagily.

Peter grinned. "Twenty-nine ninety-nine," he answered. "Not much, I grant you, but no misrepresentation, either."

He turned and caught sudden sight of Tish. His face lit. "Let me tell you," he said, "my wife and I, on our honeymoon, trekked up Mount Washington. Tish carried this herself, didn't you, honey?" Peter looked trustingly across at Tish. "Of course, that was before we found we were about to be presented with another, smaller pair of snowshoes. But it wasn't hard, was it, Tish? And no kidding, folks, when everything was assembled, it was really comfortable. Even in the rain. Right, Tish?"

Tish looked at Peter, frantically trying to figure whether she actually had to say something and lie, or whether his questions were rhetorical and meant only for his customers.

The young woman looked around and smiled warmly at her. Tish tried to return her friendliness.

"I don't think you'll be able to do any better anywhere," persisted Peter. "How are you fixed for bags?" he asked, turning quickly in another direction and guiding the couple ahead of him.

Tish stood without moving. Then, slowly but with determination, she fought her way out of the store, into the hot, acrid, gasoline-soaked air outside.

By the time Peter had returned to the car, happy and in triumph, Tish had forgotten how, once earlier, she had been so hungry.

28.

"You never even opened it!" Sara cried in disappointment. "You didn't even open the box!"

"Why should I have?" Tish asked. "I could read what it was. Really, Sara, we just didn't need brandy glasses right at the start."

"But they are so elegant," Sara remembered, holding the box to her chest. "Fragile, with wonderful silver leaf around the rims, and stems so thin you wouldn't believe!"

"Pack it, would you?" Tish said, half-irritated.

"Maybe you'll entertain Peter's boss or someone," Sara mused, putting the blue box into a larger carton. "Pretty soon, I mean, you'll have to really start playing ye olde helpmeet."

"I do, already."

Sara stood up and stretched. "I'll never understand how you got all this stuff from just a few people. I mean, an announcement usually doesn't bring in things like this."

"It's easy to be understanding at a distance," Tish guessed. "It's all nice to have, I guess."

"How many toasters did you get?"

"Three."

"Did you take two back?"

"We took three back," Tish answered. "We had one here already."

"What did you change them for?" Sara asked hopefully.

"Nothing."

"Nothing?"

"Peter thought we should get cash instead, where we could. For the baby."

"Well, that's thinking ahead, all right."

"Hand me that box, would you?" Tish asked, stretching out an arm in the direction she meant.

Sara stepped over two packed but yet unsealed crates and handed Tish what she wanted. "Want a Fresca?" she asked then.

"Desperately," said Tish. "But there isn't time. I'm trying to get all this done before Peter gets home."

"Okay," Sara said. "What do you want me to do next?"

Tish leaned back on her knees. "I don't know," she answered. "Just look around and see what we're forgetting. The movers get here so early in the morning we won't have time to think, let alone be fully awake."

Sara stepped over boxes and cartons, ducking her head in corners and around chairs. "There's not too much I can see," she announced. "Except what you've got in the bedroom. Clothes and things, and your sheets."

Tish leaned back again and then sat squarely on the floor, stretching her legs out in front of her. She wiped her forehead. September had held the heat of summer. There was still no trace that winter, or autumn even, would come to her rescue.

"What's the good word from Hank?" she asked after a moment.

"None," replied Sara. "He's spending ten days at his folks', in Michigan. Princeton doesn't open till Tuesday. I'm half-hoping he'll meet his old high-school sweetheart or someone and just not show up."

"Sara!" Tish said, struggling to stand and walking to a window that overlooked Mr. McSweeny's garden. "I thought Hank Rambler was the Big One!"

Sara grinned mischievously. "The biggest so far, anyway," she giggled.

Tish laughed, too. "I wonder if you'll say things like that in twenty years," she said over her shoulder.

"I certainly hope so. I don't intend to stop having experiences when I'm thirty-eight."

"You'll be exhausted by that time," Tish said, half turning. "You'll have lived twice as long as your years if you keep on."

"Well, Tish," Sara said slowly, "the thing is, last year was last year and life moves on. I mean, Hank was pretty terrific.

Is probably, still. But some of the newness is gone. The surprise. And we weren't developing any deep, dense sort of relationship out of bed anyway."

"You seemed to be wildly in love," Tish recalled. "And fairly happy."

"I was, I know," said Sara. "Well, I suppose I could be again, if I had to. But I'd rather branch out a little."

"I'll be right back, Sara," Tish said suddenly. "Mr. McSweeny's down there."

"Okay," Sara said, undisturbed. "I'll just lie around, trying to remember what it was like before Hank."

"Empty, I thought you told me," Tish said, standing at the door.

"Well, not entirely, I admit," Sara said with a smile, letting herself fall backwards onto the couch, her feet flying up into the air as her head hit the cushions.

Tish shook her head in wonder, and started down the steps.

But when she got to the bottom of the stairway and looked into the garden, Mr. McSweeney had disappeared. "George?" she called hesitantly.

"What?" came a disgruntled voice from somewhere ahead.

"Where are you?"

"Here."

Tish nodded her head and smiled. That was informative. She took a few quick steps toward the rose bushes and stopped. "Now where are you?" she asked.

"Same place."

"Very helpful," Tish said and walked closer yet to the garden.

What she first saw were crossed legs, seeming to grow from an old bent skewered pine on the edge of the walled enclosure. Mr. McSweeny's legs were crossed at the ankles and he was lying on his back, hands behind his head, staring at the plants around him.

Tish entered the garden proper, walking carefully on dainty brick walks that crossed and recrossed their paths.

"You look as though you've just been hit on the head with an apple," Tish teased, seeing her father-in-law sprawled out. "Failing that, what have you discovered?"

Mr. McSweeny closed his eyes and smiled.

When he said nothing, Tish decided to fill the silence. "I

didn't know today was National Do-Nothing Day," she said.
"If I had, I'd have planned our move differently."

"I'm depressed," Mr. McSweeny said at last.

"About what?"

"About everything."

Tish sat on the ground near him and wondered aloud,
"Whatever for?"

Mr. McSweeny opened his eyes and let his head roll to one
side so he could see Tish squarely. "I'm fifty-three years old,"
he announced mournfully.

"That's not so bad," Tish comforted.

"*I* don't think it is, either. But I wonder."

"About what?"

"About what comes next," said Mr. McSweeny. "I almost
quit today, Tish. Flat out. Resigned."

"Why didn't you?"

"I don't know," said her father-in-law. "Maybe because
secretly, in my heart of hearts, I keep expecting an omen.
Some sort of sign—like Kate, at forty-whatever, suddenly
needing braces. Or your having twins. My waking up one
day, staying home to start the Great American Novel."

"If you get the sign, then what?" asked Tish.

"I don't know that, either. The way I see it, one day everything becomes clear and I can see the future and the past
equally well. With that new knowledge, I'll know exactly
what I'm meant to do."

"Who says you're not meant to do what you already do?"

"No one," Mr. McSweeny sighed. "No one at all. If I
weren't so good at it, I wouldn't have these problems."

Tish smiled. "I don't see what problems you do have," she
said. "After all, you've made it. You're on top. You have a
lovely wife and family. You're as comfortable as anyone
ever could be."

"But not happy," Mr. McSweeny added. "The thing is, I
never see any people."

"I thought it was *people* who bought stocks and bonds,"
Tish said.

Mr. McSweeny nodded. "They do, but I never see them.
Up where I am, Tish, I have to administrate. Give speeches,
open new offices, make policy. The *real* people are statistics
after a while. Everything is, after a while." There was a moment of silence before Mr. McSweeny sighed philosophically.

"You know, honey, most things people fail to do are caused
by a failure to start. If I only knew what it was I wanted to
do, *I* would start."

"What are your options?"

Mr. McSweeny laughed softly to himself. "I've had two
ideas lately. One is going down to Davidson's and asking to
be a check-out boy."

"Kate would love that!"

"What it would do for me is what matters," Mr. McSweeny
said. "I'd feel more like a person again. I'd be closer to what
people care about."

"What's the second possibility?" asked Tish.

"Well, actually there are three. The second is asking John
Donaldson if he needs extra help at the garage. And the third
is going to Rutgers. Studying something like landscape archi-
tecture. I mean, I do like plants, working with my hands, feeling
the earth and knowing I can't get it all out from under my
fingernails. That really pleases me, in a simpleminded way."

"Do it," Tish said.

"I might. I might."

Tish didn't think Mr. McSweeny sounded convinced and
ready to act, but she said nothing.

"Who's up there helping you?" Mr. McSweeny wondered.

"Sara Wallace, an old friend of mine from before."

"How are you coming along? Pretty well finished?"

"No," Tish said. "It looks that way, and it certainly feels
as though we should be. But I just know there are a thousand
things I haven't done yet."

"Well, there's still time, I guess," Mr. McSweeny said. "I'll
miss you, Tish."

Tish nodded thoughtfully. "I'll miss you, too, George," she
said timidly. "You're the one person in my whole life, recent
life anyway, that always remembers and makes me remember
that I'm a human being." She stopped a moment, feeling too
sentimental to go on. She swallowed the feeling.

"Doesn't Peter do that, too?" asked Mr. McSweeny.

29.

The room was terribly bright. Tish could sense that even
before opening her eyes which, when she did, she found

difficult to do. She had the sensation of being weighted down, her legs seemed numb and unresponsive, her arms and fingers could be moved but only with the greatest of conscious effort. She felt warm, though, which encouraged her, and soon enough the ceiling—bare, clean, yet streaked with light which gave it a false texture—was seen unblinkingly.

Her mother's face suddenly broke the brightness. It was lined with worry, seemed heavier than before, older. Its eyes were otherworldly: one looked as though it had been crying, the other was demonically bright, mischievous. How strange, Tish thought, to be able to look so long and see so separately.

"Tish," said her mother softly, slowly, letting the sibilant sound ease into the air around Tish's ears. "Oh, Tish," she said again, shaking her head half sadly, half in muted I-told-you-so fashion.

"Hello, Mother," Tish said in reply. "I wasn't expecting you."

Her mother nodded as though she understood. Then Tish felt her left hand being clasped and patted protectively. Her mother seemed unable to speak for emotion of some dimly realized kind.

"Well," Tish tried saying, but found her voice had dropped to an odd conspiratorial whisper. "What's new?"

Mrs. Davies' right eye began tearing. Her left eye gleamed brightly down.

Then Tish noticed her mother's mouth. It, too, seemed divided, half turned down in sadness, half turned up in a smile. As her mother spoke, and before Tish decoded her message, she was surprised to see the words coming out slowly, first from one side, then from the other, finally through the middle.

"The baby," said Mrs. Davies sadly. "You're free," she said happily. "The baby was . . . stillborn," came the entire thought.

Tish watched the words, coming out and sliding into the air, hanging there a moment before, like heat, rising.

"Ummmm," Tish said dreamily.

"Darling," her mother said. "We're so sorry. You're so glad."

Tish tried to lean up on an elbow, on both elbows, but her shoulders seemed anchored to her bed. Now she thought she understood. Mrs. Davies stood upright, straight-lined at the bedside, watching.

There was no warning noise. Peter suddenly appeared, shoving Mrs. Davies roughly toward a corner. Tish strained to see what had happened to her mother. She had disappeared.

"Don't listen, sweetheart," Peter said firmly.

Tish looked at Peter and relaxed, sinking back onto her pillow, the sides of which seemed quickly soft and folded up around her ears. She felt cozy and warm and quite safe.

She saw Peter turn to one side. From someone in white he picked a blanket-wrapped bundle and folded it carefully in his arms. He looked down at what he held and smiled proudly. He looked then at Tish and nodded. "Good for you," he said. "Good for you."

After a long moment in which nothing seemed to move, or to happen, Peter began bending down ever so slowly toward Tish's bedside, easing gently what he held into the crook of her left arm. He arranged Tish's arm and hand with great deliberateness around something. She did not look at what she held. She looked only at Peter who, for reassurance, winked at her and grinned.

Finally, understanding that she was to do so, she craned her neck around to see what it was that had been presented to her.

A small human being was nestling there, in Tish's arm. She was surprised. "Oh!" she smiled. She was unable to do more. She could not caress the child, or smooth its blankets. In spite of thinking how to move her right arm, or how to squinch around in bed a little to be able more directly and clearly to see the child, she could not move. Instead, she looked at it only from the corner of her eye, immobilized.

The child seemed quite small. Smaller than Tish had thought a baby should ever be. Its face was flushed from breathing. It had a light dusting of golden hair on its head, straight, and its eyes seemed clenched shut against the light in the room. A tiny hand circled in the air. Tish counted carefully, and very slowly, the fingers on it. Five. The other hand sprang into action. It, too, had five fingers.

Tish felt herself smiling. She looked up at Peter. "It's a girl, isn't it?" she asked. Peter nodded with fatherly solemnity.

"Good for you," he said again. "Good for you. You did a good job."

Tish nodded. She felt gratified.

The baby squirmed in her arm. Tish had forgotten for a moment that it could move. She was surprised. She tried again to move her head to look closer at the child, but could move only slowly and with a strange creaking in her ears. Was that the bed?

As though to make matters easier, the child herself was moving, toward Tish, as though she understood the difficulty her mother was having and wanted to help. Tish smiled as the child's head began to rotate toward its right, toward her.

A weight of sensation descended. Tish was able to move, move more quickly, she knew, than ever before in her life she had moved. Her arm became alive suddenly. Her voice felt as though it were returning. It was no longer difficult or sleepy-feeling to have her eyes open. Reflexively, she looked at the child and at the same moment opened her left arm, bouncing the child from its security, and her right hand crossed her body at the same moment that she sat up partially, in terror. She opened her mouth to scream but nothing was heard. She was only aware of her own hands, the hands of the child's mother, hurling the child down from the bed and watching it bounce loudly and with a ringing echo along the plastic-tiled floor. It came to rest in a corner, unmoving.

The child's head was turned toward its mother's bed, resting now peacefully on the same side as that which Tish had first seen.

The other side, its left side, beaconed back. An enormous purple and black birthmark started beneath its fine, yellow hair and ended somewhere below its soft cotton gown. Its left eye was open and not moving.

With tremendous effort, Tish jerked open her eyes. There. It was over. She looked around. Fallen from the left arm of her chair was Dr. Spock's *Baby and Child Care.* She leaned down and looked at the page she had folded over to mark: 469. "He'll Be Happier Without Pity."

She closed the book silently and leaned back into the chair. No wonder, she thought.

She looked at her wristwatch, at the same time hearing a restless sound behind her. Slowly she stood up, leaving the light on, and turned toward the hallway. "Peter?" she called tentatively.

"What?" came his reply.

"Oh," Tish said. "I didn't know you were back. Have you been here long?"

There was a pause before Peter answered. "Not so very," he said. "The show was over about eleven."

Tish stopped in mid-step. She stood still. Had she forgotten? Again? "What show?" she called softly, half-hoping Peter wouldn't hear her.

"The new Hitchcock," he sent back.

Tish nodded to herself, and went again toward the kitchen. "Oh," she murmured. "Would you like some tea?"

"No thanks, honey," he called. "I've got a big day tomorrow."

Tish went into the kitchen and put a pot of water on the stove. Unconsciously she examined the room for the hundredth time. Some of what they had done did make her feel accomplished. The tricolored striped wallboard had brought light and order into the room. The window had been repaired. The copper skillets had been polished, hard, an entire day's task, and glittered above the stove in the beams of the recessed spotlights Peter had installed. It was true, of course, that the icebox still stood where it had for perhaps forty years. The stove, cleaned inside and out, looked about the same as it had that first day—barely able to get enough heat together to boil an egg. Still, the effort had been worth it. In spite of herself, she felt Mr. Wilson's downstairs five rooms were more and more hers, and more and more fitting.

She poured the water into a mug and dropped a teabag into it. Idly she played with the string, lifting and letting it fall back into the steaming liquid. When it was dark as coffee, she pulled the bag out and put it in a teaspoon, wrapping it tightly with its string to squeeze the remaining moisture from it. Two enormous tablespoons of sugar and some half-and-half, and Tish sipped slowly, already walking, automatically snapping the switch near the door of the bathroom.

Uneasily Tish stationed herself at the doorway to her bedroom and watched Peter slipping into bed. "I didn't know you were going to a movie," she said very quietly. "I thought tonight was for McGovern."

Peter did not look at her as he spoke. "I told you, yesterday," he said, settling into a comfortable position on his side.

Tish felt hollow in her stomach. "No, you didn't," she said.

Peter was silent. "I meant to, then," he muttered ungraciously.

"Who'd you go with?" Tish asked.

"Nobody," Peter answered. "Just some guys from the store."

"Are they nobody?" Tish asked sardonically.

"Look," Peter said, turning in bed onto his other side, "I said I told you. If I didn't, too bad. I meant to. It's no big thing."

Tish took a swallow of tea. "No, I know it isn't," she agreed. "Except that you did the same thing last week. That makes twice you've been to the movies alone."

"Not alone," Peter corrected.

"You know what I mean," Tish said. "Without me, anyway."

Peter said nothing. His arm lifted from beneath his pillow and he reached out to turn off the bedside lamp. "Turn it on," Tish snapped instantly.

Peter didn't move. Without a sound, Tish glided to the bed and turned the light on herself.

"You don't have to be married, you know," she said bitterly. "I mean, if you'd rather barrel all over town pretending you aren't, you may as well not be."

Peter groaned, and sat up.

"Don't look at me that way," Tish commanded. "Yes, we *are* going to do it all over again." She turned away for a moment, and then faced him. "Do you really expect me to believe that you can forget, whenever you want to, that you have a wife. So easily?"

"Believe it or not, it's up to you," Peter said, leaning back against the headboard. "But I can tell you one thing, Tish. I think you're getting paranoid."

"What the hell do you mean?" Tish whirled on him. Her face had lost its color. "Paranoid like hell!" she half-shouted.

"Well," Peter said, "it's not me who's suspicious all the time."

"Of course it isn't you," Tish spat out. "You're out every day, doing things. Seeing people. I'm trapped here. Just me and this godawful house you insisted on having. Me, and the Claytons upstairs. Terrific!"

Peter waited a moment before speaking again, and then he did so in a gentler, less combative tone. "You could go to classes, like you used to."

"I don't know anyone here!" Tish half-wailed.

"Well, still there's a lot to do, with the baby and all," Peter counseled. "You've got nearly everything you could want. Why don't you start doing something with it? Fix up the other room."

"Because," Tish said slowly and clearly, "I don't think it's right to have to do it alone. It's your baby, too. You're supposed to take some small amount of interest in what happens."

"Oh, I do, sweetheart," Peter said, his voice softening even more.

"Well," Tish moped, "you certainly don't seem to, sometimes."

Peter smiled a little, recognizing her tone as childish. He patted the side of the bed. "Come here," he said consolingly. "Come on."

Tish blushed for herself and put the teacup on the bedside table. Uneasily she sat where Peter directed. She did not look at him.

After a moment, Peter laughed softly, and put out his arms. Tish leaned tiredly into them, letting her head sink onto his chest.

"That's better," Peter said, stroking her hair. "Sweetheart, we're both edgy. Everything is sort of closing in. I'm working too hard, maybe. You're alone too much. But we have to remember that it won't be this way always. That what we're doing is setting up something we can be proud of later."

"Why later?"

"Not later, then," Peter said. "What we decided to do was the absolute right thing. It may not be the easiest, but it is the best. Sometimes we both forget how new we are at it, both of us. I forget sometimes. You do. We'll get better at it, at all of it."

"Are you glad we got married, Peter?"

"Of course I am. I have to be, don't I?"

"That's not funny."

"Maybe not, sweetheart," Peter admitted. "But it's true."

"Do you like me, Peter?"

"What a dumb question."

Tish pulled up and away from his arms. "I mean it, though,"

she insisted. "Do you like me, to spend time with and have around?"

Peter smiled warmly. He nodded.

"Then what I don't understand," Tish started to say. She stopped. She had promised herself she wouldn't ask questions like this.

"Go ahead, sweetheart," Peter urged. "What is it? That's not fair."

Tish hated herself even before she spoke. "Then how come you take every excuse to be away from here?"

Peter's face lost its contentment. "Jesus!" he said under his breath.

"I'm serious," Tish said. "Sara says she sees you a lot in Princeton, with other guys, bumming around."

"Fuck her."

"Well, is she right? What do you do with those people? Why can't I go along?"

Peter straightened his posture and sat upright entirely. He pulled the sheets close to his body, wrapping them at his waist. "Sara is a nosy bitch," he said. "First of all, I'm not in Princeton a lot. Sometimes I'll go out for coffee or a sandwich, and sometimes I'll drive all the way over there, just for the hell of it, to get it. With one guy or another from the store. It's no big deal. It's nothing secret or sensational or important. After all, we each have to have a little privacy in our lives. We're not the same person one hundred percent."

"Sara said she saw you with a girl, Peter."

Peter snorted. "She's full of shit," he replied angrily. "The only time I'm ever over there with anyone even faintly feminine is on a McGovern night. Jesus," he sighed, "that's where I said I'd work for the man. They expect me."

Neither spoke.

"I don't have to answer all this crap, Tish," Peter said evenly. "I can't help what suspicions you have. You can spend all day manufacturing scenes and getting jealous. But at a certain point you'll just have to choose between Sara and me, between your imagination and me. Either take what I say as true, accept me as I am, or check out."

Tish recoiled, startled. "You can say that so easily?" She kept her voice steady only with great effort.

Peter sighed deeply and again held out his arms. "Okay,

okay," he murmured, pulling Tish toward him. "Let's forget it. I'm sorry. I just can't stand the bugging." He stroked Tish's hair again, but her body was stiffened against him. "I'm your husband, honey. You've got to learn to be more trusting. I'll tell you if I'm going to fuck around."

Tish closed her eyes, still spring-tight. "It's not that," she said. "It's all of it."

"I know, I know," Peter comforted. His hand caressed her neck, massaging one shoulder.

After a few moments, Tish did relax. She felt half-guilty relenting. What she had wanted firmly settled had not been. But some control, she knew, was necessary. She had to calm down, to cease having jealous images floating before her eyes from early morning until night. Maybe she was a little paranoid. How could she be sure, she wondered. Maybe it was her.

Peter's hand held her neck firmly now, and his other hand had disappeared inside her robe and was gently rubbing the tops of her breasts. Tish sighed and leaned back, enough for Peter to be able to grasp her face and to kiss her.

She was lowered gently across Peter's body, as he bent over her, still kissing her deeply and steadily. The hardness she felt at her back, from between Peter's legs, reminded her of her triumph. The other doubt she had had for some time was unfounded then.

30.

Tish was glad she had dressed early, as she waited patiently for the deliveryman to find the proper slip for her to sign. She leaned against the front-door frame, watching stragglers or people with no first-hour class saunter along Sicard Street, to turn at the corner and head for the campus.

"Ah," she heard the man say to himself. He offered his clipboard to her and the pencil attached on a string, and Tish signed her name twice, where the man directed. She thanked him and took the thin, long parcel from his hands.

Unwilling yet to step out of the morning sunshine and back into Mr. Wilson's shadows, Tish leaned languidly back and held the package in her hands. The people she saw seemed so eager, so young and eager and unconcerned. Unaware of her movements, she put her parcel under her arm and let her other arm cross in front of her body, her hand stroking tentatively the round, unequal but firm bulge.

She continued to watch a moment more. Then, as she was about to turn and enter the house, she saw Charlotte Clayton walking briskly against the tide, returning. From her point, Charlotte too saw Tish and waved a pleasant greeting at her.

Charlotte turned up the walk and came toward Mr. Wilson's front door. She paused where a second walk branched off, which would lead her to her own entryway in the rear of the house. "You're looking very *Ladies' Home Journal*," she estimated with a smile.

"For the moment, anyway," Tish said. "Want a cup of coffee?"

"My dear," Charlotte exclaimed. "If I'd known you were up and serving, I would never have dressed! I'd just have stamped my foot."

Tish stepped aside as Charlotte passed her and went into the house. "Come to think of it," Tish said, closing the door after herself, "I don't think I've ever even heard you up there at this time of the morning. I know I've never seen you out."

"Special day," Charlotte said, turning easily and gracefully toward Tish.

"Why?"

"Today's the day I go into New York to be wined and dined and made much of by my publisher."

"Really?" Tish was impressed.

Charlotte laughed. "It's not as grand as all that," she admitted. "What I think it is is a payoff. Random House is so glad I'm writing about someone else, they keep stuffing me, like a goose."

Tish led Charlotte into the kitchen. "There's no place to sit," she said. She poured two mugs of coffee, giant ones. "We can go into the living room."

Charlotte took an immediate swallow and mumbled, "Great!" Tish wondered whether that was in honor of her coffee or the living room.

"What's that?" Charlotte asked, pointing to the package Tish still carried under an arm.

"Oh! I forgot," Tish said, putting her mug down. After some difficulty, she opened the parcel.

"How cute!" exclaimed Charlotte, grabbing the long

wooden bar from Tish's hands and swinging at the rattles and figures that dangled from it. "Where's the crib? We can put it on right now."

"No," Tish said. "I'll do it later." She took the plaything from Charlotte and placed it beneath her chair.

Charlotte watched closely. "What's the matter with it? Isn't it what you wanted?"

Tish blushed. "Of course it is," she said. "I just thought I'd wait a bit, is all."

Charlotte shrugged. "How much more time do you have?"

"Another three, three and a half months," Tish answered.

"Well, that certainly gives you plenty of time."

Tish coughed. "Actually, I'm going to send it back."

"Oh?"

"Yes. We have so many things now," Tish explained. "We'll never be able to pay for it all."

"Let Peter worry about that," advised Charlotte.

"That's the trouble," Tish said honestly, looking down at the floor. "I don't think he ever worries about it. He just sees what he thinks a baby should have and charges it."

"Lucky baby," Charlotte said.

"Maybe."

Charlotte looked up quickly, over the rim of her mug, and then decided to say something else. "I hate getting up in the morning."

"I never hear you working," Tish said.

"Well, I *try* to be considerate. After your baby arrives, I'll move my typewriter into the front room. I figured now, though, you'd rather not hear the slamming and snapping and swearing that goes into a book."

"Who do you swear at?" Tish wondered.

"Myself mostly. Sometimes Freddy. Sometimes Random. Sometimes just men in general." She laughed. "They all swear at me, so why not?"

"What are you working on now?" Tish asked, feeling suddenly like the perfect interested matron at tea.

"Exposing," Charlotte answered. "I'm doing a number on how, in spite of incredible waste and mismanagement and murderous office politics, books that make a difference some-how—mysteriously—keep coming out of one particular publishing house."

"Which one?"

"That would be telling," Charlotte hedged happily. "Enough to say it's one owned by an electronics firm. Part of a conglomerate. That's their trouble."

Tish nodded, hoping that her nod indicated that she understood what Charlotte was saying. "Is there any more coffee?" Charlotte asked, standing up. "I made a foray to that gruesome little diner on Easton, and my stomach is so full of acid and grease that a little more caffeine can't hurt. No, sit there. I'll get it."

Within what seemed to Tish a very short time, Charlotte was back, carrying the pot and her own mug. Without first asking, she stood near Tish and refilled her cup, putting the pot on top of a nearby magazine on the floor. Almost subconsciously, Tish was aware how competent Charlotte seemed. Tall and dark but with an Irish coloring, dressed the way Tish felt she would like to if only she weren't laden with her eternal surprise.

Tish took a thoughtful sip of her coffee. "How do you and Freddy ever find time to do things?" she asked. "I mean, if you work all night, and he teaches all day."

Charlotte smiled. "He's not out all the time. He spoils me terribly. Comes sneaking home at lunch with food and wakes me up, pampering me the entire time. I adore it. That's why I had to go out to the diner. There's nothing even faintly resembling food upstairs. A magician would throw up his hands in despair."

Tish smiled politely, but she was already shaking her head in puzzlement. "Maybe I'm just old-fashioned," she said slowly, "but I always thought a husband and wife should be doing things together."

Charlotte's eyes widened a bit, and her cup came down from her face. "But hasn't Peter told you?" she asked. "Didn't he explain things?"

Tish was more confused. "What things?" she said, uneasily.

Charlotte smiled reassuringly. "It's nothing deep or mysterious, I guess. But Freddy and I aren't married."

"You're not?"

Charlotte shook her head. "We were. Once."

Tish laughed self-consciously. "Then I certainly don't understand," she admitted.

"It's not so tough to grasp, really," Charlotte said. "We were married, for four years. But things got a little out of hand. Freddy found himself among his cronies, and I found my own. Pretty soon we were saying hello in the mornings, period. Sometimes he didn't come in at night. Sometimes I didn't."

Charlotte paused, but Tish had nothing to say.

"One day, we just decided that what we had couldn't be called a marriage at all, not in the usual sense," Charlotte continued. "It was more than just being into Women's Lib, or believing in the sacredness of privacy. We liked the same things, and some of the same people. But we seemed only to like them together when we were apart. Oh my!" Charlotte said. "That sounds horribly complex."

"I'll admit that," Tish said.

"In any case, one morning we happened to be home at the same time. And thinking about the same things. So, we decided to call it. Eighty-six the whole thing. Which we did. I took the midnight ride to El Paso."

"Weren't you upset?"

Charlotte sat motionless a moment, remembering. "I was," she admitted at last. "But I decided that was a hangover from my childhood. Believing that divorce is an admission of defeat, I mean. What I finally decided it meant was better understanding, a freedom to act."

"But what about now?" Tish asked.

"Well, now things are different, and exactly the same," Charlotte said, waving her mug in one hand, carefully. "What I mean is, Freddy and I found that in spite of all the things we did separated, for some strange reason those infrequent early-morning hello's were important. They seemed to give us anchors. We had a home, you see, without even realizing that we'd made one. It seemed necessary to us both, in order to go off and be ourselves."

"You don't mean——?" Tish started, and then hesitated.

Charlotte nodded. "If you want to know were we both sleeping around, the answer is yes. I mean, at least I was, and I don't doubt that Freddy was, too. We never discussed it, person by person or affair by affair. These things happen, and life goes on."

"I couldn't live that way," Tish said.

"Yes, you could, Tish," Charlotte answered. "I'm not saying you would, by choice. But you could if you had reasoned things out the way we have. I'm not preaching, but

Freddy and I feel pretty much the same way about love."

"That's the first time you've even hinted at that," Tish noted.

Charlotte nodded, agreeing. "Well," she said slowly, "sometimes people feel without verbalizing. We do, Freddy and I. Independently, we both came to understand that we did love each other. And that that gave us the freedom to love other people. That's what the early-morning hello's were all about. We had to come back and say hi to each other because we liked each other. We trusted each other to use good judgment and never embarrass the other person. And we never assumed anything."

"What do you mean, never assumed?"

"Rule Number One in any relationship: never assume," Charlotte said. "Never assume anything. For example, if you're married and your husband disappears for a few hours unexpectedly, if you begin instantly to assume he's out playing around, you make your own life hell. The assumption doesn't bother him at all. Whether or not he's hard at some lady, he doesn't know, and won't, until you let him have it when he gets back. Then, of course, you inflate his ego beyond belief. Further, no man likes a jealous woman. What matters is not whether he was actually out screwing, but what it meant to him. If it meant nothing, you haven't lost anything at all. You've strengthened your relationship. Instinctively he understands you understand, and he's grateful and warm in return."

Tish had begun suddenly to perspire. She stood up and walked across the living room, grateful for the small flow of air that was stirred by her movement.

"I guess this is pretty heavy for early A.M., isn't it, Tish?" Charlotte said with genuine concern in her voice. "I'm not criticizing what anyone does. What kind of marriage people feels fits them. I couldn't."

"I really am old-fashioned," Tish said quietly. "I think all that freedom you talk about would kill me."

"Not if I'd been able to get to your head before Peter got to your crotch," Charlotte said firmly.

Tish smiled. "My mother got there," she said ruefully. "I guess what I feel is what she does, or wants to."

"Does she have a good marriage?" Charlotte asked. "On her terms, I mean."

Tish stopped pacing. "I guess so. Now that I think of it,

she's mostly in charge, so she must feel satisfied."

"What about your father?"

"I guess he doesn't mind," Tish said. "He makes noises, but it's Mother who runs things."

"Do you feel sorry for him?"

Tish thought about this for a moment. "I don't see how I can," she said. "If he doesn't, why should I? He got comfortable."

Tish took another step. "Peter's family is different, though. There it's his father who manages everything."

"Really?" Charlotte asked, a new interest in her tone.

Tish nodded. "It seems that way to me, anyway," she answered. "Peter's mother secretly wanted to break us up, just the same way my mother did. Probably still does. But Mr. McSweeny wouldn't allow her even to try."

"Good for him," Charlotte said.

"I guess," Tish tacked on.

"My lord!" Charlotte shouted, jumping up. "Look at the time!"

"Do you have to go?"

"If I want to catch the ten fifty-five bus, I do, Tish," she answered. "A freebie is a freebie, even though it costs you a couple bucks to get to it."

Charlotte carried her mug and the coffeepot back into the kitchen. Tish followed her, keeping step as Charlotte preceded her then toward the front of the house.

"Charlotte?" Tish said haltingly.

"What, honey?"

"Weren't you jealous the first time?"

Charlotte leaned against the door. "Terribly," she said. "I was hurt and angry and determined to strike back. I didn't, of course. Not right away. First what I did was make Freddy's life absolute hell. That made me feel good for a while, even though I couldn't sleep. Triumph is not always a restful emotion." Charlotte stopped, looking at Tish and wondering whether she wanted to hear more.

"Go on, please," Tish urged.

"Well, making a short story of it, then, after a lot of soul-searching and replaying and sessions in which I was both the interviewer and the interviewee, I arrived at a new frame of mind. The important thing, I found, and I admit this was before I found out that Freddy and I did seem truly to need each other to the extent we do—the important thing to remember is that you can't be unfaithful if you're unhappy."

"You can't?" Tish had no idea what Charlotte meant.

Charlotte put an arm on Tish's shoulder. "I went out one night, bound and determined to sleep with the first man who asked me," she said. "I sat in some terribly dingy bar and waited, thinking I was gorgeous. I tried imagining I was a new hooker on the beat. What happened was that nothing happened. I was unhappy and it showed. People don't pick up unhappy people. They've got enough problems of their own."

"Yes, but how could anyone ever be happy being unfaithful?"

"In time, it's easy," Charlotte said. "As soon as I understood that Freddy and I were, somehow, in some fashion, necessary to each other, that gave me the home base I needed. I felt more secure. Freddy would always, sooner or later, turn up if I needed him. Till then, I was on my own. What he didn't know wouldn't damage him, and vice versa. People are a horrible breed, I guess," she said, shaking her head. "Nothing seems quite so much fun unless you're doing it on the sly. Open infidelity is a bore. Hiding it adds excitement. That is, if you insist on thinking of what you're doing as infidelity. We don't. Not any more."

"I don't know what you could call it, then," Tish said, half-scolding.

"My God!" Charlotte threw back her head and laughed. "Am I glad there's a little morality in the next generation, anyway! I'm sorry," she added, becoming more serious. "I'm not pushing sex around, Tish. Really I'm not. Everything depends on your attitude. You do what fits you best. Just remember, never assume."

Charlotte gave Tish a quick, friendly kiss on the cheek and opened the front door. "Thanks for the coffee," she said. "I loved it. Now I'll try to learn how to make it, and we can do this again, upstairs. Bye."

Tish moved to the door frame. "Bye," she called. "Good luck!"

She closed the door again and stood motionless in the hallway, wondering if Charlotte was truly as happy and well adjusted as she thought she was.

31.

There was a short stretch along the canalside that ran level and was empty of pitfalls and tree trunks and high grasses. Tish looked ahead and saw it and closed her eyes. Delicately, slowly, she walked a few feet without looking, feeling through her closed lids the sun above light her face, when leaves and clumps of pine boughs allowed. Carefully she put out one foot, feeling tentatively before placing all her weight on it, and then the other. She held her arms out at her sides, shoulder high, smiling as she imagined what she looked like from the other side of the water.

There was almost an hour before she was to meet Peter at Palmer Stadium. The first Saturday of October had started badly—clouds and a headachy dampness—but surprisingly it had cleared later into a perfect autumn afternoon. She hadn't really wanted to go to a football game, but now she minded less. At least it wasn't cold or uncomfortable.

She opened her eyes and stopped moving. At her left, a canoe silently wandered downstream, the man at its stern merely keeping his paddle in the water as a rudder, happy enough, it seemed, to let the small boat go where it would. Tish pulled her wool skirt around her legs and sat gingerly on the grass to watch.

As the canoe disappeared behind some overhanging branches, Tish remained seated. She was almost covered in sun, and comfortable, and feeling momentarily lazy.

She was also, momentarily, as she braced herself carefully by putting her hands flat behind her on the ground, feeling proud. For last evening, acting on Charlotte Clayton's non-assumptive clause, she had held her tongue.

Earlier in the day, after Peter had left the house, around eleven, a telephone call had disturbed her housework. She had turned off the vacuum, counting the fourth ring by the time she was able to reach it.

"Hello," she had said.

"Is Peter McSweeny there, please?" It was the voice of a woman, businesslike but young.

"No, I'm afraid he's out. Could I take a message?" Tish had said, going instantly cold and then, almost as quickly, hot and suspicious.

"No, thanks very much," the woman had said. "But there

is one thing. If you speak to him, would you ask him to call Pack-a-Camp? We thought he might be unwell."

Tish didn't know what to say. "Isn't he there?" she asked, now concerned.

"Not yet," the woman said pleasantly. "I'm sure he'll show. Probably had car trouble or something. Thanks very much."

"Bye," Tish said, hanging onto the phone, though at the other end the caller had replaced her receiver. It could be car trouble, Tish had thought, if Peter had taken the car.

She had put the phone down finally, and stood in the hallway, thinking. At least she needn't be jealous. The caller was from Peter's office. She felt relieved. Until she realized that Peter wasn't at his office, and that there was no way of knowing where exactly he was. Maybe there was a second, another, a real other woman somewhere. If he'd been in an accident, surely she would have heard by now. If he were thinking of looking for another job, he might have mentioned it to her.

Tish had shrugged then and made what she knew quickly to be an adult decision. There was nothing she could do. There was no information she could get. There was no reason to get angry, or apprehensive, until she knew for certain what any of this meant. And, she had decided with a nod to herself, she was not going to ask.

She hadn't. She had waited for Peter at the end of the day, somehow going about her chores and errands cheerfully, even though she knew the cheer false. Then Peter had called. He would be late. Go ahead without him. Tish spoke evenly and without, she hoped, traces of anything she might actually feel. She had her dinner. She watched Walter Cronkite. She read, or started to reread, Dr. Spock, having decided that one book on baby care was more than enough and that there was no reason to confuse herself.

She had watched a film on television. She bathed, put on her robe and nightgown, and took last week's *Sunday New York Times* crossword puzzle to bed for company. She had never completed one, but it kept her mind occupied, and she had a feeling of learning a little something as she struggled.

Peter came in near midnight. Tish had fallen asleep, sitting up.

She realized as she sat at the water's edge that that had

been a very happy thing, indeed. If she had been totally alert and wakeful, she couldn't ever have not said what she wanted to. Instead, she had dreamily said hello to Peter, put the paper on the floor near the bed, and crawled more comfortably under the bedcovers. This morning, while making plans to meet at the stadium, getting breakfast, and seeing Peter off for a half-day's work, there hadn't been time to be the shrew she felt she honestly wanted to be.

Tish stood and dusted off the back of her skirt. Slowly she began walking back toward her car, near the Griggsville store. Taking a quick swipe at a bush as she passed, she suddenly laughed aloud. What, she had wondered, would happen if she could get Charlotte and M.O. Olivera together, face to face, to talk about their ideal marriages? Would that ever be fun!

Walking down the slight hill, Tish could see Peter standing among a crowd of people at Gate 15. She smiled as she approached, thinking that Peter was one of the best-looking men she had ever seen, young or old.

She went to him and took his arm. "Ready, gang?" he called back over his shoulder.

Tish turned, too, to see Poncho Olivera, his younger brother Tommy, and another boy she didn't know coalesce into a group. Poncho passed quickly and said, "Hi, Tish," as he went through the gate, pointing to a blue tag he had hung on a coat button.

"Where are we sitting?" Tish asked as they too passed the guard.

"The press box," said Peter, looking down at her happily. "Poncho's dad got us passes. We could sit anywhere, but I thought it would be more fun up there."

"Terrific!" Tish said, hoping that it sounded sincere.

Poncho led the four of them around to another entrance, one which had its own guard even though it was more or less open. The guard stood warily beneath the final flight of steel steps leading up into the air and then across a bridge-like buttress and up again, farther, farther than Tish could see.

She stopped at the bottom of the stairway. "Do we have to?" she asked. "Isn't there another way up?"

"It's not so hard, Tish," Peter encouraged, stepping ahead

of her. "Look, just follow me. Keep your eyes on the back
of my head, and don't look down."

Before she could object further, Peter was on his way up
the steel construction. Tish put out both hands and grasped
the cold banisters. The first flight was only a dozen or so steps.
That she could certainly handle.

Carefully, understanding that the climb would be a long
one, she began. Within a few seconds, she stood atop the
first section. She watched Peter cross the bridge and took a
deep breath, starting out to follow. Without meaning to, she
saw below her fans streaming in and out of Palmer Stadium.
Already she could smell beer and hot dogs.

The walkway turned left, and so did Tish, coming soon
to the bottom of the real stairway. She looked up, and saw
the final reaches far above, covered in shadow under the
stone of the stadium. Peter had climbed steadily and slowly,
remembering Tish was behind, but without stopping or
looking back. By this time, he was nearly at the top of the
next flight.

Tish knew she was on her own. Closing her eyes for a
moment, she put one foot on the bottom stair. Then she
pushed off with her other, and the climb was on.

Up and up, fearful of every step, unable not to look down
because of the open steel slats, through which she saw people
below moving in a blur and heard their voices. Tish's breath
seemed to come only with gigantic effort. She began inhaling
on a schedule, to keep her mind from the height. She watched
her hands, first one and then the other, grasp the railing ahead
of her, felt the muscles in the front of her legs begin to
tighten.

She came to a landing, the final one. But here the railing
disappeared into the walls of the stadium, and she had to
maneuver a turn and the final few steps without aid. Every
nerve was alert, every muscle shook with effort and fear. She
looked ahead and saw Peter silhouetted at the top of the stairway, standing framed by the light of the stadium beyond,
waiting for her. The final few steps were of wood, and this
for some reason stayed in Tish's mind as she took them . . .
this and the emptiness behind her.

Peter extended his arm as she came to the top of the stairway. "That wasn't so bad, was it?" he said cheerfully.

Tish murmured that it wasn't. She was too busy trying to

make her heart slow down and to breathe without gasping to say anything more.

She was standing in a long, narrow enclosure that opened ahead into a cement trough-like room. From where she rested she saw the coffeemakers and plastic cups, sugar and cream substitutes on a long, low table to her right. And windows on her left, looking down into the stadium. Finally able to feel secure, she took a step into the room. "No wonder they have coffee," she said breathlessly to Peter. "You deserve a reward for just getting here."

"Come on," Peter urged, "let's find some place to sit."

Poncho met them at the door of the press chamber. He pointed to a long row of tables and chairs just below a raised dais-affair at which several men sat behind typewriters and scorecards and coffee cups. "We can sit anywhere there isn't someone else who should be here," he said. "There are a few places way down at the end."

Peter nodded and pushed Poncho forward into leading the party along a walkway. They sat finally overlooking the ten-yard line and goal posts at the south end of the stadium. Tish stood a moment before her chair, looking down onto the green field. She remembered again the climb and the distance and the space she had felt open at her back, and she shuddered.

Peter sat on her right, with the three boys to his right. Programs had been placed at each chair. Tish settled in, huddling herself, still thinking about the climb but beginning now to see the field clearly. Two teams had just taken their positions for kick-off. "Who is Princeton playing?" she asked.

"Columbia," Peter answered.

"Are they supposed to be any good?" Tish asked.

"Who?"

"Columbia."

"Not too," Peter answered.

The game began. Columbia may not have been good according to Peter, but for the first few minutes they dominated the game. "Want to make a bet, Peter?" Tish asked.

"What?"

"Columbia will cream Princeton," Tish said firmly. "They just look like they know what they're doing."

"You're on. A quarter."

"Done," said Tish. It was the last comment about sports she made during the afternoon. For in the middle of the next play a thought hit her with astonishing force. It wasn't enough to have climbed Everest without either equipment or oxygen. She had also to descend.

At one point in the second quarter, Tish stood to look down the seemingly endless rows of seats before her. Going down the cement aisles was hardly less frightening a prospect. She was trapped.

"Coffee?" Peter asked. Tish nodded. She was trying to think about what was happening around her. A man on her left was clearly loaded, shouting indecipherable encouragement to Princeton's eleven below, waving a clear plastic glass and, from time to time, giving Tish benefit of damp refreshment.

At the end of each quarter, with surprising speed, boys younger than Tish scurried along the passageways of the press area, distributing play-by-play recounts of the previous fifteen minutes. Tish was impressed.

Once a hand reached over her shoulder and placed a foil-wrapped and warm package before her. Tish held the thing in her hand, for the warmth rather than because of any hunger she might feel. The day was clear, but also cool. The press box was roofed and in shade, and thereby less pleasant than sitting on the Columbia side would have been.

Throughout the game, Peter talked excitedly to Poncho and the two other boys. Together, as a team almost, they rose and sat in encouragement and disappointment. Once Peter put his arm around Tish's shoulder and squeezed her, but that was more for Princeton's score than for affection. He would have hugged anyone within range, Tish thought.

Tish opened the foil of her hot dog. She wasn't hungry. She was suddenly tired and nervous and feeling left out and alone. She pried open the bun. Neither butter nor mustard nor relish adorned the small, soft-looking thing. Nonetheless, she took a bite. It stuck in her throat. She washed it down with cold coffee and wondered if there was a ladies' room up this high.

From time to time, she tried paying attention to what was happening in front of her. Although she knew how football was played and why certain things happened, she found she didn't care that much. After all, Princeton wasn't her school. Columbia wasn't. It was a far cry from urging your own team on, knowing that the guy who caught the final pass was going to be in Sara's playroom later that night, smiling and being schoolboy-modest among admiring girls.

In the third quarter, something caught Tish's eye. Directly across from where she sat, she saw a small, soprano-sounding section, dressed oddly alike in green. Girl Scouts? she wondered. Boy Scouts? A gaggle of children from a bussed-in school, or an orphanage, or a hospital? The idea warmed her a moment, and she smiled hearing the distant enthusiasm of small voices: "Hold that line! Hold that line!" right through the snap of the ball and the gain of several yards by the opponent. That would be fun, she decided, in a nice family way.

As though waking from one bad dream too quickly into another, Tish found herself on her feet, threading past chairs and spectators, following Peter and the boys toward the steel staircase after the game.

She talked to herself as she walked, deciding that the trip down couldn't be as bad as the one coming up, simply because each perilous step meant you 'had less far to fall on the next step. Going down, she could look straight out into the air. She needn't watch every step, and feel every step in the front of her legs.

Uneasily, she maneuvered the wooden staircase and turned. Peter and Poncho and the other two boys were bouncing down below her as though they were descending an ordinary, everyday stairway. Again she put out both hands, gripping the railings with more strength and determination even than she had on the upward journey.

Before she knew it, she was on the ground.

Peter took her hand in his, and the five began wedging through the crowd, passing velvet-covered sandwich-boards covered with pennants and dolls and chrysanthemums only beginning to turn brown at their edges.

"Where's the car?" asked Peter.

"Way at the end of Prospect," Tish answered, trying hard to keep up.

Peter nodded and led the group to the right, passing families and nattily dressed couples along the way.

In the car, Peter pulled into traffic with a screech of his tires. "I hate this part of it," he said to one and all. "The secret is to get away a little early, I guess."

He became impatient, delayed behind traffic, and took a sudden right turn on a road Tish had never known existed.

Steering with conscious effort, Peter speedily headed toward Route #1.

The Colonial Diner was not very different from any other restaurant of its kind: aluminum and tile and stainless steel and red Naugahyde stools at the counter. A smell of home fries in the air, in every corner. Individually adjustable jukeboxes at each booth, and sugar containers of thick glass, covered and coated with sugar at their spouts.

Against a window, with Peter on her right, Tish had ordered an enormous meal. She was ravenous, and she accepted it instead of fighting. A club sandwich on white toast, with side orders of french fries *and* french fried onions, a vanilla shake and coffee. Poncho's brother had listened open-mouthed, until Poncho reminded him that he had heard his own mother order that and more at any number of meals during her pregnancies. Peter laughed and said it was a good thing Tish had married a rich husband.

Tish ate without listening to the others replay the game, or discuss the possibilities of certain seniors for making the grade in pro-football. She chewed and swallowed with single-minded-ness, tasting little but alert to the fact that with each mouthful she felt somewhat more solid and less inclined to be dizzy. The memory of her afternoon's ascension was still present.

Peter finished his sandwich and took his last swallow of milk, leaning back and rubbing his stomach. "Well," he said, "I feel better but I'd rather have good old ND's peanut-butter sandwiches and a bowl of soup."

"You did, yesterday," Poncho reminded him.

Peter chuckled. "That was the damnedest thing," he said. "From the very moment I woke up yesterday, all I could think of was that it was Friday, and on Friday it's peanut-butter and soup. God," he shook his head, "you'd think Notre Dame's menu was the Four Seasons'."

"Better than fish cakes and tea," said Tommy Olivera. "That's what you get every other Friday. You were lucky yesterday, Peter."

Tish sat, listening to the boys replay events of the day before. Of Father Gavin and his tendency to sneak up and surprise the unsuspecting. Mr. Cain, the math genius, bent double with arthritis and with a temper to match. The girls who hung around the football field after school, "selling it," Tommy observed, to anyone who would buy after practice.

"Peter," Tish mumbled. She nudged him with her arm and slid across the Naugahyde toward him.

He understood and pushed to his right, and Jerry O'Brien, the silent fourth, understood, and moved to his right and stood. Peter followed and Tish rushed past them both, heading for what she hoped was the corner of the diner in which she would find the ladies' room.

32.

Tish was embarrassed as she opened the door. She hadn't known she would be. Instead, she had thought that seeing Mr. McSweeny alone again after such a long time would give her enormous pleasure. And relief. What she felt now was clearly nerves, and embarrassment, and very, very small.

"Hi," she managed to say, looking quickly into George McSweeny's eyes and then standing aside so he could enter.

Mr. McSweeny returned Tish's nervous smile with a warm, broad one, and stood in the hallway, waiting. When Tish closed the door and did not move, or speak, Mr. McSweeny took a step toward her. "Aren't you even going to pretend to give me a kiss?" he asked.

Tish blushed anew and on tiptoe pecked at his offered cheek. "That's better than nothing, I guess," Mr. McSweeny said, taking off his overcoat.

"Here, I'll take it," Tish said, and did, leading Mr. Mc-Sweeny into the living room where she had arranged a tray with coffee and mugs, and some Danish fresh that morning from a neighborhood pastry shop.

"That looks great, Tish," said Peter's father, approvingly. "I gather you managed to shepherd young Lochinvar out of the house at dawn."

Tish relaxed a little. "I almost didn't," she admitted. "He said he felt a little feverish. That perhaps he would call in sick?"

"But he didn't."

"No," Tish said. "I told him he could do what he wanted, but that today was the day I did the heavy work, and unless he wanted to help, he had better do whatever it was some-where else. That did it!"

"Not particularly helpful, though," Mr. McSweeny noted.

"Well, for this once I don't mind," Tish said. "Cream?"

Mr. McSweeny nodded. "And two sugars," he said, taking a chair and settling in as he took the mug from Tish's hand.

Tish poured her own coffee and then sat gingerly at the edge of the couch. Neither spoke. Mr. McSweeny took a sip of coffee and lowered his mug, looking alert and interested. Tish had trouble meeting his eyes.

Finally, after what seemed a very long moment indeed, Tish coughed. "Before you came," she started, "I had so many things to say. Now, suddenly, they all seem so unimpor-tant, and silly."

"Sometimes the light of day makes everything clearer, and not so threatening," said Mr. McSweeny gently.

Tish nodded. "I'm glad you came, anyway," she said. "Will you be very late in the city?"

"The chairman can always be a little late, if it's important enough," said her father-in-law. "As to that, they have to take my word that it is."

"Maybe I should have asked you to come by after work," said Tish, filling time. "Except that we haven't any liquor in the house."

Mr. McSweeny did not speak. He waited. He nodded at Tish, and smiled to encourage her. He stopped smiling, though, when he sensed she was at last about to say something that was important to her.

"I'm alone too much, George," she said finally.

"We all are, sweetheart. Except when we desperately want to be."

"I don't mean that way," Tish explained. "I mean, well, every day and nearly every night."

"Every night?"

"Most," Tish reconsidered. "Not that I mean . . . well, Peter comes home, is what I mean. But only after he's worked late, or campaigned for McGovern, or seen a movie. Some-times he just has drinks with someone. Like Fred, upstairs."

"Fred?"

"Fred Clayton," Tish said. "He and his wi—— and Char-lotte have the apartment above. Sometimes he runs into Peter on Peter's way home. He teaches, at the college."

"Oh."

Tish smiled. "Does that mean you get the picture, or that you can't think what to say?"

"Both, I guess, Tish," Mr. McSweeny said. "Why do you think Peter spends so much time away?"

"I knew you'd ask that. George, I *do* feel guilty. I don't know exactly what I've done, or why I should feel that way. But if Peter is away purposely, then something must be my fault."

"Being as honest as we can, that might be true."

"Well, it *has* to be true!" said Tish, now entirely open. "Why else would he do it? I admit, sometimes, I do sound like a fishwife when he finally appears. But I can't help it. I *do* want to know where he's been, and what he's been doing."

"And with whom?"

Tish nodded and ducked her head. "I don't think he's really doing anything," she said quietly. "I really don't. I just know he's not doing all that much around here, either."

Mr. McSweeny tried to make his little laugh unoffending. "That was going to be my next question. You outfoxed me."

"The thing is, I don't understand what's happening. Sometimes I think I'm paranoid. That's what Peter says. He says I think too much, that I spend all my time picturing all sorts of terrible things he could be doing. He says if I keep doing that, he's convinced I'll get irrational one day. Then, of course, he hits: what would he do with a baby whose mother was a crazy lady?"

"You must be joking," Mr. McSweeny said kindly. "Or he is."

"He means that. I mean, you don't just go around using certain words for the fun of it."

"You have a little jealous streak," Mr. McSweeny estimated. "That's not mental disease. It's flattering sometimes, too. Maybe you are spending too much time thinking about this, honey. You won't be able to, when the baby comes."

"But that's not why I want the baby to come quickly," Tish said. "Do you know, lately all I want the child for is company."

Mr. McSweeny stood and poured himself more coffee. He remained standing.

"I don't know that I should say this, George, but sometimes, most of the time, I think Peter is unhappy he's married.

He acts certain ways. Nothing dramatic or sudden. I wish there were things like that. But *I* feel married. I feel married all the time. He has to be reminded to feel that way. He has to be reminded that I'm around at all."

"You must be exaggerating, Tish. Just a little."

"I don't honestly think I am," Tish said defensively, looking directly into Mr. McSweeny's face. "He's begun cutting work. Sometimes he doesn't go at all, and he doesn't tell me where he's going, or where he's been when he's back. The office will call. Very polite and I guess trying to be soothing, at the same time. But he hasn't arrived, and if I hear from him, would he please call in? The silly thing is that the office thinks he's sensational, even now." Tish stopped, and took a breath. "One day, George, I know for sure he spent entirely at Notre Dame. Jesus, I know he's not very old, but what does he do that for?"

Tish was standing now, too, and her voice spoke of oncoming tears as well as puzzlement.

"Did you ask him that?"

"How could I?" Tish answered quickly. "Every time I open my mouth he tells me he hates nags. Or that I'm using a tone of voice he doesn't like to hear. That's the most frustrating thing of all. Not being able to say what you feel for fear he'll get angry."

Mr. McSweeny put his mug on the mantel and took a step nearer Tish. He put his arm around her shoulder. "I hate to sound pompous," he started, "but a lot of marriage is like that: worrying about other people's feelings."

Tish moved away. "I know that," she said. "But he doesn't . . . doesn't that have to work both ways?"

"Ideally," Mr. McSweeny allowed.

"Last week," Tish said, "we went to a Princeton game. George, Peter didn't even remember I was pregnant. We had to climb a horrible steel staircase, open and you could see through it. Peter didn't give it a thought. To him it was an adventure. Just follow me, he says, and off he goes. No help, no worry, nothing! Then, to top it all, he spends the whole day as though I weren't even there!"

The tears had come, and the anger.

"We didn't have to get married!" Tish cried. "I told him he didn't have to. I wanted the abortion. It was Peter, god-dammit, who insisted! Duty and responsibility and forever doing the right thing! The right thing would have been to do what I wanted in the first place!"

Tish turned away from Mr. McSweeny, and tried to stop herself, swallowing her tears. There was silence in the room.

"You put me in an awkward position, honey," Mr. Mc-Sweeny said. "Peter is my son, after all."

"I know," Tish answered, now surprisingly calm. "Just explain all this, make some sense of it for me. I don't care if I'm to blame. Just explain him to me."

Mr. McSweeny frowned, feeling now inadequate and not wise. "If you like, Tish, I can talk to him."

Tish shook her head quickly. "That won't do any good," she said. "He'll think I put you up to it, and come back and accuse me of nagging at him through his own family. Just explain, George, whether I really am going nuts. Whether I'm too deep in this to see clearly. Whether my worries are dumb and silly. Maybe there is something going on here that I can't understand. Just explain why he does what he does. That's all."

Tish's voice had lowered, and she felt drained.

Mr. McSweeny nodded as though accepting her commission. Then he spoke. "I can't. Honestly, Tish, I can't. How can I? It's your marriage. Your husband, more that now surely than my son."

Tish still looked expectantly at her father-in-law. "Maybe you should spread out a little, Tish," Mr. McSweeny suggested. "Do the kinds of things you were doing in Princeton. Meet some new people. Form some new interests."

"Then you do think I'm imagining everything? Taking things too seriously?"

Mr. McSweeny only shrugged.

"I'm sorry, George," Tish said quietly, sitting again on the couch. "I'm being unfair to you, asking you to baby me and give comfort and explain life. I know that's unfair. It's just that . . . that, well, I *do* feel trapped. I don't even know if I can stand the sight of the baby when it arrives. I don't feel anything toward it. I'm too wrapped up in trying to get through to Peter to have any energy left for that."

The father in Mr. McSweeny swam to the fore. "That will change, sweetheart, as soon as you actually hold the child."

"So people say," Tish admitted. "Maybe I just resent Peter,

being in the outside world and all. Maybe our marriage got to be too settled too fast. Maybe I can't adjust to that, that everything's not hot sex and flowers all the time."

Mr. McSweeny smiled down at Tish with a mixture of wonder and sadness in his eyes. "Tish, I just wish, for one moment anyway, that I were Peter. You're so young and so vulnerable, and yet sometimes so goddamned grown up I'm astonished. It would be nice to take care of you."

Tish grinned at her father-in-law. "That's a very sweet thing to say. Thank you, George."

"I wish I could say something that made sense, honey," Mr. McSweeny continued. "But I can't help feeling that sooner or later you'll find your own way through the woods. You'll be grateful you did, instead of someone else leading you through."

Tish nodded. She put down her mug and rose. "I've ruined your day," she said.

"No, you haven't. I missed seeing you."

"Even though all I do is shout and cry?"

"Even then," Mr. McSweeny said, bending down to pick up his coat and putting it over his arm. "Even then."

He embraced Tish with both arms, giving her body sudden warmth and, he hoped, strength. Tish walked him to the door.

"Say hello to Kate for me," Tish said in farewell. Then she smiled. "Without, of course, letting on you were here."

Mr. McSweeny gave Tish a quick kiss. "It doesn't mean I'll be able to do anything, perhaps," he said, "but if you get lonely again, call."

Tish smiled, and waved at her father-in-law as he walked toward his car.

Closing the door behind her, Tish walked to the threshold of the living room and surveyed it. Well, she thought, if crazy is what I'm going to be, then crazy is what I'm going to be. She resisted the impulse to cry for herself.

33.

Tish slipped into the bathroom as quickly as she could and pushed the lock, testing to see that it held in almost the same motion. Then, leaning her head against the closed door, she sighed hugely.

The door could not keep out the sounds from the other room. Laughter, extended and meaningless at times; solid rock; glasses being filled with ice; talk. Words and more words, she felt, and almost none of them making sense.

She opened her eyes to see where it was she stood. The bathroom was grayer than any dirty snow she had ever seen in New York. There was a forty-watt bulb over a cracked mirror over a sink so stained that it resembled nonobjective painting. A half-spent roll of paper toweling sat atop the dirty toilet. The floor seemed to have been purposely tracked with mud and soot, and only the desire to keep inside what she had eaten at dinner, or rather what she had nibbled when she found she wasn't likely to have dinner at all, kept Tish from pushing back the striped, molding plastic shower-curtain.

Standing in the center of all this, she could only smile forlornly. "The best-laid plans," she muttered, putting the top down on the toilet and sitting on it cross-legged. Her posture was complex: her back straight, bending just slightly where the weight of the child seemed to be draining her energy most heavily. The muscles of her left side hurt, and she massaged them briefly.

What a terrific celebration, she thought. Peter's birthday and here I sit in some godawful junkie's apartment. She stopped herself. That wasn't altogether fair, and she felt she should correct her own thought. She didn't know for certain that Gee Woods was a junkie. It was only that he acted that way. And that he kept such weirdos around.

Peter had hurried home at the end of the working day, excitedly telling her about Gee's party. "Don't pay much attention to old Gee," he had cautioned, before she could object to the plan. "He's a little like a beginner with a shotgun. If he points at something and pulls the trigger, he's bound to hit at least part of the target. Gee thinks he's fantastically sexy. So, using the scatter approach, he propositions each and every girl he meets. Young, old, pretty, disastrous, it's all the same to him. Just laugh if he says anything, and he'll probably be satisfied," Peter said. "Secretly, I think he's impotent."

"Peter, wait!" Tish had finally been allowed to get in. "It's your birthday."

"I know, but we can celebrate tomorrow."

"I learned something new, though, to cook for supper, I mean," Tish said. "It's supposed to be wonderful and festive and . . ." She stopped. Peter had already walked past her and was stepping under the water that poured from the new shower-head.

Tish knew instantly that Peter would expect her to be ready to go when he was. But what was she to wear? Who was likely to be at the party? Where did this Gee Woods live, anyway? How old was he? Who was he?

"Just a guy at the store," Peter told her as they drove east. "Nothing very special. He's friendly, though, and tries hard. I always think that no matter where Gee Woods is, he's in over his head."

When Tish and Peter had found the right building, and climbed the three flights of wooden, ill-lit stairs to enter Gee's apartment, Tish saw quickly that Peter's estimation had been double-edged: Gee Woods was one of the smallest young men she had ever seen. She felt Amazonian standing beside him. Which she had been able to do for only a very short time before Peter had pulled her across the drably furnished living space toward a temporary bar. There were half-gallon jugs of wine there, and a case of beer, its covering ice dripping slowly onto the floor. Peter handed Tish a jelly glass and poured some white wine for her.

"Pretty heavy, huh?" Peter said happily, looking around. Tish followed his eyes. There were so far only seven other people in the room: two scruffy-looking boys and four rather more sophisticated-looking girls. Plus Gee, who was standing at his doorway, looking out into the hall, shouting encouragement to new arrivals.

"No smoking, Peter, please?" Tish had said then.

Peter turned, surprised. "What?"

"I mean, we have to drive back and everything. Okay?"

Peter's face clouded. "I suppose so," he grudged. "If you really think it's as bad as all that."

"I don't," Tish explained. "It would probably just be the better thing to do. Or not to."

Peter flashed a sudden grin. "You're just jealous," he said. "You can't because of the baby."

"True," Tish admitted. "But I'd feel safer, too, later."

"Oh, wow!" Peter said, shaking his head. "I'm dating a member of the social security corps!"

"Dating!" Tish had laughed, pointing to her stomach. But at that moment, Gee Woods had returned, towing three people, introducing them by their first names.

The party had then begun to look more like a party. People jumped up to check the stereo; joints were handed round; people stood near the bar, arms around each other, whispering and then laughing. In one corner a very serious bearded man was plainly boring two slim, attractive girls whose eyes roved hungrily across the room, looking for available men. The clearly available bearded man spoke more and more intensely into the glass he held in both hands.

Peter had been pulled away from Tish to meet someone else Gee thought was "simply unbelievable, simply not to be believed!" Feeling somehow as though she were the one calm moment in a storm, Tish ambled across the room, overhearing bits of conversation. Once, a girl came up to her and stared hard into Tish's face. "You married?" she had asked.

Tish's smile was forced but pleasant. There was something in the girl's searching look that made her shiver. "Yes, I am. My husband's over there," and she had pointed.

But the girl, hearing only the first affirmative message, had turned swiftly and for some reason angrily away, and when Tish turned back to her, after pointing at Peter, her finger was of interest only to herself.

An hour passed. Occasionally Tish stationed herself near Peter to hear what he was saying and to listen to others. But later, as she made another pass at being part of Peter's group, she had become uneasy. It seemed to her that everyone was stoned. I'm overreacting, she thought. But she couldn't rid herself of the feeling that she alone in the room was cold. Even Peter seemed to have reached a contact-high. People would grab his shoulder and bend his ear toward them, whispering nonsense and Peter would nod, understanding instantly, and sharing. He laughed at things Tish thought not only weren't funny, but were just plain dumb.

At that point Tish's uneasiness became anger and boredom. From the state of things, she could tell the party was going to be a long one, probably an all-night affair. She was tired. She had worked harder than usual that day, and longer. After all, she had kept repeating, Peter's birthday came only once a year, and this year, for the first time, it was hers to share.

Before giving up entirely, though, Tish had taken one last moment to look around the room, half fearing, half hoping to see a friendly expression, a welcoming nod or wave. What she saw instead was Gee Woods closing in on her.

"Tish, right?" he said, laughing at his own confusion.

Tish nodded.

"You're his, right?" Gee pointed over his shoulder at Peter.

"Right."

"Well, it looks to me like you've been abandoned," Gee said in a whisper. "Why don't we slip away somewhere? To talk."

"About what?"

"Anything," Gee said. "About *my* wife, for instance."

"Your wife?" Tish's surprise was real.

"Sure," Gee said petulantly, as though he had run into disbelief on this point before. "I've got a wife. And three kids, too, if you want to know."

"Where are they, then?" asked Tish.

"I don't know," Gee shrugged. "I was trying to remember the other day. Whether I got lost from them, or they got lost from me. Doesn't matter. We never got on too well."

Tish laughed slightly, feeling uncomfortably superior. "Well enough to have three children."

"Hell," Gee said, "anyone can do that. The important thing is to meet someone who really understands you. I have a feeling you're a very . . . a very sympathetic person, Trish."

"Tish."

"That's what I mean," Gee said quickly. "You could have gotten angry." Gee brought his glass to his lips and looked at it in shock. It was empty. "What say we wander over to the bar, load up, and then go outside. Okay?"

Tish looked quickly at Peter, bent over again listening to someone's confession. "You go ahead, Gee," she said. "I've got to make a little . . . a rest stop. I'll meet you. Okay?"

"Sensational," Gee muttered. "Not to be believed."

Tish smiled to herself and laughed softly, sitting in the bathroom. It certainly was not to be believed.

She sighed and shifted. She couldn't hide here forever. Maybe she could signal Peter she wanted to go. She could, she knew, but his reaction to the signal was what was in doubt. Still, it would be worth a try.

She stood and for a moment faced the mirror, rearranging her hair as best she could without a comb. The heat in the other room was intense, and that plus the dampness of a wet October night had combined to make her hair start to curl at the ends.

She stepped back from the mirror, having done what she could, and inhaled deeply. Then she unlocked the door and pulled it toward her.

As she stepped into the living room, she heard a woman's voice. "Your birthday!" Instinctively Tish turned toward the voice.

What she saw made her knees buckle. One of the two girls who had been bored by the beard had escaped and was, at that minute, exploring Peter's mouth with her tongue, pasted up against him, grinding her body into his, and being firmly held in return. Her eyes were closed. Peter's eyes were closed.

Tish whitened with anger. She ducked her head and passed the embracing couple, not looking up, not stopping. She crossed the room without looking back and poured herself a glass of white wine. When finally she did turn, the girl was still at it.

Tish saw her drink jump uneasily in the glass she held. She put her other hand around the glass to steady it. It was only a partly successful effort.

She looked up as she heard Peter shout, "Oh, wow!" and she saw him throw his head back and laugh loud and long, still hanging onto the girl. She stood now flatfooted beside him, waiting for him to stop. When he did, she raised a hand to his face, stroked it, and said something to Peter that Tish couldn't hear. Peter laughed again, a little less loudly, and looked down at the girl in partial disbelief.

Tish turned away. Phrases began to whirl through her mind. She ducked them. But they returned, being then substituted by other, different, louder words which sounded harsher and angrier. Her head seemed not to be hers to control any longer. Already she was debating Peter, arguing with him, screaming at him. She wanted to do something to the girl, something dreadful, but she couldn't think what. Frantically, a thought flew into her mind that it wasn't the girl's fault.

What did she know? She probably didn't even know Peter was married.

But Peter knew he was.

Tish stared out the window, looking down into a garbage-littered back yard. More than ever before, she wanted to leave. For a moment, she didn't care whether or not Peter left with her. Let him shack up with that tramp, she decided angrily.

But she turned back into the room with a thoughtful, worried, hurt expression in place of the anger she felt. She toyed with her drink. She had stopped thinking. She seemed suspended. She wanted Peter to look for her. To find her. She would tell him she was ill. That she had cramps. That could he please take her home.

"There you are," Peter said, suddenly standing beside her and pouring some wine for himself. "I lost you."

"Bullshit!"

"What?" Peter's face dropped and he held the glass and the jug suspended, staring at her.

"Just what the hell was that all about?" Tish said, keeping her voice low and steady, but feeling it shake in her throat.

"What are you talking about?" Peter asked, beginning to sound defensive, the more because he wasn't yet certain what it was he was supposed to have done.

"All right," Tish said angrily, turning full-face to him. "I went into the john. When I came out, that girl had her tongue in your mouth. And you were kissing her back! You were, Peter McSweeny. I had time enough to see and to walk all the way over here, fill a drink, and have it before you even came up for air!"

"What are you talking about?"

"See that girl?"

"Where?"

"There, for Christ's sake!"

"Yes," Peter said, understanding now. "I see her. So what?"

"So what?" Tish put her glass on the window ledge. "Are you supposed to be married or not?"

"What does that have to do with anything?"

"Just answer the question."

"Look, Tish," Peter said calmly, which infuriated Tish

even more, "it's my birthday. She wanted to give me a birthday kiss. So she did. It's no big deal."

"She didn't give you a kiss," Tish said hotly. "You gave her one, too!"

"Well," Peter shrugged with a smile, "what was I supposed to do? Tell her no? Tell her she wasn't my type? Hurt her feelings?"

"Don't be a smart-ass with me, Peter McSweeny," Tish said. "It's a very easy thing to avoid a moment like that. If you want to."

"A moment like what?" Peter asked. "For God's sake, all I did was get kissed."

"Peter, I am your wife."

"Does that mean I can't even kiss another girl, or look at her, if I want?"

"What it means is there is supposed to be some loyalty between us. If you'd wanted to, you could have . . . you could have laughed, or something, and made a joke out of it. You didn't have to get so involved!"

"Don't shout."

"I'm not," Tish answered. And she knew she wasn't. "Did you make a date with her, Peter? For later?"

"Oh, for Christ's sweet sake! I'm getting out of here!" Peter put his drink on the bar and walked toward the front door.

34.

Tish stood before the stove, her mug in hand, sipping thoughtfully. She had not slept well and, finally, after hours of uneasiness and physical discomfort, she had decided to get up. She looked now at the electric clock above the sink: seven twenty. Ten minutes more and the alarm would sound.

She poured hot coffee into the mug and added sugar and cream. Her doctor had advised she take in a few less ounces of dairy food each day so that her weight could remain controlled, but she didn't particularly care about that this morning.

The only words spoken after their departure from Gee Woods' party the evening before had been Peter's: bitter, sarcastic, unanswerable. As they had parked the car and before, or while, he was turning off the engine, he muttered loud enough barely to be heard, "Well, happy birthday, Peter!"

Tish had gotten out of the car and walked directly into the house and the bedroom without a word, feeling righteous and angry and guilty and sad all at the same moment. She had prepared for bed, omitting to brush her teeth, and had turned out the lamp before Peter had had time even to hang up his jacket.

What was important now, she felt, drinking slowly, was to make contact again with Peter, but carefully. She didn't mind apologizing for her outburst if he would admit she had been right. Besides, what was she to do with all the food she had eagerly prepared the night before, in honor of Peter's birthday?

She heard the alarm from the bedroom. She listened carefully, but she couldn't tell if Peter had stirred or not, whether he was getting up slowly and making his way into the bathroom behind her, or whether he had decided to sleep in.

It didn't really make any difference, she decided. She knew Peter would never apologize for kissing the girl. He clearly hadn't thought it was anything he had to be ashamed of. He couldn't understand apparently how Tish felt seeing the two together like that, what it had done to the small confidence she still had in their marriage.

And what, after all, *was* so terrible about being kissed? Tish shook her head, angry all over again. It wasn't just that. It was the fact that he had not only kissed back, but had prolonged the entire moment. It hadn't been just a chaste, well-meaning birthday greeting at all.

Tish's posture stiffened. Behind her, she did at last hear Peter moving. She prepared herself for silence, for not speaking out as she wanted so desperately to do.

"Good morning, Mrs. McSweeny," came the voice from the doorway.

Tish nodded. "Good morning," she whispered.

"You're still mad."

"I can't help it."

Peter made no reply. Instead, Tish felt his arms around her waist and felt his breath on her neck. "It was my fault," he said softly. "It was."

"I should have controlled myself better," Tish said, still looking away but also still being held.

Peter raised his head. "No," he said. "You shouldn't. You were right." He turned her to face him, looking earnestly at her. "After all, Tish, if you can't say what you feel to me, who can you say it to?" He smiled.

"Do you really mean that?"

He nodded.

"Oh, Peter," she said, "there are so many things I've wanted to say. I've been afraid to."

He looked surprised. "But why?"

"Because you always think I'm nagging."

"Well, you do a lot, sweetheart. If I can say I'm sorry about last night, you can at least admit that sometimes you do exactly that."

Tish swallowed. "All right," she said. "But if we could talk things over, quietly and reasonably, then I wouldn't have to. What makes me so angry is when I say something, you listen but you never say anything back."

"I like to think about things."

"But it seems as though you're just ignoring me," Tish explained. "You can see how that would be, can't you? How frustrating that is. That's when I get angry, Peter, when you just don't seem to care enough to talk back."

Peter raised his hands to her face, framing it, and looked steadily at her. "If I promise to behave more like a sensible human being, and listen, and talk—though sometimes it's hard for me, Tish. I'm not used to it—will you promise not to be quite so jealous and suspicious? I'll be the husband and father, and you be the wife and mother, and we'll trust each other. Okay?"

Tish looked back into Peter's face. "For real," she said slowly, "or just for make-believe, for now and then?"

Peter's eyes looked as though he had been called liar. His face paled, and his grip on Tish's face grew firmer. "You've got two choices," he said, forcing his words through clenched teeth. "You can believe, or not. It's up to you."

Tish didn't look away. "It's only partly up to me, Peter," she answered. "I want the husband and father more than just after an argument."

Tish still looked steadily at Peter. Suddenly, she remembered her mother's pronouncement of many months ago:

that she had become quite a strong young lady. She was
surprised at how tough, actually, she was being. And she
knew now that if she continued to be, she and Peter would
be back where they had been the night before.

Peter still held her, seemingly unable to speak. "I'm sorry,
Peter," Tish helped. "I'm being unreasonable and cruel. I'll
be mother and wife, and you be husband and father, as
best you can. That will do just fine for me. Really it will."

She said it knowing she was lying, but clearly it was what
Peter wanted to hear. His face cleared and he grinned a
little. "Okay, Mom," he said. And then he pulled her closer
and kissed her on the mouth.

Tish pulled away after a moment. "Peter, share with me,"
she asked. "Take me with you. Don't leave me here to be
a mother all alone. Please?"

He nodded but did not open his eyes again as he pulled
her toward him.

35.

November 8

*Dear Diary: as I take pen in hand to write . . . doesn't
that sound dumb!*

*Forgive me, D.D., but starting all over again is a little
embarrassing, although I don't know why. I've thought
about you often. In the past five months, when I've
been alone or unhappy, instinctively I thought about
turning to you and spilling it all out, just to feel better
and, hopefully, get some perspective. But I never did.
I guess I decided that during the bleak times (and there
have been plenty of those!) I should be able to handle
things myself. So, purposely, I've waited until I was in
the right mood, when things finally seem to have settled
into a happy pattern. And they have.*

*The past few days have been wonderful. Peter and I
seem to have hit our stride at last. We do a lot of the things
we did before last June: we go to movies, we've eaten
out twice, he brings me silly little surprises, we've made
love—rather a strange kind, though, being all blown
up as I am—and once I even went to McGovern
headquarters in Princeton and helped phone voters.*

*(Poor Mr. McGovern. Last night was so depressing
for us both, even though only Peter was able to vote,
and that just barely, that we went to bed at nine fifteen.
There didn't seem to be any reason to stay up watching
the returns, unless, of course, we wanted to get even
more depressed.)*
*My mother has made some sort of peace, I guess, and
has visited once and phoned twice. Nervous, probably,
about the baby, though that's still a couple months away.
And we had brunch at the McSweenys' last Sunday, just
the four of us . . . Bosey having fled back to school
(hooray, say I!).*
*Anyway, things are finally nearer what they should be.
Or rather, to what I had hoped they could be.
Sometimess, I admit, I can sense strain in Peter. As
though he is conscious all the time of doing exactly
the right thing in the right way. But I figure the more
practice he gets, the better he'll be at it, and then things
will just be wonderful, automatically. While you were
away, so to speak, D.D., I had my own little bout with
the conscious. I had almost decided I was going nuts.
I did dumb things; I said horrible things; I used all those
awful words I never thought I would. But I was angry,
in those days, and frustrated. And I'm not any more.
Peter and I don't talk so much about things as I'd like,
but we do try every once in a while, and that helps me
keep the pressure bearable. I still get jealous . . . in
my head. I'm quite convinced I make myself that way,
although I don't know why. I wish I did. If I could find
that out, then life would really be clear sailing.
Today was sort of fun, D.D. After Peter left, M.O.
called and wanted to come over for a while. I haven't
seen her in weeks. What happened, or the real reason
she wanted to visit, can be told very simply. She almost
ran up the sidewalk, kissed me hello, walked into the
living room, and at the top of her lungs shouted that
lovely four-letter word ending in k. Not once, but a
whole string! Then she turned around and saw me
staring and smiled—I couldn't understand it. Back
goes her head and she lets loose again, this time with a
selection of four, five, six and seven-lettered words
generally associated with sailors.*

*Well, being on the alert for signs of my own mental
disintegration, I was naturally convinced I was witness
to M.O.'s. Not so. She twirled around in the living room
with this enormous grin on her face and then stopped.
Suddenly she was quite normal again, and asked for
coffee. As we went into the kitchen, she explained
everything. Her husband can't stand for her to use any
swear words and apparently, every once in a while, M.O.
just feels she has to or she'll crack up. If her kids are
around (and whenever aren't they?), then she feels
trapped. She just happened to think of me and came
rushing over for satisfaction.*

*Well, I said I was glad to help, and then we had a silly,
womanish half-hour chat, with M.O. all the time
throwing in these salty exclamations, probably wearing
herself down and feeling better each time one slipped
out. I think I'll ask Peter if we can afford a tiny cassette
recorder for M.O. at Christmas. It would save her gas
money—and my nerves!*

*Charlotte came down this afternoon, carrying a suitcase,
and asked me to keep an eye out for Fred. She's off for
two days in New York to do battle, as she says, with her
copy editor and her galleys. Sounds glamorously hard
to me. I said maybe we would ask Fred down for
dinner tomorrow night. Peter came home and I made
chicken and dumplings, for old times sake. Then he
went into Princeton to help close down the McGovern
office. He asked if I wanted to come, but I've been
feeling very pregnant lately, so I declined. It's nearly
ten now, and he'll be back at any minute. I'm glad we
had a chance to catch up, D.D. I promise I won't submit
you to anything but happy news from now on.*

36.

By eleven thirty that night, Tish was sitting propped up in
bed, a glass of hot chocolate on her bedside table, sleepily
trying to concentrate on Dr. Spock. She had come to enjoy
settling in with the doctor, because he always made her feel
that, in spite of her fears and the feelings she had of knowing
next to nothing about what was going to happen, she could

handle whatever arose. That she was going to be, surprising even herself, a competent, happy mother.

"You know more than you think you do," he wrote. Tish had read the opening chapters over and over again, drawing strength and comfort from Dr. Spock's confidence in her. "Don't be afraid to trust your own common sense. Bringing up your child won't be a complicated job if you take it easy, trust your own instincts, and follow the directions that your doctor gives you."

Tish smiled, thinking about her doctor's advice to lay off so much milk and cream. Hot chocolate was something she had always had as a child, in the winter, of course, but also whenever she had been in bed with a cold, or perhaps measles. It was comforting to her. It made her think she was being taken care of, that someone was waiting on her. Even if her only servant was herself.

She closed the book and snuggled down against the pillows. Having a baby, she thought, might not be as bad as all that. She hadn't been ill. She was healthy. She was glad in advance she had decided on anesthetic. She agreed with M.O. Things were tough enough with it, so why ask for more trouble? And she was grateful to Peter's father, who had promised she could stay in the hospital for a few extra days, resting. As his gift.

Tish opened her eyes. Almost twelve.

The past days had been so busy. She had meant to ask Peter to sit down and help her think about a baby's name. Boy or girl, Tish didn't really care. She was just suddenly aware that naming the child hadn't really been seriously considered. She and Peter referred to it always as The Kid. "Kid" McSweeny. She laughed.

Swinging her feet out from under the covers, Tish sat on the edge of the bed, putting on her robe. She stood and went into the kitchen, pouring more milk into the saucepan, filling a second mug with chocolate. Peter would probably be tired and a little sad when he came in. It might cheer him up to find a treat.

She went into the living room and switched on the television set, not bothering to select a channel. She would keep awake watching whatever happened to swim onto the screen. She waited. It was Dick Cavett. She smiled again to herself.

McGovern had been trounced, and here was Cavett, about to be. She didn't think she would miss him, particularly since she had begun to think he was a little bit of a smart-ass lately.

By the time the show was over, Tish had made two trips to the kitchen, and one to the bathroom. She was now sitting staring at the beginning of a late movie with Maureen O'Hara and John Payne, about the Marines. She had begun finishing off the quarter-gallon white wine that had been left from dinner. More chocolate would really make her uncomfortable; wine was less filling.

From time to time, she stood and walked to the front windows, looking out on deserted Sicard Street, seeing a few parked cars and an occasional brush of light from a car turning at the corner.

She decided against telephoning Princeton. The McGovern office there probably didn't even have a phone any more. Besides, that would seem too much like checking up on Peter. If he was delayed, he surely had some good reason. Perhaps he had offered to drive people home from there. Or maybe he and a few of his friends were having a final cup of coffee or a beer somewhere. One thirty wasn't dawn, after all.

But three o'clock was approaching it. She had opened the front door for air, feeling warm and uncomfortable as she paced the living room. Twice she had walked out to the street in her slippers and robe, and looked up and down. Walking back to the house she had glanced up and seen that Fred Clayton's house was dark.

Pride kept her from phoning her own family, or Peter's. But at four, she had decided that at least she could call the Princeton hospital, in case there had been an accident and she hadn't been notified. She had had this idea for hours, but had hated giving into it. She dialed. She was connected with the emergency admitting office. No one by the name of McSweeny had been brought in that evening.

If Peter had had car trouble, he could have phoned and said so. Or perhaps taken a late bus back into New Brunswick. It wasn't such a long walk from #27 to Sicard Street.

Consciously, as though swallowing down a piece of food she hated, Tish would not allow herself to think what she had been thinking to herself for hours. She had promised. She had decided she wouldn't ever give in to hysteria and anger and frustration and doubt and fear again. If what she thought had happened, and by five she was certain that she knew exactly what it was, there was nothing now she could do about it. The damage had been done. The question to resolve was how she would treat the event. If event there had been. She wanted badly to believe she was wrong. But she didn't, not really.

In spite of the feeling that it would be better for Peter to come home and find her asleep, or pretending to sleep, she had made a breakfast for herself at six. She was not hungry. She forced down the food. Watching the eggs fry to just the degree she liked, and turning 'bacon, buttering toast, all this kept her occupied and alert. She hated to waste what she had made. Finally, though, she threw into the garbage the second piece of toast and a good amount of cooked egg-white.

She was standing in the kitchen, pouring coffee, when she heard the front door open and close. She could tell from where she stood that Peter was standing motionless, his shoes probably in his hands, listening to see if he had disturbed her. She was going to give no clues.

She heard Peter tiptoe down the long hallway and stand in the doorway of their bedroom. She heard him turn and walk back to the front of the house. Calmly, she leaned against the stove and took a sip of her drink.

"You're up," he said, standing at the kitchen door.

Tish nodded that that indeed was true. Without thinking, she looked at the clock on the wall. Seven thirty-five.

Peter stood in the doorway, not moving, seeming uncertain what to say, or how much, or how to begin. Tish turned her back and reached for a second mug. She poured coffee into it and handed it to him, moving past him into the dining room without touching him. She sat at one of the two places at the table, carefully putting a paper napkin beneath her mug to protect the table's finish.

After a moment Peter too turned and came into the dining room. He stopped just behind Tish's chair. "Aren't you going to say anything?" he asked in a low voice.

Tish shook her head. "Would it change anything?" she said reasonably.

"I guess not." He put his mug on the sideboard and stood behind her, his hands at his sides. "Are you going to do anything?"

Tish sat without speaking a moment. "If you mean, do I intend to become New Jersey's youngest divorcee, no, I do not."

Suddenly Peter was on his knees at Tish's side, clutching at her and speaking rapidly, the sound of tears in his voice. "Jesus, Tish, I didn't mean to," he began. "It just happened. Everything was so rotten and then everything was better and people were around, and I don't know . . . I don't know, I guess I got carried away, and . . . I really was at the McGovern place. I was, really, Tish. But it was so depressing, and everybody hardly spoke as they moved things around and threw stuff away, and then afterwards, well, some of us thought maybe going out might make us feel better. I mean, it was just a friendly sort of idea, you know, getting together for consolation and all. There was this girl there, she'd been sort of bugging me, well, bugging isn't the right word I guess but she'd been kind of after me all summer and I just . . ."

"You don't have to tell me this, Peter," Tish said with her eyes closed, her posture as straight as it had been when first she had taken the chair.

"Yes, I do," he said. "I've got to, Tish. I've got to try to make you understand . . . well, not maybe understand, but see anyway that what happened didn't have anything to do with us, with you and me. It didn't have anything to do with our being happy and married and . . ."

"Did she know you were married, Peter?"

"I don't know. Maybe. I don't remember. But that's not important, honey. What's important is that I came home, that I'm here, that I know I did a rotten thing. That I promise, and I really do, Tish, I promise, I swear to God, this will never, ever happen again. I promise you that, sweetheart. What happened just happened. It was just a thing, just a one-night stand, is all. It didn't mean anything. She was after something, and so I gave it to her. That's all it was, just a sex thing, just that, nothing like what you and I——"

"Christ Jesus!" Tish screamed, standing up suddenly and looking down at Peter. "Are you compelled to tell me all this?"

Before Peter could recover his balance and stand, Tish had run past him, through the kitchen and into the bedroom beyond.

PART III

37.

*I am not breaking my promise to you, D.D. I am not
going to fill your pages and ears with moans and cries
and tears. In fact, I am not even going to tell you
everything that has happened lately. I haven't told
anyone else. I'll probably go to my grave without doing
so.*

*I am sitting up on my side of the bed. It is past midnight,
well past. Peter, beside me, is sleeping, looking innocent
and untroubled. Isn't it incredible how people look so
different in sleep . . . so incapable of doing the kinds
of things they actually do.*

*Tonight is the first time in almost two weeks that I've
admitted I'll sleep in the same bed with him. It's not that
I'm angry. I feel quite detached, sober, reasonable.
The reason I won't tell you all the brutal details, D.D.,
is that I'm certain that in years to come, if and when I
reread all I've written, I won't have forgotten a moment
of it. So there's no need. Also, of course, suppose
someone did stumble on this. Whether or not I knew it,
I would be humiliated, and suddenly it occurs to me
that dignity is important.*

*For the sake of honesty, however, I will admit that Peter
and I have had, recently, an argument. A serious one.
In fact, I can't imagine there will ever be one quite so
serious. Not certainly one about which I will still want to
write.*

*It's enough to say that Peter is in the wrong. Whether
or not he felt pushed into doing what he did by me I
can't say. Perhaps he did. Although before we seemed
to be doing wonderfully well, as you know.*

*What I've had to decide, D.D., is where we're going
from here. It's been my decision. Entirely. Peter, of
course, wants to stay together. He wants another chance,
a time to prove what he refers to as his better side, the
feelings he has of affection (what a formal word!) and
responsibility and husbandly duty. I'm less interested in
all that than in reality. And so I've made what I hope
is a sensible, pragmatic (where did I learn that word?)
decision. We are going on. We'll have the child, of
course, and stay together through that and afterwards.
No one is on probation. After a while, and how could it
be otherwise, we'll see if things can return to normal.
The baby, I imagine, will help. As for me, I've turned
inward a little. I now at last begin to feel something for
the Kid. Probably because my feelings for Peter are
different now than they were. I actually look forward
to having him now. The strangest thing is that I've been
thinking a lot about a woman's role in a marriage. Maybe
I'm becoming pre-liberated. I don't know. I do know
that my position is one I've fought against mentally, but
haven't had the guts to say anything about out loud.
Through fear of losing Peter, of being alone, of being
thought tough. But from now on, things are going
to change.
(I've just reread that. It sounds to me like I'm not
pre-liberated as much as pre-castrating. That isn't what
I have in mind. What I mean is that I, too, count. I,
too, have a freedom to protect, a sense of right and
wrong that has to be considered. And from now on,
I am determined that Peter will take these things
into account.)
I don't want him softer than he is. I want him more
understanding. I want him to live the roles he assumes,
to live the words "responsibility," "duty," "affection."
I finally understand, after what's happened, how much of
a strain he, too, has been under. But he's had his
releases; I haven't. And, objectively, if I had to give
sympathy to someone, I'd give it to me.
The past ten days or so have been very hard on us both.
Peter has been attentive, but wary of being overly so.
He's trying to find a position he can adopt, I guess,*

*toward me. He wants now to pamper, and to share,
and to talk. We've seen very few people since that one
Morning. I think because we both fear other people will
see us and immediately understand what's been
happening. That's foolish, of course. But true. For
me, anyway.*

*There are, I admit, other considerations, other things I
thought about when I decided to stay. First and
foremost was my own pride. My own image, I guess
you'd have to say.*

*My reluctance to admit to my family, or to Peter's, that
we weren't really able to handle what we thought we
could. Then there's Sara, and M.O., and the Claytons,
and anyone who has come to think of us as a couple.
Of course, there's the Kid, too, and what's best for
him/her (although I find myself now thinking of him
only as a him). There's my anger, at Peter, and at
myself. I have to be able to handle that, and live with
that, too.*

*Practically speaking, if I didn't stick around, where
would I go? I couldn't stand going back to Mother and
Daddy. Peter's mother won't even feed me, probably.
I don't happen, at the moment, to be the world's most
employable citizen. And I don't have a wad of my own
to lean on.*

*Having written all this, it suddenly strikes me that my
decision—to stay—is the right one, no doubt, but made
for all the wrong reasons. Charlotte would kill me if
she knew. But she doesn't, and no one else does, so no
matter what happens from here on in, I'll have only
myself to blame or thank. Question: Is it at that point
that one becomes mature?*

*Newsy Notes from All Over. The baby has begun to
make himself known. Which is to say he kicks a lot. In
the back of my mind is the certainty that he's not going
to be a full-termer. That he is impatient to get out and
may surprise us all. There's been a good deal of
play-acting over this event. Peter likes holding my
stomach from time to time, feeling the movement.
And I find myself constantly talking about it whenever
I talk at all to anyone. I suppose it's a way of keeping*

one's mind off other things. In fact, there's a good deal
of acting going on in our family all the time now.
Maybe it will stop when the Kid arrives. Today, for
example, we had accepted an invitation for brunch with
Peter's family. (I hope this isn't going to turn into a
weekly event.) Of course, we had to show the
McSweenys how wonderful everything was. How
successful Peter is at work; how organized and happy
I am as his wife. How we are deliriously happy at the
very idea of the Kid appearing. I don't think I ever
properly appreciated Bloody Marys before. My total
was, I think, four and half, maybe five. It certainly
made the afternoon more pleasant. Oops! D.D., the Kid
is awake. I take that back, he's been awake ever since
lunch. Maybe it was the booze. Just what we need:
an alcoholic to round out the family. Incidentally,
we've decided to name him George, after Peter's father.
There are two good reasons for that. I like George, a
lot. Also, George has money, a lot. That sounds
mercenary. It is. It is also honest, practical, sensible,
and farsighted.
I've been holding my breath, D.D., for a minute or so.
The Kid couldn't be that anxious. But this certainly feels
different. I wish Dr. Spock had written a little something
about detecting real from imaginary signals. He goes
on about everything else, including how to make the
father feel important when the baby arrives. But no one
mentions (at least he doesnt) how to tell when the
baby himself decides to feel important.
You don't suppose it actually could be the booze?

38.

It was. At least, Tish thought it was. Her first words, back
in her room after delivery, were, "Wow! Those were some
drinks!"

She had whispered this, dreamily looking up at Peter
who bent solicitously over her bed. His expression was drawn
and concerned, and even in her fogged state Tish felt his
need to be reassured. She tried her best, and smiled. He
beamed back, leaned down and kissed her lightly.

"Is he healthy?" she asked then.

"Beautiful," Peter answered, still glowing. "He is the most beautiful little girl you've ever seen."

Tish nodded, as though the news were no news at all. "No kidding," she said weakly, "I've got a terrific hangover."

"Can you keep awake long enough to think what you want to call her?"

Tish did not move. She seemed to consider. "What do you think?" she dodged.

"We may as well sail into the teeth of the storm," Peter said. "If he was going to be called George, why not let her be Kate?"

"Catherine," Tish tried it out. "Catherine . . . Anne?"

"Touching all bases," said Peter, grinning.

A few hours later Tish awoke. Peter was sitting by her bedside, reading Dr. Spock.

Tish still felt exhausted, but also that she ought to make some effort, for Peter's sake, to amuse, to reward him for his worry and attentiveness. "Learn anything?" she asked weakly.

Peter looked up, startled. "Um-hmm," he said. "That a breast-fed baby is less likely to be a thumb-sucker."

"Terrific," Tish noted. "If I can hold out, we'll have a non-neurotic kid."

Peter closed the book. "There's quite a crowd gathered to do homage," he said.

"Oh, God," Tish moaned.

"You don't have to see anyone, if you don't want to."

"Are you kidding?" said Tish. "Who's there?"

"Your family, and mine."

"Together?"

Peter nodded.

"What did we name him?"

"He is called Catherine Anne McSweeny."

"Oh," Tish said. "Right. Any complaints?"

"Not really," Peter said. "I think your mother feels it should have been Anne Catherine. But she'll get over it."

"Oh well," Tish sighed, trying to pull herself up into a more formal position. "Hand me that bag, would you?"

Peter did. Tish took out a pocket mirror, a brush, and her lipstick. Hesitatingly, as though it were taking whatever strength she still had, she tried to make herself look fresh and alert. "How do I look?" she asked finally, fearing the worst.

"As good as you did that first night at Sara's," said Peter.

She smiled in response, disbelieving but not caring. Gingerly, she lifted one hand and slowly moved it along the sheet to her stomach. She seemed to be feeling the air above it, as though making certain that nothing was left of what she had carried around for seven months.

She nodded and motioned to Peter to help arrange her pillows so she could easily see her visitors.

"Ready?" he asked.

"This is the first time they've been together since the wedding," Tish said, a worried catch in her voice.

Peter opened the door and motioned into the hallway beyond.

Tish's mother was first through the door. She smiled all the way to Tish's bedside. "Darling," she said, leaning over and kissing Tish's forehead. "She's a beautiful baby!"

"I'm glad," Tish said.

She looked past her mother and saw her father standing some feet away, embarrassed to move closer. She smiled long-distance at him. Slowly he approached the bed and silently leaned down to kiss her. When he straightened, Tish saw tearful eyes in a reddened face.

"I'm all right, Daddy," Tish comforted. "Really."

"I know," he answered in a whisper. "I brought you a few things."

Mr. Davies turned and reached behind him. Opening a huge blue shopping bag, he brought out first a pink blanket, then a pink snowsuit, a Raggedy Ann doll, and a silver rattle. And a panda.

"I've been sort of . . . picking a few things up . . . on the sly," he admitted.

Tish laughed. "Did you know all along it was going to be a girl?"

"Just a hunch," said her father. "There's more stuff on the way."

Tish reached out for her father's hand, and was still holding it as the McSweenys neared her bedside.

"Thank you," said Mrs. McSweeny. "It will be nice having a Kate to start all over again."

Tish nodded.

From her purse, Mrs. McSweeny pulled out a tissue-wrapped package and handed it to Tish. Surprised, Tish took it, but she didn't feel she had the strength to untie its wrapping. She handed it to Peter.

He tried carefully untying the ribbon and finally gave up, pulling it apart quickly with a little "snap." Then he opened the tissue, but did not take out what was within. He gave it all back to Tish.

Slowly she pulled a silver porringer out. On its side was engraved, "C. A. McS., Nov. 20, 1972."

"How could you get it so fast?" asked Tish.

"Well, dear," Mrs. McSweeny said, "I had it on order at LaVake's. When Peter called and told us the baby's name, I phoned them, and then picked it up on the way here. They're very obliging."

"It's lovely," Tish murmured. "Thank you."

Mr. McSweeny reached around his wife and handed Tish a rose, just the blossom on a stem.

Tish laughed. "It can't be *your* rose," she said. "In November?"

"Freeze-dried," he answered with a wink. "It'll probably disintegrate in ten seconds."

"No, it won't," Tish said. "I doubt it ever will."

She held the rose, and the porringer. She was embarrassed to look up at her family. She felt that at whomever she looked, the rest would be momentarily unhappy. Instead, she closed her eyes with a smile.

"Well, folks," Peter announced, "that's it for the four o'clock show."

Tish was asleep again before her last visitor had quietly slipped out of the room, closing the door with great care and slow silence.

39.

November 20

Not really. Not really the 20th, I mean, D.D. It's Sunday, the 26th. But because I have a whole week to catch up on, I started on the day Kate was born, so I'd have enough space (although I notice I used a little of

*the 20th last time). That, naturally, is the big news.
Kate. I saw her for the first time nearly a whole day after
I'd had her. She was premature, of course, and she had
been incubatorized, if such a word exists, not so much
because she needed it—she's enormous!—but just for
safety, in case of.
She really isn't a beautiful baby. But it comes to me
that no baby, objectively, can ever be beautiful what
with crinkly skin and maybe a rash or two and eyes
that barely open and then only in a nonfocused way. You
can convince yourself, I suppose, that what you've
done is given birth to a genius, to maybe another Candice
Bergen, but it's no easy job. Still, she's terrific-looking
and cute and healthy, and I think that's sensational!
My room in the past week has become a greenhouse.
You wouldn't believe the smells. Sometimes I've had to
ask the nurse to open the window, just to get in some
clean air. The problem, of course, is that after a few
days, things start to go bad. I've asked the nurses to look
around for other mothers who haven't got so many
flowers, and to distribute them anonymously in the dead
of night. I feel I've got so many things I didn't really
need or expect to have, some of them could be shared.
Peter and I have begun to think we made a mistake,
naming Kate Kate. Suddenly his mother is all over us.
And just as suddenly my mother has become combative.
She's damned if she'll see her granddaughter molded
by that woman! She hasn't said this in so many words.
Yet. But the feeling comes through loud and clear. I
begin to feel like I'm part of a television comedy. I
suppose in time, when Peter and I get home and feel
less like children ourselves—have you ever noticed that
when your parents are around, you can't help but feel
like a child?—we'll be able to make a stand and avoid
some of the tension and the bickering that will probably*

November 21

*follow. I hope so. I must be careful about letting one
or the other baby-sit. The one who follows is sure to
make some devastating assessment of the other's*

*character. Simple, direct, and nasty. I could have a very
confused child on my hands.*

*Bosey sent a night-letter which arrived the day after I
saw Kate for the first time. "I think you're both crazy,
but brave. Hooray for you. Love." That girl is just too
smart for her own good. That's something else I'll have
to watch: "Aunt" Bosey's influence. In spite of how
smart she is, or how smart she thinks she is, I'm
convinced she's going to end up an addict of one kind
or another. Not dope so much as men. Liberation is all
very well, but you still have to have some sort of
selective process. Bosey's a lot like Sara was, like I used
to be, I guess, to be honest. How old I feel at seventeen,
looking at her.*

*"Uncle Tommy" though is a different kettle of fish. He
keeps bouncing over on his bicycle, looking at Kate
and holding her as though she were fragile enough to
shatter, but being very proud that he can hold her
without damage. He's very funny, really. He talks to her
—as a matter of fact, he's the only one who speaks
to Kate as though she were an adult; everyone else
baby-talks—and teaches her and cautions her and looks
after her as though she were his own daughter. It's
nice to see. I think he is going to be a sensational father
himself one day. Kate's real father is pretty interesting
to observe, too. Peter runs over from the store at lunch,
and he's here every evening. He keeps bringing things,
for me or for Kate, I don't think it matters one way or
the other as long as he never arrives empty-handed.
Kate now has about two dozen dolls and clothes she
won't be able to wear for years. In between Peter and
my father, who I suspect is spending his life savings on
the sly, Kate is ready for* Vogue.

*Peter is wonderfully attentive, which is nice. He's
behaving like the perfect young new father in any movie
you've ever seen. And I do my best to pretend I'm the
perfect movie-mother. There is some strain, to be
honest, because now that I'm more myself, I do
remember things. But I'm trying, and I know Peter is.
I find that in spite of myself I am beginning to believe
him. He hasn't made any promises that I'm to guard.*

*And I haven't, either. But clearly we're both determined
to do what we should, to really live and behave as though
what we were doing came absolutely naturally. Some of
it does. I have to be honest. Some of the little jokes we
have, and some of the talks—about Kate, about the
family, about being glad we did the "right thing"—
have been constructive, solid ones, and I'm grateful that
Peter is finding that talking is not so difficult or binding.
He loves to go on about his vision of "the family."
About his role and responsibility to his new daughter,
and to me. And it's fun, I admit, to listen to some of
the crazily-painted pictures he draws in the evenings. He
says he's painted the back bedroom, even though we'll
only be there a few more months. And he's put up the*

November 22

*crib and the playpen and the bassinet. He's ordered some
Disney decals for the walls, and believe it or not he has
been sewing curtains for Kate's room, too! Can you
picture that? That fantastic man, all muscle and brawn,
sitting by candlelight, sewing? It kills me! I wonder how
he finds the time to do all that and work as well as he
obviously does.*
*Sara made her appearance the other day, a Magi
bringing gifts. Hooray for her, I say, because most of
what she brought was for me! A super cashmere
cardigan, rather matronly but also groovy, and even
better a super silk robe! I'll say this for her—sometimes
she's a bit wild but her instincts are right. Also, she got
a lot of kids at school to chip in and wheeled in a
baby-carriage yesterday! Oddly enough, my first
thought was about as mean and ungracious as you've
ever heard: oh, God, that means twenty more thank-you
notes. I got over that, though, because it is beautiful
and useful and lovely to see and unbelievable of her to
have done.*
*M. O. Olivera, on the other hand, comes armed with
practicality. On her first visit she brought over loads of
toys her own kids had outgrown . . . educational
things like blocks and pegs and hammers and boards*

(*she has mostly boys, so it's natural*) *and a few old but
clean and beautifully kept dolls* (*just what we need!*).
*But on her second visit, she presented me with a perfect
M.O. present: a silver cocktail shaker! I'm dying to ask
her sometime if she really does booze it up the way she
pretends, but also I don't really want to know. It's just
too much fun thinking that she actually does to know
differently. I get these terrific visions of her lying on a
sofa at the end of a day, when her husband gets home,
and saying something about what a rough day she's had
but actually being snoggered! I think she likes those
pictures, too.*
*The thing that appeals to me about M.O. is that she's
happy. Really, truly, genuinely happy. Of course, maybe
I'm being naive, and secretly she's not. But if that's so,
she's the world's best* (*and most underpaid*) *actress. I
mean, to have ten kids and still be able to joke and
laugh and enjoy having them around all the time is an
unbelievable feat. I don't think I want ten kids myself,
but I'd love to be able to be like her and face everything
calmly and thoughtfully and to be able to handle every
emergency with love and care. She's some lady!*

November 23

I can see that today (*i.e., the 23rd actually*) *was
Thanksgiving. Peter came to visit around noon. He had
been to church, he said, for the first time alone,
unforced, undirected. He felt he had so much to be
thankful for.*
*When he told me this, I nearly started crying. I don't
know what held me back.*
*I've never thought much about religion. I don't now,
either. Just every once in a while I wonder what we're
going to do with Kate. The McSweenys assume that
naturally she'll be Catholic. My mother would die!
The thing is, the nicest idea is giving a child information
about every religion and then, when she can decide
these things, letting her choose one that fits what she
believes. If believe she does. But I know kids who've*

*had that chance, and it seems to me that they miss
something along the way. I don't care so much whether
Kate or anyone really believes. But I do care that some
idea of right and wrong is glommed onto pretty fast.
Apart from the "no-no's" of growing up, I mean. Some
sort of morality explained by a third person. It's a
perspective children need, I think. (I just read that last
sentence in shock. Suddenly, at seventeen plus a few
months, I've become a concerned, philosophic parent,
an adult! I wonder if I have, deep down inside me, a
lot of prejudices and ideas that will only now begin to
surface since there is trapped in my own house some
little unsuspecting creature to absorb all those things.)
Thanksgiving, anyway, was a special day, for Peter and
for me. I for the first time since Monday got something
more than gruel for dinner. I also sneaked out of bed
and walked to the bathroom for the first time. These
little things mean a lot, let me tell you.
From my bed I can see a hill in the distance. And on
Thursday I stood at the window to see more clearly.
(To be frank, there is also a parking lot beneath my
window. I'd prefer to concentrate on the poetic, if you
don't mind.) You know what really grabbed me, D.D.?
At the bottom of the hill is a thin line of birch trees,
running daintily all across the hillside. It's turned cold
of course, now, and the autumn colors have long since
melded into winter gray. But what hit me was the
brilliance of the birches. Empty-limbed, no leaves,
probably the first to fall, the first each year to be
without. But their trunks are still white. Beautiful,
crystal, sharp, bending, seeming very fragile indeed but
with strength to return each year and start over again.
I can't really express what I want to, D.D., but I looked
at those trees for almost an hour—drawing up a chair
and staring out the window at them, as though I'd never
before noticed them or any other part of nature before,
as though they were behind glass in a zoo as a special
strange exhibit. For some reason, when I finally got
back into bed, I felt very, very calm and peaceful and
rested. I don't think I've ever had such a sleep as I did
that night.*

November 24

*Fred and Charlotte Clayton came by on Friday. I still
think about how they operate, and I still think I'm glad
it's not me. Although I admit there are certain standards
they have which, every once in a while, are sort of fun
to think about applying to myself. I never would, of
course. I guess I am firmly cemented into what is called
the Great American Middle Class. I don't feel bad or
guilty and small-minded. I just think some things are
worth trying to hang on to, trying to live with and by.
It's terrible, now that I've written that down. I see
clearly that even though I tell myself I'm not criticizing
Charlotte or Fred, I really am.*
*Oddly enough, I think seeing me here, in the hospital
with Kate, might make some weird difference in their
lives. Fred's, in particular. And what I worried about,
as we talked, was that he not be disappointed by
Charlotte. He's a sweet man, and she's fantastically
bright and intuitive. Maybe she'll sense a change
in him, if there really is one. I hope so. They're
obviously good together. And frightened, I think.
And thoughtful. Charlotte says she's been looking after
Peter and feeding him at night, as well as putting things
in our fridge downstairs for when I come home.*

November 26

*Well! I just dropped off, without even feeling it coming.
Maybe it was the mention of "home" that did it. I
doubt that. I'm keen to leave and all, but I don't have
any illusions that the next few weeks are going to be
anything but very tough, indeed.*
*(I skipped November 25, D.D., because it's getting late
now, and I know that if I get home overtired, Kate will
feel it and so will Peter. Besides, the routine here, apart
from visitors and surprise gifts, is pretty routine. So
really there isn't so much more to report. Also, to be
honest, I think I'm getting writer's cramp . . . or
early arthritis!)*
Dr. Spock keeps saying to plan to have some extra

*help around the house for the first few weeks when you
go home. Terrific: if we had extra money, we'd have
extra help. Actually, I feel pretty strong. And I am
young. It may be exhausting, but I really think I'd rather
do it myself.*

*I just had a really dumb thought. Here we are, Peter
and I, having to get married because I was pregnant.
When that used to happen to someone else people
counted backward and guessed the answer. It used to be
girls would say that their babies were just premature.
But mine actually was! Kate is pretty big for a
"five-month-old" kid. A lot of people are going to
be awfully confused.*

*I'll tell you something, D.D. The last couple days
I've actually felt sort of confident about things. I admit
that the last time I felt that way, disaster was just
around the corner. But being realistic, I doubt anything
as terrible as that is likely to happen. At least, not for
a very long time. Peter seems determined to be what I
want him to be, and what Kate needs him to be. And
I'm determined, too, to be what Peter wants and needs.
Maybe a marriage needs this kind of awful start to get
better afterwards. I mean, if everything went along
perfectly at the beginning, what fun would it be later,
just living and reliving all that perfectness? This way,
as we get older and surer of ourselves, we have a chance
to learn and share and grow more together than we
would if we had actually started out that way, in love.
"In love." I'm an honest lady, D.D. I still don't know
whether that applies to Peter and me. But I am
beginning to think that maybe it might. Kate would be
a very lucky girl.*

40.

Tish was bending over her small traveling case, stuffing her
nightgown and Sara's cardigan into it. As she packed, she
mentally made notes about her own strength, how her legs felt
and whether she could walk around her apartment as she
hoped, and whether when the need arose she could move
quickly to Kate's bedroom and crib.

Her departure day was a bright one, full of autumn gusts and flying leaves, the last of the season. She had eaten a full meal, having tea instead of coffee for a change. That had been a conscious decision. After all, she felt, this *was* the first day of a new part of her life.

She heard a soft knock on her door and turned, smiling, ready to see Peter at the agreed-upon time. It was Dr. Neider instead.

"All set to go back to the front?" he asked pleasantly.

Tish grinned in response. "Just waiting for the ambulance wagon," she said. "Probably having a tough time getting through the flack."

"Not unless Peter is flying," corrected Dr. Neider. His gray hair was rumpled and stood around his head wanting to be a halo. He always looked to Tish as though he had just come back from six months in the Antarctic. She also sensed a moodiness in him, a desire to be liked, loved, and obeyed. Frankness was something he wanted only occasionally.

"Did you have a good time here?" he asked.

"What a funny question," Tish said, and then remembered it was important to please him. "If you mean was the experience a painful one, I'd have to say that it was, as far as I remember. Then again, it was heavenly, lolling around day after day with only one little problem attached."

The doctor nodded. "How do they feel?"

Tish brought her hands up to her breasts protectively. "I never thought a baby could do such damage."

"You'll get used to it," Dr. Neider encouraged. "What time is Peter due?"

"Eleven," said Tish. "You said you wanted the bed shortly after that." The doctor remembered. "You can have the room now, if you want. I can wait downstairs."

"There's not that much rush. Besides, we like to keep the babies warm and undisturbed until the last minute. It would just mean an extra walk down the hall for you later."

There was a ringing of bells, a different sequence of tones heard from the hall. "That's me," said the doctor, taking Tish's hand. "Come see me in about a week."

Tish held the doctor's hand firmly. "Thank you," she said. "I have a feeling that without you everything wouldn't have been so easy, and so successful."

The doctor's face broke into a satisfied smile. "That's the

feeling you're supposed to have," he said. "It may not be true, of course, but I think it is."

He turned and went through the door. Tish stood a moment without being certain what to do while she waited. Finally, having checked and rechecked the room to see that everything she had brought was accounted for, she drew up a chair to the window and looked out. Her birch trees stood as they had before, nodding in the breeze, looking as though they were made of wire.

By eleven thirty, Tish had grown a little uneasy. She paced a few steps and then forced herself to sit again. She wanted to call Pack-a-Camp to see if Peter had left for the hospital. But she hesitated. She knew the hospital had probably made out her account. All calls had been logged and charged. One more would no doubt confuse and anger the bookkeeper downstairs.

At ten minutes to twelve, Tish picked up the bedside phone. "This is room three-eleven," she said. "Would making one more call ruin your billing system?"

She was told it would, but to keep track of how many times she used the phone for outside calls. She promised to keep scrupulous count, and dialed.

Peter had not been in the office all day, a woman told her. In fact, they had tried to reach him at home this morning, but there had been no response.

Tish put down the receiver. No doubt Peter had been up at the crack of dawn, doing things, arranging for baby food and bottles and toys. He was probably on his way only now, having adjusted everything to his satisfaction.

At twelve thirty, Tish began to feel hunger and nerves simultaneously. She wondered if she had to wait much longer whether she could get one more lunch. She decided she would have to sit there without, for that too had no doubt been toted up and would only aggravate the hospital personnel.

Her mother would be glad to come by and take her home, if only she would phone. But Tish didn't want to do that. After all, being held up in traffic, stopped somewhere on a parkway, wasn't exactly a national disaster. There was no need to disturb anyone else.

At one, she dialed Charlotte Clayton.

"Tish!" Charlotte said. "I didn't even hear you come in. How are you feeling? How's Kate?"

"I'm fine, and Kate's fine, and we're still at the hospital."

"Whatever for?" asked Charlotte. "Is something wrong?"

"No. It's just that something has held up Peter and we haven't any way to get out of here."

"Want me to come get you? I'd be glad to."

"Really, Charlotte, I'd be terrifically grateful if you could. I'm getting flashes of guilt occupying this room when someone else is probably holding in a kid by willpower alone."

"Be there in ten minutes," Charlotte said. "Will you be downstairs, or should I park and come up?"

"Park and come up," Tish instructed. "They don't let the children out until the last minute, until they know they have some way of leaving."

"Be there in a flash," Charlotte said, hanging up.

Tish sighed. She was certain she was overreacting, but suddenly she wanted to be gone from that place, to be in her own home where at least, if Peter were away, she would have things to occupy her time and mind.

"Hello. This is Three-eleven again. I've made my last call. There were two."

The operator thanked her and said she would relay the charges to the accounting office.

"There's only one thing," Tish said hesitantly, hoping that her lie would be undetected. "My husband has been delayed. Business. I've asked someone else to come get us. Can I leave without actually paying you now?"

The operator promised she would relay the question to the proper department. She told Tish to stay in her room, that someone would phone with permission or denial.

Tish hung up the receiver, sweating. What would happen if the hospital insisted on being paid before she and Kate could leave? She had about ten dollars in her purse, period. She had heard apocryphal stories about tangles of this kind, about how hospitals hounded and hounded and then would never close an account, hanging onto a family as a ferociously hungry dog does to a bone. Well, she decided, they could chew forever on her family, for all they had was a particularly delicious kind of air to taste.

She paced slowly, practicing sounding indignant and powerful in her mind for the benefit of the accounting office. Charlotte knocked.

"All set?" she asked, poking her head in through the door.
Then she walked farther into the room and picked up Tish's
suitcase.

"Ready," Tish said. "You're an angel for coming."

"My dear," Charlotte said, holding the door open for Tish,
"there are some days when to write another sentence about
one incredibly stupid editor or another is simply no longer fun.
This is one of them. I'm grateful to *you*."

41.

"I still can't believe how nice they were," Tish said to
Charlotte, after putting Kate to sleep in her crib. "I was armed
to the teeth, in my mind, anyhow. Just waiting for one mean
word or look."

"Clearly today is your lucky day," Charlotte said. "Yours,
and your father-in-law's."

"I had completely forgotten, you know?"

"Still, hospitals are not normally noted for charm. They
were very nice, in any case."

"I'll never be able to thank you enough," Tish said, easing
Kate's door nearly closed and turning into the hallway. "I
was going crazy just sitting there, waiting."

"Well, Tish, sitting is something you'll probably have to
learn to like a little. At least for a while. How do you feel?"

"Tired," Tish admitted. "I don't have the strength even to
unpack."

"Can I get you something?"

"A cup of tea would be great," said Tish. "I'll just go collapse up front."

Which she did. She was tired and edgy. She struggled to keep
the worry from her voice. She was grateful that Charlotte had
not yet asked what could have delayed Peter. Tish had no idea
what she would say. Or whether she would be able to say
anything coherently at all.

She looked at her wristwatch. Nearly three. Kate would
be awake in an hour probably, hungry as a lion. After that,
Tish thought. After that I can call my parents. Call the
McSweenys, too. Checking in doesn't sound like checking on.

Tish leaned back in the chair and closed her eyes. Peter
really had been busy. The nursery was a brilliant room, full

of warm colors and toys, clean as it could be. He had arranged everything in the kitchen Tish would need. He had even put talcum and liquid baby-soap on a ledge near Kate's bassinet. And an enormous pile of diapers, real ones. A box of Pampers stood nearby, no doubt for experimentation. Tish hoped Kate would be a rash-free baby. The idea of a pink, red-faced, screamingly uncomfortable child who required constant changing and powdering was not enchanting.

"Here you are," Charlotte said, maneuvering slowly into the living room with Tish's mug and one for herself. "I put milk and sugar in it. I hope you take it that way."

"You're terrific, Charlotte," Tish said, smiling. Charlotte sank onto the couch. "How does it feel?" she asked Tish. "After seven months, to be slim and beautiful again?"

"I don't feel either, yet," Tish said. "I've lost a little weight, is all. It's going to be an uphill struggle getting really slim again."

"Where could Peter be, do you suppose?" Charlotte wondered. "He couldn't have forgotten what day this was, could he?"

"Well, I wouldn't think so," said Tish. "But he has been frantic at the store. They've been asking him to take over one of their other shops, in Mountainside."

"Really?" Charlotte was impressed. "He sounds like an embryonic tycoon."

"The good thing is that he likes what he does so much," Tish said, feeling the words come out one after the other in a surprisingly calm and sensible order. "It would be awful if the only job he could have gotten was one he hated."

"There's nothing worse," Charlotte agreed. "Listen, I put a huge pot of homemade Scotch mutton-broth in your fridge. All you need to do is make some eggs or a couple of sandwiches, and your first home meal is a triumph. I've got to get upstairs and try to do something for *my* husband," she laughed. "Sometimes I think he really is that again. Anyway, for Fred, for supper. You'll be okay?"

Tish nodded as Charlotte stood and put her mug on the coffee table. "I'll be fine," she said. "I've only got a thousand things to get organized, apart from feeding Kate, that is. I'll be busy till dawn if I'm not careful."

"Well, don't be," said Charlotte sternly. "Let Peter do the

heavy stuff. You should be taking it easy for another couple of weeks, at least."

Tish stood. "Can't," she said, "Nobody likes a lazy mother."

42.

November 27

The little mother is home. So is The Kid.
The sun was shining, probably still is somewhere. The house was fresh and clean. Peter did do all the things he said he would. Kate is supplied to the gills. Anything she doesn't have, she doesn't need. (Sardonically, she asked, does that mean a father, too?)
I am feeling surges of strength and then am completely wiped out. Great energy mixed with total exhaustion. It's hard to write just now, D.D. Will be back in a while.

It's now about nine. Kate is asleep, for another few hours. I should be trying to get some rest, but I think, all things considered, that would be pretty tough just now. Still, I am determined to save what strength I have for Kate, not for worry.
I talked to Mother, who wanted of course to come charging over with food and advice. I suggested she wait until "we" get a little better organized. I also called the McSweenys, to thank George for the past week and the hospital bill. All normal at that house, too. Charlotte sent down a divine soup, which is about all I've had the taste for. Happily, it has all kinds of great things floating around in it, so I don't feel guilty about not giving Kate the proper nutrients, whatever they are.

Later still, now almost eleven thirty. Kate has begun to stir, making funny little sounds and bubbles in her sleep. I sat in her room a while, just watching. Which, I admit, is not all that exciting, but tonight it's comforting. What about tomorrow?

There's no point in telling you, D.D., what time it is. It's late. I'm tired. Kate is asleep again, after having wolfed down what must have been seventeen quarts of

*milk. Maybe there's a streak of Russian in me, Russian
peasant, wetnurse, and midwife and salt of the earth.
I've done all the little things I could think of to keep
busy, and not to have to think. Right now I'm absolutely
beat. I haven't a grain of emotion left, neither tears nor
anger, nothing. I keep telling myself that I don't care.
But I do. Why? If I could answer that, knowing for
certain that it's me I'm worried for or Kate, or even
Peter, things would be a bit easier. I'm not going to stay
up pacing or worrying. I'll assume nothing, except
that Peter is somewhere safe and not doing things. I'll
give him the benefit of every doubt this time. Maybe he
went into New York to get something special, and
everything just took more time than he planned. Maybe
he got mugged. Or maybe—actually, D.D., there aren't
any more maybes.
That's not true, of course. There are. That's the most
awful part of it. Life seems only to be maybes. Am I in
particular selected to go through all this, or does
everyone? I'm tired of thinking. D.D., hang around a
while, will you? I know I once thought that keeping
you up-to-date was a childish thing and when I was
married, it seemed even sillier to confess and confide
in you when I had Peter. Well, sometimes you get
surprised. Don't desert me now, D.D. Happier times
are just around the corner. Or something.
Why is this night longer than the other?*

43.

Tish sat up in bed, wild-eyed and uneasy. She looked at the
alarm. Not quite eight o'clock. Had it been Kate she heard?
The phone?

The sound came a second time, perhaps a third. The doorbell. Hastily, hardly bothering to close her robe about her,
Tish slid from her bed and padded through the kitchen and
the dining room to the front hall. She understood without
actually noticing that the sun was shining.

She pulled open the front door, which had not been locked.
"Poncho!"

Poncho stood on the cement stoop, smiling at her but without looking into her face. "Is Peter ready?" he asked in a low voice.

Tish remembered the day before with sudden clarity. She couldn't decide what to say. Poncho was Peter's best friend, and one of hers now, too, she supposed. That gave him some rights. She opened her mouth to say something, what she wasn't yet certain herself, when Poncho spoke quickly. "He's not home, is he, Tish?"

Tish was astonished and could only look at Poncho and nod.

"I thought so," said Poncho sadly. He half-turned and took a step down.

"Wait!" Tish said hurriedly. "Wait a minute, Ponch. Come on in."

"What for?"

"Well," Tish started and then faltered. "At least you could take a look at Kate. You've only seen her through glass before."

"Okay," Poncho said, following Tish into the house.

Wondering why she was doing so, Tish led Poncho along the hallway and quietly pushed open Kate's door. Together, they tiptoed into the room and looked into the crib.

"She looks pretty much the same to me, Tish," Poncho whispered, giving Tish a soft nudge in the ribs. "Remember, this isn't the first kid I've ever seen."

"Still," Tish said, "she is pretty, isn't she? She will be, anyway."

"She'll be a killer."

Tish turned and faced Poncho. She held his look a moment, without knowing what information was being exchanged. She shrugged finally, giving an imitation grin, and motioned Poncho out of the room.

In the hall, she said, "Want some coffee? Only takes a minute."

"I'll be late for school," Poncho said.

"So what?"

"So," Poncho agreed, smiling.

"Wait in the living room. It'll just be a second."

Tish turned quickly and slipped through her bedroom into the kitchen. As quickly as she could, she pulled a filter from a package, and put on water to boil. Measuring eight cups, she poured the coffee into the filter and then, when the water had nearly come to a boil, for she was rushing, she poured it.

Poncho had been standing uneasily near the living room mantel, unable to decide where to sit, when Tish appeared with a tray.

"Sit down," she said. "There."

Poncho did as he was told, while Tish poured coffee for them both, adding cream and sugar without asking. She handed Poncho a mug and then sat down herself.

She took an uneasy sip. "What do you know I don't?" she asked quietly.

"What do you know?" Poncho asked in return.

"Only that Peter's been somewhere for twenty-four hours," Tish said. She was holding onto her own suspicions, feeling instinctively that if she opened her mind completely to Poncho, he might avoid what she had to say, avoid the implications and then say nothing more, about anything. "You must have seen him, Ponch. What was he supposed to be ready for? When you came. Why did he need you to pick him up?"

"You mean where did he want to go?"

"All right. Where did he want to go?"

"School."

"School?"

Poncho nodded. Tish saw for the first time that he looked extraordinarily tired, as though he had been up all night. His hair was sloppily combed, which was rare, and it seemed as though the clothes he wore were selected on the basis of being handy, being on the back of a chair instead of neatly hung in his closet.

"Listen, Tish," Poncho began, "this is probably none of my business. Except that for some dumb reason, I feel responsible. Not to you, so much, or even to Peter, really. Just responsible."

"Just start from the beginning, Ponch," Tish said. "I'm a big girl. Really."

Poncho nodded but he took a moment to drink his coffee.

"Go ahead," Tish urged gently.

"Well, it's pretty screwy," Poncho said at last. "Yesterday, when school was out, all of a sudden there was Peter, suited up and ready for practice."

"Practice?"

"Football practice. We came out of the locker room and started out to the field, and he just materialized, right in front of us."

"In his uniform?"

"And with his playbook under his arm. Set and ready to go."

"But what on earth for?" Tish asked after a moment of thought. "What does he think he's going to do with his job?"

"You're probably thinking ahead of him, Tish."

"Well, what did he say to you, then?"

Poncho blushed. "That he was . . . that he was free to play football, again. That he was eligible to play and that here he was, back just in time for the final game of the season. He wanted Coach Johnson to give him his old position. He had studied the plays, he said. He was in good shape. He was raring to go."

Tish shook her head. "I don't understand, Poncho," she admitted. "How could he be eligible when he's married?"

"That's the big one, all right."

"Well?"

Poncho hesitated. "Well, I was standing around when he told the coach he had been . . . had gotten an . . . annulment."

"A what?"

Poncho flinched. "An annulment, Tish," he said quietly.

Tish stood, holding her mug.

"I must look terrible," she said suddenly, putting her hand to her hair and turning away from Poncho.

"Tish," Poncho said encouragingly, "I don't believe that."

Tish stood facing away. "Why would he say something like that? Just to play football?"

"I don't know."

"Well," said Tish, turning quickly and trying to smile attractively, "if we *are* annulled, it's the first I've heard of it."

"You're not alone there," Poncho said. "It's also the first your family heard, or Peter's."

"They know?"

"No," Poncho said. "They don't. But *I* know."

Tish's face told Poncho she had not thought as rapidly

as he had spoken. "Maybe I skipped," he said. "Let me start again." He stood. "There he was, suited up and ready to go. What he told Coach Johnson and me was that over the weekend there had been an annulment. That meant he was no longer married and would be eligible again to play for Notre Dame. The coach didn't know what to do."

"Did he believe him?"

"Why wouldn't he, Tish?" Poncho said. "I mean, who would make up something like that?"

Tish laughed a little bitterly. "Peter, I guess."

"Which is probably what he did, although I can't figure out why, either," Poncho said. "Anyway the coach was boggled. I mean, there wasn't anyone around he could ask to verify the thing. And Peter had been a pretty hot end. We *could* use him Saturday."

"So could I," Tish broke in.

"I know," said Poncho evenly. "I know. Anyway, Coach Johnson sort of had to take Peter at his word. Which he did. He alternated Peter with Mike Curtis, the guy who's played end all season."

"Unbelievable," murmured Tish.

"Well, not all of it," Poncho said. "You should have seen Peter, Tish. He was a real killer. He is in pretty good shape, still. Anyway, after the game, while Peter was showering and getting dressed, Coach Johnson came to me since he knew, I guess, how close Peter and I are. What did I think, he wanted to know. I didn't know what to say. He knew as much as I did."

"What happened then, to Peter, I mean?"

"Wait a minute," Poncho objected. "Let me try to get things in order. The coach asked if I could find out whether Peter was telling the truth," Poncho went on. "I said I could, but that I didn't know if that would make him eligible to play Saturday. The coach said he'd check that."

"What happened to Peter?"

"Nothing," Poncho said. "He showered and dressed. I offered him a lift home but he said he had his own car. So off he went."

"And that's all there is?"

"Not quite," Poncho admitted. "He told me to pick him up in the morning, for school."

"And you didn't."

"No. I didn't have to. I couldn't have found him. I knew that when I got here."

"Did you go to McSweenys', too?"

"Nope," said Poncho. "I just told you, I didn't have to. I knew."

"What, for Christ's sake, did you know?"

"Easy, easy," said Poncho. "That doesn't help."

"I'm sorry," Tish said. "I'm trying to be sensible, but it's not easy."

"Okay," Poncho said. "Here's what happened. After practice, after Peter took off, I began to sort things out. The problem was, how could I find anything out without making everybody—you, his family—unhappy or frightened. After dinner, I finally figured how. I called your house first, Tish. Your parents, I mean. I made up some story about how I wanted to visit, and did they think it would be okay? I said I didn't want to call directly, because you might be sleeping, or Kate might be. I thought they would know better than I."

"And?"

"Your mother said she thought probably I should wait a few days, until you had settled into a routine. She said it wasn't an easy thing coming back from the hospital and organizing your life from scratch again."

"What about Peter's family?"

"Pretty much the same. The same story, same answer. Neither one of them said anything about how awful it was, or how badly they felt about things, or anything like that. I guessed they didn't know anything one way or another, really, but about an annulment they would have. They'd have to, wouldn't they?"

"Jesus, yes!" Tish answered. "My father would kill Peter."

"If he could find him."

"If he could find him and if it were true, which it isn't."

"Okay. It isn't," said Poncho. "Anyway, I had a bad night, Tish. I knew I was into somebody else's business. That I was mucking around where I shouldn't be. But I couldn't stop thinking about it, or worrying, either."

"Have you seen Peter?"

Poncho shook his head negatively. "I went out once, about ten, just driving along, thinking I might see his car parked somewhere, like a diner or a gas station or something."

"Or . . . maybe, someone else's house?"

"What do you mean?"

Tish reddened. "Nothing," she answered, looking down at the floor.

"I figure he slept in his car."

"But why?" Tish half-cried out. "What the hell for, Poncho? What does he think he's doing?"

Poncho shook his head. "I'm sorry, Tish," he said after a moment. "I'm sorry. I knew he wouldn't be here. I was certain. I'm sorry to have barged in and . . ."

Tish paced in front of Poncho, shaking her head. "It's not your fault, Ponch. How could it be? You did everything you could. I'm glad you came. I didn't know where he was either, not all day. He never showed at the hospital. He wasn't at work. If you hadn't come, I still wouldn't know anything." She stopped walking. "We still *don't* know anything."

"Nope."

"What's going to happen today. I mean, if Peter shows up for practice again?"

"I don't know," said Poncho. "I haven't talked to Coach Johnson."

"Well, what could happen?"

"It beats me," Poncho answered honestly. "What can I tell you? If he does show up, and he sticks to the annulment thing, I'd say . . . I'd have to say something was pretty screwy."

"You really think . . . ?" Tish's voice was almost inaudible.

"What do I know? Who am I? My old man works on trees. My mom has kids. I just try to scrape through."

A tentative cry came from the back bedroom. "Oh, God," said Tish, walking quickly down the hallway. Within a minute she had returned. "She'll just have to wait," she announced, speaking over Kate's mewling. "Do you think I should be at school this afternoon, Poncho?"

Poncho shrugged. "I guess," he said. "If Peter shows up."

"Why wouldn't he?" Tish asked reasonably. "If he thinks you believe the story about his annulment, and that he's eligible to play, where else would he go?"

"I don't know," Poncho said unhappily. "Listen, Tish, I'm no expert at this."

"Well, neither am I!"

"I wasn't blaming you. I was just talking."

For a very short moment, Tish didn't feel like apologizing. When she did, Poncho was already planning. "Maybe you should call his folks," he offered. "Or yours."

Tish nodded.

"It might be better, you know, sort of calm him down, if he saw everybody there."

"Or send him through the roof," said Tish, looking up quickly.

"Maybe."

"What will the coach do?"

"Who knows?" said Poncho with a shrug. "He's a pretty sensible, fair guy. He'll do whatever he thinks best."

"Terrific."

Kate's crying became stronger.

"I better go," said Poncho. "I'm late, anyway."

Tish walked Poncho to the door. "You know, Ponch, we don't have the faintest idea what we're doing. Or even why."

"I know."

"Bye," Tish said, putting an arm quickly and lightly on Poncho's shoulder.

"See you," he said, walking quickly down the walk without looking back.

"Oh, Jesus!" sighed Tish, turning back toward Kate's room.

She attended to Kate single-mindedly, not allowing herself to think or ponder anything but her child's needs. Twice, once while diapering Kate, and a second time, while standing near her crib and looking down at her, Tish caught herself beginning to choke with tears. Both times she stifled the sensation, turning quickly to do something else.

Finally, there was nothing she could do but think about Peter. About what Poncho had told her. "Never assume anything," came Charlotte's dictum to her mind. It was impossible not to. No one normal did the things Peter was doing.

It was nearly ten o'clock when Tish had steadied herself enough to phone her family and Peter's. Before she could pick up the receiver and dial Princeton, however, the phone rang.

Without daring to hope, Tish picked it up. "Hello?"

"Mrs. McSweeny?" It was a woman's voice. Tish thought she recognized it but was uncertain from where.

"Yes?"

"Hi, this is Rosemary at Pack-a-Camp. Is Peter still there?"

Tish cleared her throat. "Yes," she said. "He's in bed."

"Oh, I'm sorry."

"The twenty-four-hour flu, he thinks," Tish continued rapidly. "Although I guess you'd have to say more like forty-eight hours, wouldn't you?"

Rosemary laughed. "I guess so. Well, we were only wondering. Tell him to follow instructions and get better fast."

"Yes, I will," Tish said. "Thanks for calling."

"Bye."

Tish put down the receiver. My God, she thought, just like normal people. When there's trouble, consolidate.

Not allowing herself more time to think, she picked up the phone and called Linden Lane. "Daddy?" she said. "What are you doing home?"

"I've got the flu," said her father huskily.

Tish laughed. "What's so damned funny?" her father wanted to know.

Tish was still laughing. "I'm sorry," she said, out of breath. "It's just that . . . well, never mind. Listen, Daddy . . . could you do me . . . a favor?"

"I don't know," her father said, seeming to consider. "Why should I do anything for a ghoul who crows when someone is on death's doorstep?"

"Oh, I am sorry, really, Daddy. It was just a thought. Are you really feeling that bad?"

There was a pause on the line. "Honestly, no," admitted her father with a muted chuckle. "I just felt like taking it easy for a day. Happily, this is your mother's day for good works. I've got the place to myself."

"Well, could you do me a favor, then?"

"Sure, sweetheart. What?"

"Would you come over and pick me up, say around three thirty or so? I've got to meet Peter somewhere, and he's got the car."

"What about Kate?"

"Oh," Tish lied, easily now, "Charlotte Clayton's said she'd look after her for a while. It won't be for very long, really."

"All right, honey," said Mr. Davies. "I'll come by a few

minutes before that. So I can sneak another look at my granddaughter."

"You're an angel, Daddy. Thanks. I'll see you then."

"Okay. Bye, sweetheart."

"Bye."

Oh, God! Now she had to phone Charlotte as well. What if Charlotte couldn't come down?

But she could.

Tish made a note near her bed to buy something extra special for Fred and Charlotte. Soon.

One more call. She dialed. "Hello, Kate?"

"Tish! How are you? How's Kate?"

"Couldn't be better," Tish said cheerfully. "Sleeps wonderfully, thank heavens, and eats like a bear."

Mrs. McSweeny laughed. "That must be painful."

"It is," Tish agreed, making a laugh-sound, too. "Listen, Peter asked me to call."

"Yes?"

"He said . . . he said he's got a surprise for us. He wanted to know if we would meet him at school this afternoon."

"School?"

"Notre Dame," Tish explained. "He's got some terrific thing planned, I guess. And it's happening there. Or at least somewhere nearby," she hedged, fearing suddenly to say too much and find herself trapped.

"Does he want George, too?"

"I guess, but honestly I don't know," Tish said weakly.

"Well, I doubt I could reach him, anyway. He'll just have to miss whatever it is. Any ideas, dear?"

Tish closed her eyes. "Absolutely none, Kate."

"Well, whatever it is, I'm sure it's something nice. Peter's like that."

"I know. Well, I guess I'll see you then."

"All right, dear. Around four?"

"Fine."

"Four it is. Kiss Kate for me."

"I will. Bye."

Tish put the receiver back on its cradle. Then, cradling herself, she leaned against the pillows on the unmade bed. She felt the tears forming, but fought them back, willed them into retreat. There was time enough for that, she told herself. And then she opened her eyes wide and wondered why, instinctively, she had thought she would be alone, and actually have time enough to cry, alone.

44.

Tish and her father turned off the Lawrenceville Road and into the parking area to the south of Notre Dame in silence. Their journey had not been as calm.

"What do you mean?" Mr. Davies had shouted. "He's trying to get out of all this?"

"No, Daddy," Tish said. "It isn't that. It's . . . it's, I don't know what it is. But something's on his mind, and he's having trouble straightening it out."

"The miserable rotter!" muttered Mr. Davies.

"You don't know that!" Tish defended, almost shouting herself. "No one does. That's what we've got to find out."

"I'll bloody well find out. I'll beat the shit out of him till he comes to his senses!"

"Daddy," Tish pleaded. "Please. Think of me, and Kate."

"I am, dammit!" said her father. "I have been all along. A lot more than you or your mother seem to give me credit for."

Tish had been unable to answer. She understood her father's anger, his desire to strike finally at Peter. His disappointment and love. But she felt unable to explain that she understood, at that moment.

The car moved determinedly alongside the school before Mr. Davies turned it off to the left into the lot. A lone figure in a football uniform ran quickly toward them.

Tish got out of the car as her father moved swiftly around in front of it, ready to intercept the boy.

"Hi, Ponch," said Tish loudly, to signal off her father.

"Hi, Tish," said the worried-looking Poncho. "Hello, sir."

Mr. Davies nodded curtly.

"Where is everyone?" asked Tish. "I thought you'd be out on the field."

"The coach is holding things up. He wanted to wait till you got here."

"So what's going to happen, Poncho?"

Poncho shook his head. "The coach says he'd rather let

Peter play a while. He thinks he could be upset pretty badly if he weren't allowed to." Tish agreed silently. "What he wanted you to do, Tish, was stay in your car until we get on the field. Then, after a few minutes, sort of ease over onto the sidelines. Coach Johnson thinks that maybe, when Peter sees you standing there, he'll remember everything and sort of clear his head."

"What if he doesn't?" asked Mr. Davies.

"Then I don't know, sir," Poncho answered. "I guess then we have to wait till the end of practice."

"His mother's coming, too, Ponch," said Tish. "Around four."

"Does she know?"

"I couldn't tell her," Tish said quietly. "I thought . . . I don't know, I guess I was afraid she'd be angry at *me*."

"Well," Poncho said, "she'll have to do whatever is necessary. We all have to."

"Tell me, boy," Mr. Davies said brusquely, "you really think he's not faking this whole thing?"

"I've known Peter McSweeny a long time, sir," Poncho said evenly. "I don't think he's faking."

Mr. Davies nodded. Tish saw that Poncho's words meant more to her father than her own did. She was angry for only a moment.

"Better get back to your car," Poncho advised. "The coach has been reexplaining plays and game plans till he's blue in the face and the guys are bored out of their skulls. He's only waiting for me to give him the signal."

Tish sat in the front seat. "Daddy," she said. "Come on, please."

Mr. Davies walked back around the front of the car and got in as Poncho ran up the small rise to the door of the gymnasium and locker room.

A few girls appeared from around the corner of the school building and, carrying books and laughing, talking among themselves, they approached the sideline of the field as the first members of Notre Dame's team came out.

Tish watched silently, not yet seeing her husband. "You okay, baby?" asked her father very softly.

Tish tried to smile reassuringly.

In the last bunch of players, Peter appeared. How he

looked, whether he was tired or depressed or angry, Tish couldn't tell. His helmet and padding made him a stranger to her, and it was only his height and the slight roll of his body as he walked that identified him.

Tish looked at her watch. Nearly four o'clock. Kate McSweeny would be wheeling in at any moment. She ought to be met, Tish thought. They should stay in their car, and then approach the sidelines together. But how could she tell Kate she had lied, that Peter's surprise was a little more serious than she might have imagined?

Her father smoked ceaselessly, lighting one cigarette from another, stubbing each out in the car's ashtray and then letting it fall over the side of the car through the window. Tish stared straight ahead at the field. From where she sat, she could see no action. She saw two squads moving, down and across the field and back, but who was carrying and who was tackling was impossible to discern.

A light tan Cougar swung into the parking lot, stopped, started again. The car circled the lot slowly, as though looking for a familiar space. Slowly it passed Tish and her father. Then, more quickly, it backed up. "Tish?" called Mrs. Mc-Sweeny, waving in uncertainty.

"Oh God," sighed Tish, waving back.

Mrs. McSweeny pulled her car as close to Mr. Davies' as she could, and got out of it. She walked brightly over, leaning down into Tish's window. "Hi, darling," she said cheerily. "Harry! Hello!"

Mr. Davies barely grunted, but Mrs. McSweeny didn't notice. "I couldn't reach George, Tish," she said. "I had his secretary leave messages all over his office, and on the floor, and at his club. But I guess we really couldn't count on him. Now," she stood, checking the area around, "where's Peter?"

Tish opened her door slowly. "Kate," she said, trying not to let her urgency sound clearly through her voice, "why don't you get in with us for a while? Peter's . . . he's not here yet."

"Oh, all right," said Mrs. McSweeny pleasantly, sliding in beside Tish. "Tell me, how's Kate?"

Tish nodded that Kate was fine.

"Your son's not so hot, though," said Mr. Davies.

"Pardon me?"

Tish's elbow found her father's ribs. "Kate," she said, "we think maybe there's . . . there's something a little wrong . . . something disturbing Peter."

"You mean he's ill?"

"We don't know yet."

Mrs. McSweeny stared at Tish. After a moment, she said very steadily, "Why don't you just tell me what it is you have to?"

Tish nodded. "He claims he's gotten an annulment."

"An annulment?"

"Yes," Tish said. "That he's single again, and free to re-enroll in school, and eligible to play football again. Which he didn't even like all that much before." In spite of herself, Tish found her voice quavering.

Mrs. McSweeny said nothing. She continued to watch Tish, ready to hear more.

Tish took a deep breath, trying to stifle whatever traces of emotion there were on her outside. "He hasn't been home in two days. Maybe more, I don't know. He wasn't there when Kate and I came back from the hospital. Charlotte Clayton came to get us. He hasn't been at work this week, either. We don't know where he's been."

"We?" said Mrs. McSweeny calmly.

"Poncho Olivera and I," Tish explained. "Poncho saw Peter yesterday, here, at practice. Where Peter spent last night none of us knows."

Mrs. McSweeny turned a bit in her seat, looking out the windshield. She said nothing. Apparently she felt she was not expected to say anything at all.

There was a long silence. "Well," said Tish's father after a moment, "what do you think of all that? It sounds to me like he needs the kind of thrashing your husband probably never gave him."

Mrs. McSweeny faced Harry Davies, her face cold and unsympathetic. "It doesn't sound that way to me," she said, and then, before facing forward again, she glanced at Tish.

Tish knew exactly what Mrs. McSweeny's look meant, but she didn't feel like arguing. "I think we can get out now," she said instead, making a tentative movement. "The coach said we should just casually walk over to the sidelines, and watch."

Mrs. McSweeny said nothing still, merely opened the car door and got out.

The three began to move toward the playing field.

As they approached, Coach Johnson, a short man wearing a sweatsuit and baseball cap, noticed them and nodded, making no other effort to speak or confer. Tish and her father and Mrs. McSweeny stopped some feet behind the bench, looking over the heads of the reserves at the action on the field.

Peter was playing his old position. Tish assumed this meant that whichever boy was Mike Curtis was probably sick with worry and anger. She wondered idly which form of those in front of her was his.

Peter's squad had the ball, and had just broken through the center of the defensive team for a first down. Coach Johnson trotted onto the field to have a few words with Notre Dame's quarterback.

The next play from scrimmage, the quarterback faded. Peter ran forward and cut to his right, bringing him close to the sidelines. The quarterback loosed the ball. The catch was a secure one, and the tackle immediately afterwards equally secure. Peter got up and bent over to feel his knee. As he straightened, he inadvertently glanced toward the sidelines.

Tish couldn't tell whether he actually identified any of them from that distance. But for a second, Peter froze.

Then, shaking his head a bit, he turned away and trotted back to his huddle.

Mrs. McSweeny looked straight ahead, standing a few feet away from Tish and her father.

After a moment, the squads faced off again. The quarterback backstepped quickly and fired a pass downfield, this time with too much strength and not enough accuracy. The ball sailed over Peter's outstretched arms, and landed squarely in the arms of a back on the defensive team. Immediately he ran forward. In a neat step, Peter was in his path.

The two men collided. Instead of going to the runner's legs, Peter had lunged for the man's midsection, his arms flying around the runner's waist. The fury of Peter's intense forward movement moved both men horizontally, before crashing to the ground.

Peter jumped to his feet quickly. The other man lay still on the turf.

The coach blew his whistle, and trotted out onto the field;

a group of players and two trainers, in addition to Coach
Johnson, bent over and ministered to the boy. Peter stood
nearby, looking on, looking down, shaking his head. Tish
could see him try to explain something to the coach. But the
coach was occupied with worry. Peter turned and used his
hands to indicate something to his teammates.

The injured boy was carried off the field. The coach
remained among his players, giving advice and counsel. As
he turned to walk to the sidelines, he gave Peter's shoulder an
encouraging pat.

Tish let out her breath. She felt weak. Her legs hurt. So did
her back.

The team had reversed positions, so that Peter's team, the
offensive one, could again be on the offense despite the
interception. They went into a huddle.

They broke and moved up to the line. The center snapped
the ball. The quarterback took a pace back, and then plunged
into the line, breaking through and being stopped after five
or six yards' gain.

Peter, who had not been in on the play, was smothered by
defensive tacklers. The pile arose slowly, almost begrudgingly,
until Peter, too, could stand, knee by knee.

Tish watched as again his team conferenced. They
broke apart. The center snapped the ball and the quarterback
moved quickly to his side, looking over the line of rushing
defense men, then hurling the ball just over their fingertips
into the arms of his intended receiver.

Tish watched disbelievingly as yet one more defensive
player threw himself onto a growing pile of bodies. Peter was
under that. Again.

Something was happening on the field and Tish was
frightened. There was no reason for Peter to be hit again
and again, not that way, not that hard, not by so many. He
had tried to explain, she felt certain. He hadn't meant to
hurt the other player. He had been there and had done his
job and that was that. Why didn't they understand? Why
were they sullen and angry and lethal?

She clutched her purse until her fingers hurt. Peter had
moved slowly again into the huddle, shaking his head in disbelief or perhaps because he had been stunned. Tish wanted
him out.

Coach Johnson had moved closer to the field now, and seemed to look with mounting concern at what was happening. A trainer was at his side. Tish wished she could hear what they were saying.

Peter's team came out of the huddle and took its position. This time, Peter broke from the line freely and was under the quarterback's well-aimed pass perfectly. He was also hit from three sides instantaneously.

Tish felt her insides collapse. She felt dizzy.

The coach blew his whistle and hustled out onto the grass. He called the defense team together and spoke rapidly to them. When he turned back toward the bench, Tish could see the worry and anger on his face.

Before turning around again toward the action, Coach Johnson looked at Tish. No information was exchanged between them. Neither understanding nor sympathy nor worry. The look was blank, acknowledging but noncommittal. Tish was miserable, and moved closer to her father, putting her arm through his for support.

It's like a war, she thought. A little game that changes suddenly when one person is hurt. Then people want to hurt back. Then hurt back some more.

As though in a fog, Tish watched Peter's squad line up at scrimmage. The play was called and began. Tish could not see who was the ball carrier, only that Peter so far was uninvolved in the action. She held her breath. The play ended with Peter still on his feet.

Relief began to warm her. Perhaps the coach had felt what she had. Perhaps he had been able to calm people down, bring them to their senses.

Again the ball went from center to quarterback. Again Peter was only a defensive obstacle for his team.

Then one man hit him. Two more, from behind. Tish closed her eyes as she saw a fourth figure flying through the air aimed at the mound growing second by second.

Before the tangle of bodies could sort itself out, Tish had broken from her father's arm and was standing immediately behind the benched players. "Coach Johnson," she called, but her voice was weak.

Furthermore, she had cried out to the back of a short, worried man who was running onto the field. The pile still had not untangled. An occasional arm could be seen, seeming to try to pull away from the mass and then be pulled back, almost against its will, into the fray.

The whistle was loud and piercing and long.

At last, the movement on the grass stopped. First one, and then another, player extricated himself and stood. The last man but one rose, seemingly nonchalant, turning quickly away and taking his first steps back toward his team. Only Peter was left.

Mr. Davies' arm kept Tish from going onto the field.

Coach Johnson knelt beside Peter. He waved for two trainers. The men ran to his side. After a very long minute, Tish saw all three help Peter to stand. They did not move.

I've seen this before, Tish thought, in a statue. I know I have.

Finally the four men eased toward the bench.

Mrs. McSweeny had stationed herself in front of the reserves, waiting. She seemed to be taking each step with Peter, her face strained, her arms held in half-positions of aid and comfort.

The coach pulled off Peter's helmet. Now Tish saw. He was unshaven. His hair was matted, from the helmet no doubt, but perhaps also from the night before. There were circles under his eyes, not the circles she had seen before, purposely put there in charcoal to stop the glare from the field hitting a player's eyes, but nearly as dark.

His eyes seemed vacant. When they focused on the sideline, they focused on his mother. Peter gave a sheepish grin and tried to shrug, but clearly the motion gave him pain, for he winced immediately.

Coach Johnson said something to Peter's mother. Tish strained but could not catch the words. Mrs. McSweeny nodded. She put her arm around Peter's waist and helped him lift one of his arms around her shoulder. Stepping through the reserves at a break in the bench, they began to move away from the field and back toward the school. They had to pass Tish.

"Peter . . .?"

Peter and his mother stopped. He looked at Tish. He smiled, a meaningless but pleasant smile, a polite one. "Hello," he said.

"Hello," Tish whispered. She knew instantly that he hadn't the faintest idea who she was.

A sudden movement seen from the corner of her eye snapped her to attention. She turned. Her father was moving, forming his fists, taking a step away from her toward Peter.

"Daddy!" Tish cried, running quickly to grab his arm.

Peter and his mother had stopped, hearing Tish's cry. Mrs. McSweeny turned. Easily she understood what had been about to happen. Coldly she looked back at Tish and her father, and then a thin smile came to her lips.

Tish and Mr. Davies watched helplessly as Peter was led away.

"Come on, Daddy," Tish said finally, taking her father's arm again.

"Where?" he said. "The only place I want to be is where that son of a bitch husband of yours is!"

"We'll follow them home, to the McSweenys'," said Tish, deciding against trying to reason with her father.

Mrs. McSweeny helped Peter across the field and into the paved driveway of Notre Dame, leading him slowly toward her car.

Tish and her father followed, not hurrying. Tish looked up at the school. It was ugly, truly. Having a feeling of thinking almost the same thought before, she wondered if inside, or inside a student's head, there was ever any compensating beauty.

"Tish!"

She turned. Poncho was running toward her, carrying clothing in his arms. He arrived out of breath. "You'll need these," he said. "The keys to the car are in the jacket pocket."

"Thanks, Ponch," Tish said, taking the bundle. She turned toward her father but stopped as she was about to speak. "My God! I forgot about Kate!"

"I'll go, sweetheart," said her father quickly.

"No, Daddy, she needs to be fed."

Poncho stood nearby, waiting, edging away. "Poncho," said Tish, turning him to stone, "will you call Mrs. McSweeny? Explain that I'll be over as soon as Kate is taken care of?"

Poncho nodded.

"You want me to follow you back, Tish?" asked her father. "I can stay with Kate after you leave."

"That would be terrific, Daddy, thanks," she said. She turned toward her car, carrying Peter's clothing. Mr. Davies turned toward his.

"Tish?" called Poncho.

She turned.

"Good luck," he said softly.

None of the three moved. Then, as though on signal, each turned in a different direction and began walking away.

45.

Driving madly through rush-hour traffic, Tish arrived back in New Brunswick ahead of her father. By the time he had arrived, she had thanked Charlotte and was already in the middle of feeding Kate. She had said nothing of the afternoon to her neighbor, only how grateful she was that she was there to sit with Kate. She promised she would try not to make a habit of it, to impose on Charlotte's generosity more than was necessary.

Charlotte seemed not to mind.

Mr. Davies parked his car and rang the bell, coming straight in when there had been no answering response. "Just a minute, Daddy!" Tish called from Kate's bedroom.

When she was done feeding Kate, and changing her, she came out to face her father. Neither knew what to say. Finally, nervously, Tish had told her father what to do if Kate cried, or seemed restless. Mr. Davies informed his daughter that he was not a stranger to the business of small babies.

"I'll be back as soon as I can," Tish had promised, putting on her coat and nearly running out the door.

Behind the wheel of Peter's car, however, she now drove slowly, not seeming to be directed by signs or stoplights, handling the car automatically as she turned down #27 and drove toward Princeton.

By the time she found herself in the middle of Nassau Street, not far from Peter's house, Tish had arranged her thoughts.

Clearly, she decided, Kate McSweeny was blaming her for whatever had happened to Peter. Tish admitted that, from a certain point of view, that was understandable. She would just have to be bigger than Kate, more mature, more capable, less emotional. After all, whatever *had* happened in Peter's head, or was happening now, affected them all. And that, Peter's head, was the one concern that all shared now. Getting it back to where it should be.

Tish rehearsed in her mind the kinds of things she would say. She ordered her arguments. She didn't expect to see Peter, to try to talk to him. She knew instinctively that Kate would have him secluded somewhere, and would fight like crazy to keep him alone, there, with her.

Tish gripped the steering wheel with determination. She didn't care what Kate thought, but the one thing of which she was certain, instantly clearly certain, was that Peter should not stay at the McSweenys', isolated. If he were allowed to return to the garage, if things were allowed to seem as they had *before*, Tish wouldn't stand a chance of reaching him. He wouldn't ever acknowledge little Kate that way. Or herself. Or their marriage, or home, or their life together.

Whether speedily or painstakingly, Tish wanted to bring Peter back to her reality. Not for her sake alone, or for Kate's, she decided. For his. If he truly believed all the things he had said, before they had married and afterwards, about responsibility and duty and affection, it would do him more damage to realize he was running away from exactly those things than it would to face up to them.

Tish shook her head, turning off the ignition. Theorizing did no one any good. What did she know, really, except that Peter was having trouble, that she wanted to help him? She had to, for she felt no one else knew how as well as she. And then, stepping out of the car, she knew that, too, was wrong. Not only did she not know what to do for Peter, what cure he needed, realistically and honestly she couldn't even begin to diagnose his ailment.

She looked around. There were no cars parked behind the McSweenys' house. A hollow feeling grew in her stomach but she shook it off.

She stood at the back door, ringing the bell. There was no answer. She rang again.

Fleetingly, she thought she caught a movement at a curtain of an upstairs window. She rang a third time, prolonged and loudly.

She moved back from the doorstep and looked up. Whoever had been there, if someone had, had gone. She nodded. Probably Louise, the cook. And probably Kate had given her instructions to open the door for no one.

Well, where should she go? Where had Kate taken Peter? To a hospital? To a doctor's office, a private one? To New York, to a specialist? But what kind of specialist? For bones? Were Peter's bones damaged in that last tackle? To a psychiatrist? This fast? Without an appointment? Did psychiatrists have emergency patients?

Dumb, dumb, dumb! Tish thought. I'm standing here with nowhere to go and nothing to do and I'm alone and determined and ready to fight . . . and there's no one to fight back.

Slowly, almost aimlessly, she walked back to her car. She got into it and started the engine. She had Kate. That was where she should go. Without being aware of doing so, she turned on the car radio and started to glide down to the street.

Where was George?

She turned onto the highway and started slowly back toward Princeton and to New Brunswick beyond. The radio was loud. She turned it louder.

A few blocks before reaching the campus, Tish automatically turned off to the roadside. She twisted the dial on the radio until the sound became deafening.

Other cars, as they passed, took momentary note of the disabled vehicle, and passed on.

46.

It had only been with great effort that she had been able to keep her mother from rushing to New Brunswick. Tish's father had to call home, naturally. When he went back for dinner, apparently he had explained what had been happening to his wife. That, too, was natural. And so was the instantaneous phone call from Mrs. Davies, trying to find comforting things to say and slandering the McSweenys obliquely at the same time.

Tish hung up finally, exhausted, drained. She had looked at the kitchen clock. Nearly nine. At nine, if she had heard nothing, she would call. It seemed to her a very small thing to do. But she didn't know what else, with Kate here to care for, she honestly could do.

She sat in the living room, a mug of tea laced with honey in her hands, her head back against the chair, her eyes closed.

"I'll think about that tomorrow," she murmured to herself, and then smiled. Scarlett strikes again.

What she would think about tomorrow was what in fact she would do tomorrow, or the next day, or the following. She knew she would have to line up the alternatives—with Peter, without him—soon, for her sake and for Kate's. But not yet. Maybe everything that had happened during the past two days had been muddled, unclear, confused. Maybe she was reading Peter badly. Maybe he was only stunned when he saw her at the side of the football field. He had after all just been tackled. Hard. How would anyone react when what was probably running through one's mind fastest was pain and the need for comfort?

Of course Peter knew who she was. And would remember Kate, too. And the life he had lived these past months. Mrs. McSweeny was overreacting, no doubt. And that was natural. After all, she was Peter's mother. She cared for him, worried for him, as any mother would. There was nothing evil or hard-boiled or vindictive about that.

And what if Peter had been out overnight? He'd done that before. He'd said it had nothing to do with what he felt for Tish or probably, now, for Kate. It was just something that happened, that built up and needed to be released.

Tish shook her head. Calm she could try to be, but not that calm. If, in fact, that was all that had happened, then she had better start to decide what next to do tonight, not tomorrow.

The phone rang.

Tish sighed and stood slowly. She walked without hurrying into the kitchen. She knew who it was. Not who, so much, but about what. She had been waiting. She would take whatever news there was calmly, as an adult. "Hello?" she said.

"Tish, this is Kate McSweeny." The voice was quick and bitter and sharp.

"Where's Peter?" Tish's voice rose to meet the hostility automatically.

"Is George there?"

"Where's Peter, Kate?"

"I'm looking for my husband, Tish. Just tell me, is he at your house?"

"Kate, let's make a truce," Tish said evenly. "You drove *my* husband somewhere this afternoon. He's been missing longer than yours. Where is he?"

"Here."

"Doing what?"

"Resting."

"Why?"

"That's something we'll know more about in a few days' time," Kate McSweeny answered flatly. "Now, is George there with you?"

"Has Peter been to a doctor?"

Kate McSweeny sighed. "Yes, he has. He's been given something to make him sleep. His shoulder is badly bruised, but not broken. Now"—and here she shouted—"where the hell is George?"

"I thought he was with you." In spite of herself, Tish felt a little elated at Kate McSweeny's disarray.

"He was," said Peter's mother, "but he disappeared."

Tish's mind was already smiling, already hearing her say "win one, lose one." She said nothing, ashamed instantly.

"I'll be over in the morning," she finally announced.

"Don't," said Mrs. McSweeny.

"Why not?"

"Because I told you not to," the older woman said. "Because I won't let you in."

"George will, Kate."

"We'll see."

Tish put down the phone. Mrs. McSweeny had done so seconds before.

47.

November 28

I've just finished talking to Sara. Listening to her, to be more precise. I feel like hell, but I just have to write all this down. It's too unbelievable.

*(a) Hank has called it quits. Sara said she had, and
maybe, but I doubt it. (b) Sara has discovered . . .
are you ready for this, D.D. . . . Charlie Neil! (c) Sara
has decided to be a virgin again. There was no way for
me not to listen, D.D.; I picked up the phone and she
was off. All I had to do was say "yes" at the right times,
or maybe "no," or "really?" That's called the fine art of
conversation, don't you know?*

*Anyway, Sara has decided that all her past experiences
were forced on her! That society said people her age
were supposed to be sleeping around, experimenting,
meeting people and giving freely to them as a sign of
caring for them. Now she decides she really doesn't like
all that many people. She objects to having to play a role
prescribed for her by others. She's decided that the old
values are the proper ones. And she has physically willed
herself into a sexless trance. For Charlie, she says, isn't
ready for it yet. (I can believe that!) She says she's never
noticed him before because she'd been so wrapped up
trying to prove to Hank that she was a liberated lady,
wild with sex, crazy with desire, etc., etc. Suddenly
Charlie swims into view . . . all blushes and stutters
. . . and nerves. She says his mind is fantastic, and
subtle, and that he has a sneaky sense of humor. She's
in love again, but now for the first time, the first time
for real.*

*Well. I guess life is full of little surprises for everyone.
Do you suppose, D.D., if I tried hard enough, I could
will Kate back into an egg, and myself back into a
virgin, too? And Peter back into . . . into what?*

48.

Tish had made an honest breakfast for herself. The night
before had been endless, or so it seemed with Kate needing to
be seen to three times, and trying to sleep in between. Tish
had, in fact, slept off and on, waking to Kate's cry each time
with a sudden, fearful start. The fear had subsided, but
having been there it left little pockets of panic she was afraid
to explore.

She ate because she knew she was edgy, that at some moment

she might explode in powerlessness and anger. She spoke to Kate when the child was awake, and played with her. As much as could be done with a child only ten days old.

She had made her own bed, to thwart any hangover desire to take to it and forget the rest of the day. She had bathed and dressed, and sat now at the dining room table with the newspaper before her, thoughtlessly leafing through its pages, not reading headlines as much as getting a sense of the outside world from whatever pictures there were there.

She heard the doorbell ring. She was uncertain she wanted to answer it. It rang again, and she sighed, stood, and went into the hall.

She opened the door and stood back. Her mother swept into the house. "I came without calling purposely, dear," she said as she took off her coat and picked up her bundles again, marching directly into the kitchen. Obediently and silently Tish followed.

Standing before the cabinets, busily stowing what she had brought, Tish's mother talked over her shoulder. "I brought you a few things you'll probably need," she said and then, with a self-conscious laugh, added, "and a few you would probably never think of. But I thought it might be nice to have a few luxuries around for a change. Especially after that hospital food. Besides, this will brighten things up a bit. Sterile bottles and Pampers and talcum get very unattractive in a very short time. I know. I can still remember when you and Tommy were small. How I longed for a few of those silly, feminine things, expensive ones, that used to seem so unimpo———"

"Mother, for heaven's sakes!" Tish said. "Relax."

"Me?" Mrs. Davies asked. "I'm right as rain. I knew, of course, that really, in your heart of hearts, you needed someone and that you'd never, never admit it, not even to your mother. Mothers have these kinds of instincts, dear. You'll see, when Kate is . . ."

"Mother!" Tish said quickly and sternly, but without raising her voice. "Will you please calm down? You'll drive me up a wall."

Mrs. Davies turned at this, silenced, and regarded her daughter. "You look tired, dear," she said softly.

"That's not too surprising, is it?"

"Is Kate sleeping badly?"

"No," said Tish with a soft laughing sound, "she's sleeping wonderfully. I'm not."

"Well, of course not, dear," Mrs. Davies said, turning again to finish shelving her gifts. "When Peter gets back, you'll have the kind of help you need for nighttime. I remember, your father used to grumble and grouse endlessly about whether it was his turn or mine to feed you children. Secretly, I think he liked getting up to play the martyr."

Tish smiled as pleasantly as she could, feeling foolish as she did so. She decided she would not discuss Peter's return, if return there was, with her mother. Not now. Not this morning. It was too early; she was too tired. She leaned against a wall and crossed her arms, determining to wait out her mother, to listen all the way through until finally, like a toy unwinding, her mother had come to a halt. There would be nothing more she could rattle on about without approaching finally the subject she had so clearly come to discuss.

"Well, there!" said Mrs. Davies, standing back and closing the cabinet door. "Just wait till one of those nights when you want something but can't quite think what it might be. What a lot of surprises you'll find!"

"Thank you, Mother," Tish said limply.

"Now, where's the coffee? I'm absolutely dehydrated from all this work."

Tish pointed to the pot that sat on top of the stove.

"Is it still warm?" asked her mother with professional cheerfulness.

"Mother, any minute I expect you to ask how 'we' are feeling today. Can't you relax, please?"

"Of course I can, dear, as soon as I have a cup of coffee in my hands."

Tish smiled and pushed off the wall, reaching for a mug to hand her mother. "Now, Mother, when you've filled it, and before you take a sip, take a huge, big breath and get your pulse rate back to where it belongs. I'll be in the living room, if you can come in and sit down and take it easy."

Tish patted her mother's shoulder as she left to show she wasn't angry, only tired. Mrs. Davies watched her leave the room.

By the time Tish's mother found a place in the living room that seemed to her suitable to sit, she was subdued. Tish watched her mother's movements carefully. Everything Mrs. Davies did now was slow and predetermined. The way she sat expectantly holding her cup, her back stiff with proper posture, the look on her face—clear-eyed, sensible, helpful but realistic.

Tish shook her head and smiled. "I can't believe you," she said.

"Whyever not?"

"Well, you're so ready to do the good turn, the right thing," Tish said. "Your whole body throbs with your hurry to be a mother again."

"I don't see that that's wrong, Tish," said Mrs. Davies. "I won't even be defensive. After all, things have turned out rather badly, haven't they? And whom should you turn to but your mother?"

"We don't know for certain, Mother, how things have turned out yet."

"Well, you may not, dear, but it's clear to me, from what your father's said that Peter has very simply had a nervous breakdown. It's quite plain."

"Is it?"

"Of course it is, dear, and you may as well face it. There's no point in waiting for a sudden wonderful change in him. Believe me, these things take time."

"Mother," Tish said, her exhaustion making itself even plainer in her voice, "*I* don't know any such thing. All I know for certain is that yesterday Peter was injured, and probably went into shock because of it. That's all there is, factually, to know."

Mrs. Davies put down her cup and scooted nearer her daughter. "Tish, darling," she said, "truly you have to admit things. You and Peter were never a love match. You knew that, and he did. You had plans, and so did he. Whole other lives. Kate's arrived. Peter has simply left you holding the bag, but in a rather startling way."

"You think that's all it is?" Tish asked, a little angry now. "You really think this is all in aid of his freedom?"

"Well, why not? What else can I think? What do you honestly know that's any different, darling?"

Tish stood, walking to the mantel. She turned and looked placidly at her mother. "I am very fond of you, Mother. And

I appreciate your help, really I do, and your concern. But you'll just have to accept the fact that if *I* don't know for certain what's happening—you can't. If you could will me back two or three years I know you would, and you mean that only for what you think is my own good. I understand all that. But, Mother, realistically, at this very moment I know less than nothing about what's going on. I am holding still, waiting to learn. When I do understand what's what, then maybe I'll have an idea of what to do. But not yet."

"Darling," Mrs. Davies objected, having waited patiently, "there is only one thing you can do. Come home with me. Bring Kate and the things you need. We can put you both in your old room. You'll have the kind of help you need, and company, and that's important, dear. You can't be alone with your own thoughts for company at a time like this."

"Mother, I would prefer that to listening to this."

"Oh!"

"You're a generous, loving woman, Mother," Tish hastened on, determined now to make her mother feel needed and worthwhile. "And I *do* appreciate what you're doing. The reasoning that got you here, the things you brought, your concern for Kate and me. I really do."

Mrs. Davies said nothing in response. She looked into her lap.

"Don't cry, Mother," Tish warned. Then she laughed softly. "You know, I've never seen you cry at all until this last year. And I think I finally understand how you operate. I mean this kindly, Mother, but your tears are always a tipoff to the last-ditch stand. And I doubt whether there are too many of those in the past you've lost. Are there?"

Mrs. Davies could do nothing but look at her daughter, and then smile. "My own daughter," she said. "Seeing her mother for what she is."

"Yes, generous and strong."

"That's a very nice way of putting it, dear. I promise I'll behave." Mrs. Davies stood now too. "What is there I can do for you, honey? That won't seem like interfering, I mean. I do want to help, you know."

Tish sighed and smiled openly. "You could sit around and listen for Kate while I try to get a couple hours of sleep. I think that's what I need most now, sleep."

"What about phone calls, dear?"

Tish stopped on her way into the hall and thought a moment. "Honestly, Mother, I don't think there will be any," she said after a moment. "If there are, wake me. I mean, if it's Peter or his father. If it's Mrs. McSweeny, just make up some wonderfully gruesome story about my imminent demise. That'll please her."

Mrs. Davies walked toward Tish and put her hands on Tish's shoulders. "We are on your side, dear," she said gently. "Truly. We'll do anything you want."

"Thank you, Mother," Tish said. Then she kissed her mother's cheek. "Just stay awake a couple of hours. That would be wonderful."

Closing her bedroom door and looking at the freshly made bed, Tish knew she wouldn't be able to sleep. But it had been a way of extricating herself from a scene she had been able to control, so far. She doubted whether, in a longer meeting, she would have been able to maintain that.

She lay on top of the spread and closed her eyes, wondering whether every child ended up being parent to his own.

Tish awoke slowly, surprised to find herself curled up on top of her bed. She looked at the bedside clock. It was almost noon. "Mother?" she called tentatively. There was no reply.

Slowly and with some effort, Tish swung off the bed and stretched. She went to her door and opened it. "Mother?" she called softly again.

She walked across the hall and looked into Kate's room. She was lying on her back, eyes wide open, with something resembling a smile on her face. "Learning virtue, eh?" Tish said, laughing a little.

She turned and went forward in the house. Perhaps her mother, too, had fallen asleep. But in the living room there was no sign that Mrs. Davies had ever visited. Shrugging, Tish turned and without knowing she had made a decision, she walked into the kitchen and dialed a New York City number. It was all very well to be passive, in a way. To feel that perhaps by telephoning Peter's house she would be in some way upsetting him. Not directly, she felt, but via his mother who so clearly wanted no intrusion, even from Peter's wife. But to be passive and to be considerate were different things.

"Yes," she said to a woman who announced a firm's name, and asked if she could assist her. "I'd like to speak to Mr. McSweeny, please."

She waited while her call was switched to her father-in-law's office. His secretary picked up the phone and spoke brightly.

"Is Mr. McSweeny in?" asked Tish. "This is his daughter-in-law."

"I'm terribly sorry. He's away all day. Is there anything I can do for you?" offered the secretary.

"You don't know where I can reach him, do you?"

"I'm sorry, I don't. He called in early this morning and said he would be away for the day. He didn't leave a number."

"Oh well, thank you very much, anyway," Tish said. She replaced the receiver, wondering whether this meant that Peter, too, was away somewhere. Had he been taken somewhere away from her, from Kate, without their knowing.

Screw it! she thought, dialing Kate McSweeny's number.

Kate herself answered the phone. "Hello?" she said, as though in a hurry and in a frame of mind not to be trifled with.

Tish hung up the phone quickly. She didn't want a repeat performance of last night's conversation. And if Kate was at home, that probably meant Peter was, too. And George? No, she decided, George at least would have tried to call. Who knew?

She shrugged and walked into her daughter's room. She bent down over the crib and lifted Kate carefully onto the top of the bassinet, feeling her diapers.

"Mama's own little hydrant, eh? National fire prevention week," she said, chuckling as she began to change the baby, and powder her. "I think a bath might be in order today. After all, how do you expect to make friends this way?"

Picking Kate up nervously, supporting her head, Tish carried the child into the living room. Holding her gently, she eased onto the couch and opened her bathrobe. "Now, for once, Kate, try not to be a glutton," Tish said, putting the child's head to her breast.

She leaned back and let Kate feed as she wanted. Surprisingly, Lady Macbeth came to her mind. Something about how the milk of human kindness had curdled? Tish stared at the ceiling. Could that really happen, she wondered. If she were unhappy, or edgy, or bitter, could Kate tell the difference?

At that moment, clearly Kate was either nonselective or ravenous.

The doorbell rang suddenly. "Oh God," Tish said, trying to think what to do. "Who is it?" she shouted toward the hall.

"It's M.O.," came the reply. "Hurry up. I can't hold this forever!"

Puzzled by the propriety of standing in the doorway while nursing Kate, Tish nonetheless stood. She walked toward the front door, Kate still gnawing away. Standing behind the door, Tish reached out and unlatched it. The door swung toward her as M.O. struggled into the hall, carting an enormous casserole. "Tish?"

Tish pushed the door closed with her foot. "Right here," she announced. M.O. jumped.

"Gracious!" she said. "What are you doing there?"

"It's too difficult to explain," Tish said with a smile.

"Isn't she sweet," M.O. cooed. "Oh!" she groaned then. "I've got to put this thing down." She turned and staggered toward the kitchen.

Tish had barely seated herself again on the couch when she heard M.O. swear. "Tish!" she shouted. "You could have told me!"

Tish put Kate on the couch and closed her robe. "Hang in there," she advised her daughter. "Won't be a minute." And she walked to the kitchen to see what caused M.O.'s complaint.

"I mean," said M.O., "here I spend since dawn practically, making this gigantic thing to feed your starving family, and I get here to find exactly the same thing already in your oven."

"You do?" Tish said, surprised, bending down. Her own casserole stood on the oven's top rack, heat from the darkened space flooding out into the kitchen.

"It must have been Mother," she explained, feeling the excuse a lame one.

"Nuts!" M.O. said. "It's clear you've simply got a magic oven!"

"Oh, M.O., I feel terrible."

"Well, don't," M.O. said, cheering herself up as well. "These things are always better after a few days." She opened the refrigerator and found room for her pot by reshelving a few things. "There," she said proudly, pushing the door closed. "Now, I'll take a cup of kindness."

"It's right there. Go ahead. The idea of one more cup of that stuff makes me feel weak."

Tish hurried back into the living room. Kate had fallen asleep, dribbling as she breathed. "Damn," Tish whispered, picking her up gently, hoping not to awaken her. "But I deserve it."

She took Kate back to her crib and returned to the living room, armed with paper toweling. M.O. was sitting in an easy chair, sipping and smoking.

"Cute little thing, but rude!" Tish said, trying to wipe the couch dry. "*I* never did anything like that."

"Of course not."

"It's nice to see you," Tish said, sitting down. "Really."

"Good," M.O. said. "How are things?"

Tish looked quickly at her visitor. "You mean you don't know?"

"I know. At least, I know what happened yesterday, at practice. Poncho is very depressed."

"Everybody is, I guess, except maybe Peter."

"Have you seen him?"

"No."

"But why not?"

"His mother thinks whatever is wrong is my fault. She's guarding the gates like a hound."

"You're his wife, Tish."

"I'm about to make the same statement," Tish answered. "As soon as I can. Actually, I've been trying just to hang together."

"Kate seems healthy," M.O. offered. "That's good."

Tish nodded.

"You know, Tish, the old man and I were talking last night. I'm sure you won't want to do this, but we thought you should know the possibility is always there. We've got an enormous amount of room at our place. The kids are terrific with babies. You'd be free to rearrange things as soon as you were able."

Tish looked at her hands. *Please, don't let me let loose now,* she prayed. But when she looked up at M.O., there were tears in her eyes. "Oh, M.O.," she said, "that's really . . . terrific, no kidding. I appreciate it so much."

"Nothing's worse, honey, than being left out," M.O. said softly. "In our house, that's impossible. You're part, or you starve."

Tish smiled weakly. "I'll remember, if I ever . . ."

"Relax, honey. I'm not the family. You don't have to be brave in front of me."

"Oh, M.O., I'm not brave, I'm not!" Tish got out.

"Like hell."

Tish could hold things in no longer. Her tears fell faster now and she sat there letting them stream down, not wiping or sniffling.

"You know," she started to say, twice. "You know, M.O., for a while, I thought it was me who . . . who was going . . ." But without warning Tish's tears stopped, and she began to laugh, at first softly. "I thought *I* was going nuts!" Meaninglessly, she was giggling.

M.O. smiled, and tried to laugh a little, too. But Tish's laughter far outstripped hers.

"Egad!" Tish gasped, "I'm an hysterical woman! Finally! I've grown up!" And she doubled over, holding her stomach, her laughter continuing to shake her without ceasing, until finally she rolled on her side, almost in pain. "Oh," she said. "Oh, my, oh, my!"

Tish lay there, on her side, looking at the ceiling, trying to bring her breathing back to normal. "Maybe I am crazy," she said wonderingly. Then she sat up. "I mean, who else would get the giggles over her husband's breakdown?"

M.O. lit a cigarette. She was uncertain what to say.

"You know, M.O.," Tish said, starting to chuckle again, "you're supposed to leap up and slap my face for me. Then I sit up, stunned into reality again, and thank you for it."

"Next time," M.O. said with a grin. "I was never any good at theatricals."

Tish inhaled enormously. "Well, there probably won't be a next time," she said. "At least, I hope not."

"Well, being practical for a moment, honey," M.O. said, "there's one thing you can call on us for, anytime."

"What?"

"Babysitters. I've a sleep-in staff of four who are old enough to handle that."

Tish nodded. "Maybe, in time, I'll call, M.O. That's terrific."

M.O. sat in her chair, watching Tish. "I'm not the world's most subtle lady, Tish," she said. "Is there anything you really need to let out? That you haven't been able to talk to anyone else about?"

After a moment, Tish tried to explain. "The problem is I don't even know how to start talking about things. I sit here, waiting. Waiting to hear what really happened. What anybody can do. What I'm supposed to do. Whether, in fact, I'm going to be allowed to do anything."

"Don't wait too long, honey," M.O. advised.

"I know," Tish said. "But really, I *don't* know what's happened, how serious it might be. It's tough to go to war without knowing why, or whom you're fighting. Maybe it's me that's the enemy. Maybe it *is* my fault, whatever the matter is."

"I doubt that," M.O. said. "It's easy to say and tough to do, Tish, but the one thing you've got to remember is to believe in yourself. As long as *your* head's in order, and your feelings, you never have to worry about making bad decisions."

Tish smiled. "Is that a promise?"

"Eighteen years long, and successful, that promise," was M.O.'s guarantee.

49.

November 29

Questions considered in the past few hours (nope; I'm hedging again, D.D. Questions considered, off and on, since yesterday morning).

(1) Is Peter's problem my fault?

(2) If it isn't entirely, how much is?

(3) Could I have seen it coming?

(4) Could anyone?

(5) Could it have been prevented?

(6) Can I ever again react and speak and feel without worrying what effect all that will have on someone else, someone I might care for, like Kate?

*One bloody great circle, D.D. Just when I've finally
come to some firm conclusions, something else comes
to mind and I have to reconsider everything.*

*Should we have had Kate? Yes. Should we have gotten
married? Maybe not. Should I have aborted and kept
my mouth shut? Yes.*

*The problem lies in the fact that between the first yes
and the second one, there is a no. That doesn't make
any sense at all.*

*We should have had Kate because she's here now and
she's wonderful. Without having her, though, without
seeing her and playing with her and getting to love
her, we wouldn't have missed her. That's cruel but true,
for if not Kate with Peter, then no doubt later Kate with
someone else. Not quite the same Kate perhaps, but a
Kate nonetheless. Do I feel guilty? No. I should,
probably; I don't. I can't find it to feel alone responsible
for all this. But I suppose, being honest, that I am.
From the beginning. After all, as M.O. once said, I
needn't have told Peter anything at all. And if I hadn't,
he would still be running loose and free and healthy and
happy and hunky today.*

*I stopped for a minute, D.D. Headache. I've been
thinking so hard, trying to see so clearly. And I have
to say I don't think I'm getting very far. Everything
revolves around something else.*

*There is one thought, though, I've had that seems to
stick around. If I hadn't been so selfishly concerned
with what marriage meant to me, if I hadn't been so
eager to make our life together into what I wanted, all
this might not have happened. It might have, but I
might have been able to see more clearly (scratch that
"more," since I didn't see at all) what was happening
to Peter.*

*But neither did anyone else. M.O. didn't, or Peter's
father, or anyone. All we did was philosophize about
marriage, about adjusting and the strains and the time
needed. Everything seemed so normal in terms of what
we thought we saw and experienced. If Peter did
something I thought was weird, there was always a
good reason . . . either I myself had brought it on,*

*or he was taking time to readjust his view of things, or
our roles in marriage were still being defined. Or
whatever.*

*And all the time none of us really saw what was going
on at all. Does anyone, ever, anywhere, see that clearly?*

50.

It was the new, early darkness that made her so hungry,
Tish thought, spooning Irish stew onto her plate. It was
barely six. Kate had been fed some time ago and was, like
an obedient child, sound asleep again. Standing at the front
window, seeing students make their cautious way home in
semidarkness, Tish had grown emptier by the moment.
Nerves and hunger being identical to her, she had decided
to have an early dinner.

Next to her place, at the dining room table, was one of
Peter's books. It was a supposed diary of a young man's experiences with drugs. Not an addictive experience but a controlled one, under the tutelage of a legendary Mexican Indian.
It certainly seemed to start out slowly, Tish thought, flicking
a page. The college boy was making no progress whatever.
He had been unable to convince his mentor that his desire
to learn about drugs was genuine.

"Oh, for heaven's sake," Tish muttered, reading a speech
of Don Juan's. "What do you care? Give it to him."

She turned the book over and looked out into the darkness
beyond the dining room window. She felt she wanted something more but she was undecided what. She stood, pushing
back her chair, and carried her plate into the kitchen, and
ladled more stew onto her plate. Then, smiling, she took two
pieces of soft, fluffy white bread and covered them in an eighth
of an inch of butter, soft butter. Thus prepared, she turned to
go back to her place.

The telephone rang.

Tish put the side-plate with the bread and butter on the
counter, and picked up the receiver. "Hello?"

"This is Kate."

"Hello. How's Peter?"

"Coming along just fine, thank you very much."

"He is? When can I come over? Tonight? I could leave in about ten minutes. I'd really like to, Ka——"

"Is George there?"

"Again?"

"Don't be smart, miss. Is he there?"

"No, he's not. Kate, I'm coming over."

"He won't be here."

"Why not?"

"Because we'll just leave."

"What the hell do you expect me to do?" Tish shouted into the phone.

"Don't raise your voice to me."

"Oh, for Christ's sake! All *right*, *Mrs*. McSweeny. Have you any idea what your son's wife is supposed to do while waiting around for you to miraculously cure him of who knows what disease?"

"I should think you'd choose to be bright and witty at some other time."

"Kate, I am not kidding around. What am I supposed to do?"

"George will be in touch."

"What does that mean?"

"Just what I said. George is supposed to talk with you. I have nothing more to say."

"Well, I have," Tish said quickly. "If George had one ounce of sense, he wouldn't come home tonight, or tomorrow, or the next, either!"

Trembling, Tish put the phone down. She looked down at the plate she held in her hand. Swiftly, she marched across the room, put her foot on a plastic lever, and dumped its contents into the garbage. On her way out of the kitchen, however, she collected the bread and butter and had already begun to eat as she walked into the dining room.

She pulled back her chair and sat down, trying to feel comfortable. She reached for her glass, and took a swallow of milk.

"George will be in touch." The sentence repeated itself in her mind. About what? There was no point in getting excited, Tish told herself. Whatever he was going to say he was going to say. Nothing she could do would change that. But what was it he was supposed to talk to her about?

Instantaneously, Tish knew.

By eight thirty, Tish had reasoned everything out.

She would not be difficult, or demand too much. Child support, of course. Kate had a right to that. And perhaps a token amount of money, just enough to build on when she had found a job. It should be enough, at least, to take care of the expense of having someone sit with Kate until she was old enough for nursery school.

She would take Kate to her parents', but only until she had found her own, small, reasonable apartment. Peter could visit, if he were able to and wanted to, on weekends, and he could have Kate for a time each summer. They would try to remain cordial, if not friendly.

Depressed, but also somewhat relieved, Tish sat in the dining room, waiting.

The phone's ring, when it came, did not startle her. Slowly, in one motion, she stood and walked unhurriedly to the kitchen. "Hello."

"Hi, Tish."

"Hello, George." She looked at her wrist. She could probably snare Charlotte or Fred for an hour, if George wanted to meet somewhere else.

"I'm sorry we haven't had a chance to talk before now, sweetheart," said Mr. McSweeny. "Life has just been too fast for all of us lately."

He certainly sounded chipper, Tish thought without begrudging him his mood. If she were he, she would suggest a neutral spot, somewhere where she couldn't get hysterical and fight or argue.

"You still there, Tish?"

"Yes."

"We have to meet, to talk a while," Mr. McSweeny said. "Would it be all right if I came over there, say in about twenty minutes?"

Tish looked at the clock above the stove. That would be around nine fifteen. Why not? She was going nowhere.

"That's fine with me, George," she said after a pause.

"Wonderful. Oh, and Tish, if you've got anything in the place to eat, heat it up. I haven't eaten all day, and I'm on the ropes."

"Fine, George."

"See you in seconds, then."

"Right." She replaced the receiver.

She stooped and twisted a dial on the stove.

No doubt he was being cheerful hoping she would be the same. Well, she wouldn't be. She couldn't. What had she to be bright about? She would give graciously what she knew he sought. She smiled bitterly. Peter would have said she was doing the right thing. She was handling responsibility. She had a sense of duty.

She also had a ten-day-old baby. And a throat that was beginning to ache.

51.

"That smells wonderful," Mr. McSweeny said, throwing off his coat. "You don't mind if I sneak a look at Kate first, do you?"

Tish smiled thinly. "Go right ahead."

She watched her father-in-law tiptoe down the hall and go into Kate's small room. She leaned against a wall, waiting for him to return.

"You know," he said approaching her, "she really is beginning to look human. A little." He laughed and patted Tish's shoulder as he passed and went into the dining room. "I'm so hungry I'd eat the table itself."

"I hope it will be tastier than that," Tish said.

"I didn't mean it that way, sweetheart. It's just that I've been on the go all day, and haven't had a chance to eat. Probably good for me, though." He took a sizable bite of the stew. "That is good, Tish. Really. Peter's been very lucky, I see."

Tish nodded as she sat down at the other end of the table. "How is Peter?" She managed to keep her voice steady and low.

Mr. McSweeny took another bite. "Give me one more minute at this, okay?"

"No, George," Tish said, surprising herself. "I won't. No one has bothered for two days to tell me anything. I'm tired of waiting."

Mr. McSweeny put down his fork and sat back, looking down the table at her. "You're right, Tish. You're perfectly right."

Tish said nothing in return. Her silence, she felt, said more than enough.

"It's not as bad as all that, sweetheart," said Mr. Mc-Sweeny.

"Why isn't it?"

"Well, these things can be fixed, you know," said her father-in-law. "It may take some time, but things aren't irreparable."

"What exactly isn't irreparable? It seems to me you're in very good spirits for someone whose son has just gone round the bend."

"But it's not so bad as that, Tish."

"For God's sake, then, tell me what it is as bad as!"

Mr. McSweeny nodded. "Now I don't pretend to be a psychologist, Tish. My way of saying things may not even be accurate. But what the doctors have said is . . . well, the reasons for Peter's breakdown—and that's the word they use, breakdown. It can't be as bad as you think, can it, if they just call it that?—anyway, the reasons for it are clearer to them than the right way to treat him is."

"Which means what, George?"

Mr. McSweeny stood from his place and began to pace in front of the dining room window. Tish understood he did not now want to have to look into her eyes.

"What *they* think, Tish, is that . . . that Peter's been fighting, inside, this whole thing."

"Our marriage, you mean?"

"That, and having a child, and having to go to work. Having to forget all about the plans he'd made, about finishing his childhood, I guess, in the way he thought he would."

"What about all his talk about responsibility, then? What was all that?"

Mr. McSweeny understood. "He really thought that, Tish. I'm sure he did. His head told him what he had to do, what course he had to take to keep his own respect and his obligations to you. Apparently, his emotions just didn't agree."

"I see," Tish said softly.

"Actually, and this really gets me, when the doctors examined him yesterday at the hospital, from stem to stern, they found that he was heading for an ulcer. Part of his stomach lining had eroded. A break was due at any time. Imagine that. Ulcers at eighteen!"

"Imagine that," said Tish.

"Anyway," Mr. McSweeny continued still pacing, "the doctors told us that Peter has probably been repressing all his natural instincts and feelings in favor of what he felt he should feel. Where he is now, I guess, is back in the old days. Safe, single, unhampered."

"Like me, you mean?"

Mr. McSweeny was stopped by Tish's tone. He looked at her. "No, Tish, not like you. I know that."

Tish nodded, satisfied in a way. "Go on," she said.

Mr. McSweeny seemed momentarily ill-at-ease. "Well . . . the doctors think that what needs to be done is . . . show Peter that what's happened is a positive experience.".

Tish stood up quickly. Her voice was flat but edged. "George, you begin to sound like a medical journal. I'm not understanding any of this. Just tell me what you want me to do. You want me to divorce Peter? Is that it? I will if it's what he needs. I've thought it all through. I can't exist in limbo. I need to know, or be part of knowing. I'm no good sitting here with Kate just wondering and unable to actually do anything. Just tell me what you and Kate have in mind, and let's settle it."

Mr. McSweeny stared at Tish. She held his look, feeling exhausted and dispirited and in a hurry finally to get matters concluded.

"Tish, Tish," he said, taking a step toward her and then stopping. He looked at her a moment more and then moved all the way across the room to take her in his arms. "Honey, you're way off. That's not what we have in mind. Not any of us. Believe me, you're wrong."

Tish pulled out of his embrace gently but firmly, giving him a weak smile as she stepped back. "I'm a big girl, George," she said. "Don't go through hell trying to break it easily. No kidding. Just say it straight out."

Mr. McSweeny continued to stare at her. "You're fantastic," he said finally. "I am not breaking it to you easily, Tish. None of us has ever even thought about divorce."

"Not Kate?"

Mr. McSweeny frowned. "Not any more. I gather you've

had some conversations with her. Well, I apologize for her, Tish. Truly I do. I guess not everyone is attractive all the time, under all conditions. Kate is simply more human now, more like the rest of us."

Tish smiled to herself, doubting whether in fact Kate Mc-Sweeny could be pushed aside so easily. She sat down again. "All right, George. If I'm wrong, tell me what it *is* you have in mind."

"All right," Mr. McSweeny said, fertilizing his own enthusiasm as he began to speak. "First of all, Peter." Tish nodded. "First of all, the doctors think whatever damage is done can be repaired. They're not even sure what damage has been done, whether it's real or serious or not. They think Peter has pulled his security blanket over his head, wishing himself back into the spot he was before all this happened."

"That, of course, is not possible."

"True. He probably knows that, too, Peter. But he needs to find his own reasons for thinking that it is. He needs to understand that although some of his plans have been changed, what has happened instead can be worthwhile, can be meaningful in completely different, but still valuable, ways."

"How does he go about doing that?" asked Tish skeptically.

"With a lot of help, Tish," said Mr. McSweeny pleasantly. "Yours, and mine, and little Kate's. And the doctors', more than anything else, their help."

"You mean he's going into analysis?"

"I guess you'd say that, if you were making it simple."

"Is he to be isolated? Is he going to live at your house, in the garage?"

"No."

Tish was puzzled. "Not here?"

"Not yet," said her father-in-law. "I've found a clinic, near New Haven, where they'll take him for a few months anyway. Where he can work intensively on this."

"George, this all sounds too easy to me," Tish said. "Too simple. How . . . how ill is Peter?"

Mr. McSweeny looked at the floor. "A little worse than a nervous breakdown," he admitted.

"Will I get to see him before he goes away?"

"No."

Tish nodded. "What about us, George?"

"You and Peter?"

"Kate and me."

Mr. McSweeny coughed. "That's the hard part, Tish."

Here it comes, Tish thought. He had been lying after all.

Mr. McSweeny stood in one spot, looking at the carpet, not moving. He spoke without raising his head. "The hard part depends on you, Tish. It's unfair but I'm afraid it's true."

"Go on." Tish was ready.

Mr. McSweeny looked at her finally. "It's the aloneness."

"That's not new, George."

"I know that. But it has to continue. For a while, anyhow."

"George, what happens if Peter, when this is over, decides that he doesn't think what we've had is a 'positive experience'? What if he decides I'm a nice enough person, but not to spend a lot of time with? What if he decides that Kate is cute, but not that cute?"

"You really think that could happen, Tish?"

"I don't know. I suppose not."

"What happens if you feel that way some day?"

Tish looked at Mr. McSweeny with new interest. "What happens if somewhere along the way you meet someone new?" her father-in-law asked. "While Peter's away, perhaps. Tish, do you love Peter?"

"Do those questions go together?"

"No."

Tish nodded. "I love Peter. I've had time to think, to find out really that I do. Yes."

"Now, what about the first question."

Tish shrugged. "What can I say, George? I don't know what's coming from day to day. That sounds hard. It's not meant to. These last few months haven't exactly been your everyday happy honeymoon picnic. But I don't feel inclined to junk everything and look around."

"You'll be able to visit Peter, you know."

"I will?"

"Yes. I can't say when," Mr. McSweeny said. "But the doctors want you to, too, to help Peter. If you can."

"You mean if I still feel like it?"

"That's what I mean."

"I'll still feel like it, George."

"Good."

"There's something very unfair in all this, you know."

"I know."

"I just wanted to make sure you did," said Tish. "I'm not a martyr, but I am human. I don't want people to forget about me or Kate."

Mr. McSweeny's face broke into a sudden grin. "Well, we're not! Believe me, we're not. I've been running around like the headless chicken for two days trying to make certain of that."

"How?"

"Well, Tish, remember what I said about waiting for some kind of omen, a signal that would tell me the time had come to break out and start all over again?" Tish nodded. "This is it!"

"Peter's illness?"

"Absolutely. When I got home last night and found out what had been happening, I had a lot to swallow. All I could think to do was get in my car and take off. Sort things out. Try to see where Kate and I had failed, had helped make the breakdown inevitable, if it was. How you might be to blame. How having the baby had been the final peg. I couldn't get anywhere that way, Tish."

"Neither could I."

"Then, later, driving along, I had an odd sensation. All those years, when I was in town making money and climbing, all that time I'd never learned anything about my family. Men are like that, having to work hardest when their children are smallest. Suddenly, one day you're confronted by an adult, and you wonder what you've missed, where he came from. And now, here's a second chance."

"You lost me."

"What hit me, Tish, was that this must be the omen I'd been waiting for. Then I began to wonder about you and Kate. How you were going to get on without Peter. Which led me to Pack-a-Camp."

"What?" Tish couldn't help but sound confused.

"I drove over last night and had a long talk with Peter's boss. He's very high on Peter, on his work. He'd been after

Peter to gamble on managing a new, smaller shop somewhere."

"Peter told me."

"*Well!* I thought to myself."

"You?"

"Why not? I've got experience."

"In camping gear?"

"In life! That's what counts."

"That's exactly what Peter said once."

"Must have picked it up from his old man," Mr. McSweeny said. "This all sounds selfish as hell, Tish. But suddenly, being needed, having to pitch in to help my son, got turned around to where I was helping myself. Lots of men want to change, but not many actually get the chance. Here's my chance, Tish. For you and Peter, even more for myself, I can't afford to let it go."

"You're going to work there?"

Mr. McSweeny grinned and shook his head. "Had to sell the man, just a little. Fifty-three isn't eighteen. But that's where I was last night, and all day today until just after I spoke to you. We're open every night till nine now because of Christmas." Mr. McSweeny's grin sobered. "I'm not committing myself to a fairy tale, Tish. Realistically, even though I want that change, I'd be foolish to think that taking Peter's job is really the right thing. At the moment it works, for all of us. I've arranged a leave from New York. They can get on without me, probably for a very long time. They'll sort out their problems as I sort out mine. One day we'll all know what it is we want. Peter will know. I will. The company will."

"George, I'm not quarreling with what you're doing, with what you've done. I'm happy you're happy. But what about Kate and me?"

"Whatever I make comes to you and Kate, every week, on schedule. If I don't find myself right away, if I feel uneasy about moving onto something more permanent, I'll stay until Peter can take over again. If he wants to."

Mr. McSweeny paused. "There's something you have to know, Tish. You're never going to be abandoned. You're part of our family now. You're in this with us, as long as you want to be. You'll be able to see Peter, and write to him, and probably have him around occasionally before he's really back to normal. As long as you want to be his wife, you are.

I've made that very, very clear to my Kate. That you are Peter's wife and to be treated with respect, not as a child.

"And if . . . if sometime you come to me and say you can't hack it any longer, that you want out—well, I, for one, promise I'll never call you names or cut off credit or any of those things people do. You're a fine young woman. I know that. There's an enormous amount of life ahead of you. I also know that you'll fill that time as you think best, after you've felt and thought and reasoned. That's enough for me."

"George," Tish said, standing swinging his hands in hers and feeling just a little sentimental, "you don't have to go through all this."

"I know that. I want to."

"All right."

"I'd like to visit you and Kate often," said Mr. McSweeny. "For Peter's sake, when he's healthy again, and now, for mine. If you'll let me?"

Tish nodded.

"Sometimes we could have lunch together?"

"All right," Tish said, turning her eyes floorward.

"And I'll help you find another place, too, when the time comes."

Tish nodded again.

Mr. McSweeny pulled Tish to him and held her a minute. He bent his head toward her ear and spoke in a half-mocking accent. "Remember, you heard it here first: Life is like a poker game, Tish. You can be dealt a fiddly-wa-diddly but you get to turn in three cards. You never know when the new ones are going to match."

52.

November 30

I just traumatized Kate. She was so adorable this morning, after her bath, and so happy, I took Peter's Instamatic out and took her first baby picture. The flash terrified her. All her life now she'll be Greta Garbo or Jackie Kennedy—suspicious, hunted, alone. Hee-hee. It's just ten in the morning and I'm strangely alert, keyed up. I realize, looking back on my last few entries, that

*I haven't been altogether honest with you, D.D. Not
dishonest so much as selective. For the record then: today
Peter is being driven to a clinic somewhere in Connecticut.
His mother is taking him. George is at work at
Pack-a-Camp—I suspect at sea and worried and feeling
nervous. He's done what he says he's always wanted
to do, but I think, secretly, he's frightened. He says he's
happy, and he tries to sound happy. What I know for
certain is that he wants to be happy, more than anything.
Kate and I are alone. And you know what: suddenly,
maybe because of the sunshine, today being alone doesn't
bother me.*

*Not that things are shaping up. Life around here is as
formless as ever, and as much guesswork. Only now I
realize that that's the way it's going to be, for quite a
while. Maybe, in my sleep last night, I got used to that
idea. Kate, happily, slept wonderfully last night, too, for
three and a half hours at a clip. She's very helpful and
concerned, I suspect, which is nice. (Now that is dumb.
She's totally insensible and selfish as all babies are. But
it makes me feel warmed somehow to start thinking of
her as having human feelings.) And what about me, you
ask. No, I ask. Well, I don't really know except that
today is very definitely Scarlett O'Hara's tomorrow.
Here I am, at least till April, with Kate and the Claytons
upstairs (that's lucky, anyway). If I'm lucky, I'll
probably see Peter once a month, and then only under
some sort of supervision. I don't think I quite understand
yet what exactly is wrong with him. But maybe that's
not so important as settling in to the fact that something
is wrong and that it needs to be fixed and that it will
take time. I'll tell you what's scarey: when it is fixed,
whenever that finally is, how will he feel about Kate and
me? What do you suppose I can do in the meantime to
make certain that when he's himself again he'll look at
me the way he did when we first knew each other?
One thing, of course, is exercise. I've let myself go, as
they say, and at seventeen! Not that badly, of course,
just enough to look a little flabby. Maybe I'll find out if
there are exercise classes or modern dance in New
Brunswick somewhere. That might help.*

*I realize, reading that, that my first concern is my own
exterior. How's that for selfish?*

Well, why not?

*Because that isn't fair to Kate or Peter, that's why. The
radio just started playing "An American in Paris." I
wonder if I'll ever get there. One of the comforting
thoughts I had last night, D.D., was that sure, life lately
hasn't been glamorous. But there's more ahead than
behind. If not Paris now, then next year. Or the year
after. Or in five years (I'll only be twenty-two then; or
ten, at twenty-seven). I'm a baby! Sort of. And I'll tell
you something else: I'm glad.*

*Not glad about everything, you understand, but about
a lot of things. Glad about Kate, when I didn't think I
ever would be. Glad to have had Peter which, awful
though it sounds, is exactly, and all, I started out
wanting. Glad and grateful for George and M.O. and
Daddy and even Sara.*

*I made a list last night, after George left, of pluses and
minuses. You've just heard the pluses. The minuses are
(the envelope, please!): not finishing high school or
getting into college—fixable at a later date; having the
responsibility of Kate from now until forever—sharable,
I hope (how I hope!) at a later date; this apartment—
exchangeable later. That's not so bad. The rent is paid
until tomorrow (hoo!), there's food in the kitchen, Kate
has what she needs, and there's not much I need that
I haven't got.*

Except—

*But I won't allow myself pity. I'm through complaining.
If I don't understand, I can ask. If I still don't
understand, I can wait. It is a world in limbo, I know,
and last night I thought I would hate that. But it's my
world, and while I didn't exactly choose it or shape it,
I did, a little, and so the only person I can come crying
to is myself. And I am not the world's most sympathetic
listener.*

*The thing now to do, D.D., is make some sense of all
this. To start constructing a life that makes sense even
if in the greater sense it can't really. Does that make
sense? Well, it does to me.*

*I thought this morning about calling George at work
and suggesting that he and Kate come have dinner here
tomorrow. They could see little Kate, we could patch
things up, and I'd have two whole days to cook.
(Naturally I'd decided to have chicken and dumplings.
Apart from the fact that I can eat what's left for days,
it's cheap . . . sort of.) Then I changed my mind. I'm
not really ready for that scene yet. Starting small is
starting sensible.
So I called my mother. For lunch, today. She tries hard.
If she can, I can.*